T0244887

Readers Love AMY LANE

Swipe Left, Power Down, Look Up
"A dose of much needed sweetness, humor, and an excellent HEA…"

—Rainbow Book Reviews

The Rising Tide
"If you're looking for a well-written urban fantasy with hot sex, this one will do it. Nicely."

—Sparkling Book Reviews

Weirdos
"The 80 pages is just as sweet as you think and pulls on your heartstrings… It did mine."

—Paranormal Romance Guild

Shades of Henry
"If you want emotions, character drama without it translating into a third-rate show and a romance that makes you feel tingly, go ahead with Shades of Henry."

—Leer sin Limites

Bonfires
"This book is for everybody, for the gay and the straight, for the open minded and the close minded, for the brave and for those who are afraid! Everybody."

—OptimuMM Book Reviews

By Amy Lane

Published by DREAMSPINNER PRESS
www.dreamspinnerpress.com

By Amy Lane (cont'd)

Published by DREAMSPINNER PRESS
www.dreamspinnerpress.com

Published by DREAMSPINNER PRESS
www.dreamspinnerpress.com

BOWLING for
TURKEYS

AMY LANE

Published by
DREAMSPINNER PRESS

8219 Woodville Hwy #1245
Woodville, FL 32362 USA
www.dreamspinnerpress.com

This is a work of fiction. Names, characters, places, and incidents either are the product of author imagination or are used fictitiously, and any resemblance to actual persons, living or dead, business establishments, events, or locales is entirely coincidental.

Bowling for Turkeys
© 2024 Amy Lane

Cover Art
© 2024 L.C. Chase
http://www.lcchase.com
Cover content is for illustrative purposes only and any person depicted on the cover is a model.

All rights reserved. This book is licensed to the original purchaser only. Duplication or distribution via any means is illegal and a violation of international copyright law, subject to criminal prosecution and upon conviction, fines, and/or imprisonment. Any eBook format cannot be legally loaned or given to others. No part of this book may be reproduced or transmitted in any form or by any means, electronic or mechanical, including photocopying, recording, or by any information storage and retrieval system, without the written permission of the Publisher, except where permitted by law. To request permission and all other inquiries, contact Dreamspinner Press, 8219 Woodville Hwy #1245, Woodville FL 32362 USA, or www.dreamspinnerpress.com.

Any unauthorized use of this publication to train generative artificial intelligence (AI) is expressly prohibited.

Trade Paperback ISBN: 978-1-64108-796-4
Digital ISBN: 978-1-64108-795-7
Trade Paperback published November 2024
v. 1.0

Mary, if you don't see yourself here, I do. Mate—you put up with so very, very much. Johnnie, Geoffie, Julia... you are all terrible people, the worst, most distracting of workmates, the most gawdawful roommates I've ever encountered. But you are all very, very GOOD dogs, and the best friends I could hope for.

Acknowledgments

I'd like to thank everybody who takes a look at Julia, our reactive, panicky, social disaster rescue dog, and laughs. "There's one in every crowd." Julia's that one. And she's hard. But she's so worth it. Thanks for helping us teach her a better way.

Author's Note:

Three years ago a friend found a tiny dog wandering the streets until her paws bled. We took her in and named her Ginger and loved her, and she loved us. And then in a panicky moment, she took off from the dog boarder's and got herself killed. We were devastated. But we knew that our other dogs, Geoffie and Johnnie, needed a friend. Johnnie isn't getting any younger, and Geoffie still has a good five years of thinking she's a young dog to go. So we went to a shelter and came home with Julia. She is... exactly as described. She will chase the squeaky... FOREVER. She hates cats, squirrels, and most dogs. And isn't all that fond of people who won't scratch her belly. She's weird and quirky and misanthropic... and will let Geoffie clean her ears and her eye-goop for hours at a time, because she's smart enough to know a good friend when one licks the crud off her face. Dogs are like people—not every dog will be perfect, and it would be weird if they were. As long as a dog gives you something to work with, the worst dog can still be the best friend. And no dog is a bad dog—sometimes they can be reactive disasters, and sometimes they can be careless crap machines—but that's still a good dog with a few... personality features. Julia is a good dog with some personality features, and she comforted us when we were desolate and sad. Good dog. Goooooooood dog.

A "Get Out of Bed" Surprise

"GET UP."

"Mariana, no…." Milo knew he shouldn't have answered the phone—he *knew* it. Sure, Mariana Roberts was his forever bestie, the keeper of his secrets, and the sister of his heart, but… but… but *oh my God*, she was *so* much a lot!

"Mariana, *yes!*" she retorted with her usual terrifying determination. Mariana had been forced to drop out of college in her third year so she could help support her mentally ill sister. She'd taken a job on a hospital phone line and now made way more money than Milo did with his degree in graphic communications, and she often claimed that her major was in fixing people's lives.

She'd managed to fix her sister's; Serena now lived in an assisted care facility, where Mariana visited at least twice a week, and she apparently had friends and hobbies and was happy.

Since Mari was often cheerfully single—and Milo was *not* cheerfully *anything*—that left *Milo's* life to fix, and sadly, he was giving her a *lot* to work with.

"But Mari, it's *Saturday*," he whined, and knew it for a whine. "It's my day to lounge around and—"

"And skip out on lunch with your bestie, you bastard," she snapped.

He winced. "I'm sorry. You're right, I shouldn't have bailed on you—"

"Twice. You bailed on me *twice* since the breakup, and I get that I had to work overtime in September, but it's *October* now, and we haven't seen each other since your vodka-and-ice-cream pity party and… and *dammit*, Milo, I'm worried about you!"

Milo glanced around his duplex in a daze, noting the dead plants he'd meant to water, the laundry he'd meant to do, the dirty dishes he'd meant to wash. Hell, he was probably out of coffee, and he wasn't sure if there was anything in his refrigerator to eat. How was he supposed to "lie in" when there wasn't enough here to keep him alive? "Two months?" he asked, feeling stupid. Did Stuart break up with him two months ago? "It hasn't been two months, has it?"

Her sigh was eloquent. "Yes, baby. It's been two months. Now wake up and get out of bed!"

He did what she told him to because that was the pattern they'd established in high school. Mari made the plans, Milo carried them out. She was good at it, he thought wretchedly, trying to find a bare place on the carpet to place his feet.

"I'm awake," he told her crossly. "I'm out of bed. Now what?"

"Come answer your door, asshole. I've been here for ten minutes."

Milo's eyes went wide, and he cast desperate glances around his once-neat little duplex in panic.

"No," he almost whimpered, seeing the piles of dirty laundry draped on every surface of his bedroom. He was wearing his last pair of boxers, and his T-shirt was getting a little ripe. He knew without looking that the sink was piled high with dishes, his living room awash in a sea of takeout, and his kitchen table piled high with bills.

He was pretty sure his power was about to be turned off.

"Oh yes," she said grimly. "You thought you could curl up and die that easy? You've got another goddamned thing coming. Now come open your door. We're coming in."

"Wait," he said desperately, although the long habit of following Mari's orders seemed to have morphed into an actual magical compulsion. He was walking. Wow, had his laundry actually spilled into the hallway? And what the hell was that smell coming from the bathroom? Holy jebus, when had he last eaten? The food on the dishes in the sink was... well, uncomplimentary colors.

The only clean thing in the place was Chrysanthemum's food and water bowl on its little placemat in the corner of the kitchen, waiting for Stuart to bring him back. Milo almost paused there, but Mari squawked from the front door.

"Get out here, you coward! I'm not going anywhere!"

Which was how, through the wreckage of a life he'd once been proud of, he slogged, hating himself more with every step.

What kind of loser let his life get this disgusting in so short a time?

By the time he opened the door for Mari and hung up his phone, he was almost in tears, ready to confess to the sin of giving up completely and beg for her help to clean up his mess.

But Mari was not alone.

"Here," she said, shoving a leash into his hand. "Go sit on the couch while I go get shit from the car." She stood on her tiptoes and peered past his shoulder, her bright brown eyes inquisitive and judgy. "And it's exactly as bad as I knew it would be. Jesus, Milo, you couldn't have called me before it got this bad?"

"I didn't know it had gotten this bad," he said muzzily, staring at the creature on the end of the leash. Lean and muscular, with the head of a pit bull and the body of a... kind of stocky Chiweenie? The dog had short white-yellow hair with flat pit-bull eyes and Chihuahua ears.

She was staring at him quizzically from under a cat-eared headband.

"Mari?" he called to her as she hustled out to her sedan, which sat right behind his in the driveway. "What in the hell is this?"

"Your dog, Milo," she called back. "She's here to replace Chrysanthemum."

Milo glanced down at the unimpressed dog wearing the cat ears. "I don't remember asking for a dog," he told the dog. "I don't remember putting in an order."

The dog nuzzled his shin, and he bent down and fondled her ears. She gave him a tentative look of "like," and he fondled them some more, which is what he was doing when Mari hustled past him, her arms full of grocery bags—one of which was emanating a very... promising smell.

"Now sit down, Milo," she commanded. "I've got your breakfast—or lunch or last night's dinner...." She peered at the mess in the sink with a practiced eye and then squinted at the takeout containers in the living room. "Oh, Milo," she said with a sigh, "you haven't eaten in *days*, have you."

"Maybe three," he hazarded. He had a distant memory of somebody putting a sandwich in his hand as he sat at his desk during his one mandatory in-person appearance at work that week.

"Yeah," she sighed. "I'm sorry I was so late. Now sit down on the couch. I'll give you some food—you too, Julia—and we'll have a talk before we tackle this place."

Milo opened his mouth, and she said, "But in return you have to take a shower and brush your teeth."

"Okay," he said, cowed. He glanced down at the dog. "Julia?" he asked, and the dog didn't twitch a whisker.

"That's what the shelter named her," Mari said cheerfully, setting the bags down before getting to work doing something bustling and organizational. "My sister's roommate's brother called me up to ask me if I could adopt an animal, but, as you know—"

"You have the county allotment of cats," he said dutifully.

"I have *over* the county allotment of cats," she agreed. "Mostly because Georgie has snuck me a couple of extras." A ginormous breakfast burrito, with chorizo and hot sauce and about a dozen scrambled eggs wrapped inside with tater tots, appeared in his hand, and he doggedly munched while she went back to the kitchen.

Mari worked from home too, which gave her lots of time to clean cats and feed cats and make rugs and beds for cats and generally pour all the love in her formidable soul into the apparently *more* than five cats that had taken over her small house.

"Georgie?" he asked, lost already.

"Serena's roommate's brother, who is sort of a derpy hottie, and we may end up sleeping together," she told him bluntly. It was a trait that had cost her more than one boyfriend, but then, Milo knew none of those guys were good enough anyway.

"You have two more cats—" Oh Lord, this burrito was everything that was right with the world. Every word he said was through a mouthful of eggs.

"Three," she said. "He's got a thing for cats with one leg or no eyes or tails that have been chewed off. I'm telling you, if you can resist a cat with a chewed-off tail, you're a monster, and I want nothing to do with you."

"And yet," he said, watching as Julia—freed of her leash—was currently rolling in a pile of blankets that were possibly the only clean things in the duplex, "you didn't bring me a cat, which I know how to care for—"

"A"—she said, still bustling. He couldn't look at her anymore. She seemed to be simultaneously putting dishes in the dishwasher, cleaning up takeout containers, and stacking mail on his table—"cats need very little in the way of care. If I gave you a cat, you would feed the cat and let it crap on all your stuff and forget to feed yourself, and then when you died you'd be glad the cat survived on your eyeballs. No. A cat is not high enough maintenance for you right now."

"And B?" he asked, watching as Julia found one of Chrysanthemum's toys under the pile of blankets. Tentatively she shook it and was rewarded when it squeaked. Her eyes opened in joy, and she shook her head, squeaking it some more.

"Julia was found two weeks ago," Mari said, her voice getting a little lost among a clatter of kibble in a stainless-steel bowl.

Julia stopped her assault on the squeaky toy enough to trot into the kitchen, searching for the source of that familiar noise.

"So...?" He sounded dubious—and he was—but he still watched the creature to see if she would eat and drink from Chrysanthemum's bowls.

"See her tummy?" Mari said patiently, bending to fondle Julia's ears as she came to eat. "See the elongated nipples?"

Milo grimaced. "I didn't want to say anything in case it made her self-conscious."

"How very kind," Mari told him, and she may have rolled her eyes at him, but she was continuing to pet the dog, so Milo couldn't see. "But yeah. She'd had a litter, and she *mourned* her litter for her first week and a half, and Georgie said she was getting depressed, because maybe she got dumped because the puppies were cuter and everything she loved had just gotten, you know...."

"Yanked away," Milo said, suddenly desolate. Because that's what it had felt like when he'd gotten home that first week in August to find that Stuart had taken all his stuff, including his ugly table lamps and his weird art on the walls and the half-grown cat Milo had gotten them to celebrate their first anniversary three months earlier.

"Yeah," Mari told him, suddenly bending over the back of the couch to hug him. She dropped a kiss in his greasy hair, and his eyes were blurry for a whole other reason besides hunger. "Just like you," she said softly. "And that's why I brought her."

Milo took a gulp of air, hoping he could maybe not cry. "Why the cat ears?" he asked.

"Because you've never had a dog before," she told him. "I thought maybe they'd make it easier to adapt."

Milo nodded and felt another sob coming on. "Oh Jesus. Mari, can I go cry in the shower?" Because he *really* needed the shower.

"No," she said softly. "You acted so together in August. I should have known you weren't. You cry right here."

And he did, Mari's arms around his shoulders, until Julia, still crunching on kibble, jumped onto the couch and rested her chin on his knee.

EVENTUALLY MILO stilled, wiped his face on his filthy shirt, and managed to struggle up to excuse himself to the bathroom.

When he got there, he flushed the toilet (which helped with that awful smell) and scrounged up a towel that wasn't mildewy before jumping in the shower.

He had to wash his hair with hand soap because he was out of shampoo, but at least he still had toothpaste when he got out. His beard tended to be scraggly and patchy anyway, so the electric razor took care of that, but unfortunately all that self-care forced him to *look* in the mirror.

Ugh. No. His face was thin to the point of gauntness, his cheeks sunken, his eyes—which were usually an attractive almond-shaped brown—also sunken, his skin practically green.

Yeah, he wouldn't want to shag himself either.

Out in his kitchen he heard Mari, still clattering, and thought of how busy her life was, and how she'd taken a special day here to wade through his trash and do a wellness check on her jerk of a friend who had blown her off for a month.

At his door he heard a tentative scratching sound, and surprised, he opened it.

Julia was sitting there, staring up at him with those oddly shaped flat eyes, her cat ears still firmly in place. He couldn't tell if she was reproachful because he'd locked her out or irritated that he'd gone somewhere she hadn't, but something told him the two of them were now bound inextricably in the mutual endeavor to make sure Mari hadn't wasted her time.

"Well, old girl," he said softly, bending to scratch her behind the ears, "I think we're about to become a thing."

She snorted and walked toward his bedroom in a slow, stately gate unlike any Chihuahua or Chiweenie he'd ever met. He didn't even want to look to see what he had clean.

"OH MY God," Mari said when he emerged, carrying a load of laundry. "I can't... I can't even...."

"Bella Vista Broncos," Milo said grimly. "I swear to Christ, they're the only clean things in my drawers."

"Who keeps their gym clothes from high school?" she demanded. "Milo, you're *twenty-eight years old.*"

"They were almost the last things in the drawer," he said. "Everything else was from before my growth spurt in eleventh grade." He glanced down at his bright blue sweats, grimaced, and in a conspiratorial whisper, added, "I'm going commando."

Mari put her yellow-rubber-gloved hand over her eyes. "Oh my God."

He scowled defensively. "Remember those times in college when I carried you over my shoulder to your dorms?" he asked. "You've puked on my ass, Mari. *Puked on my ass.*"

She took her hand off her eyes and grinned at him. "That's my Milo," she said, and he could swear she had hearts in her eyes. "I knew you were here somewhere. Good. Now I've already got a load of your bathroom stuff in, so set that down on the washer and go through your bills. Jesus God, I can't even believe you held down a job in this mess."

Milo tried not to groan. "Well, God bless working from home," he said frankly before going through the connecting door to the garage and doing what she'd suggested with the laundry. When he'd climbed back up into the kitchen, he surveyed the mess again and let out a breath. "Believe it or not, I think I've gotten a few promotions."

"Aw, my poor little graphic artist," she chided. "Did you get all lost in your head to avoid your broken heart?"

"I'd tell you to go to hell," he said, although they both knew he wouldn't, not in a thousand years, "but...." He glanced around his duplex, thinking about the carefully chosen area rug and the leather furniture, the bright contrasting tiles on the floor, and the big holes in the wall where Stuart's hideous "art investments" had been.

"I don't know, baby," she said with a sniff. "You've been here for two months. How's the view from hell?"

"Boring," he said, thinking about the artwork. He had his own in the garage. He should put that on the walls tomorrow. He resolved to do that. By himself. "Lonely," he admitted, sitting at the table with a sigh. She shoved his empty recycling bin next to him in a helpful manner.

"You want some music?" she asked. "Or a movie for background noise?"

"The *Star Trek* reboots," he said promptly.

"Three comfort movies coming up," she said.

They knew the dialog by heart.

MARI COULDN'T stay over on his couch that night because, in her words, she had eight furry food-vacuums she had to care for. Apparently two of the new ones needed medication too.

But by the end of the day, he had clean clothes for a week and more in the laundry, a clean kitchen, a bedroom he could walk through, and groceries.

And a dog.

Julia had followed them both throughout the day, watching them with interested, calculating eyes, and accepting their shows of affection with a sort of genteel grace.

It wasn't until they sat down in the evening, both physically tired from cleaning and emotionally exhausted from hauling Milo inch by inch from the quagmire of his depression, that she showed any real personality at all.

"I'm sorry, Mari," Milo said as she leaned on him and they watched the sun set through his newly fluffed and aired curtains. "I didn't mean to suck up your time. You barely have enough as it is."

"Shut up," she mumbled, digging in. She wasn't tall or wide, but she had a sort of weight about her that was, he suspected, entirely muscle and determination. It probably didn't show up on a scale, but when she nestled, she *nestled.* "I should have seen it in August. I was busy, and God, Milo. You're such an easy-care friend most of the time. *I'm* the one who needed the trip to rehab in college. *I'm* the one who needed her hand held at the abortion clinic when Calvin the creep bailed on me. This isn't a sorry. It's not a you-owe-me. It's me being your Mari and you being my Milo, okay?"

He swallowed. "You'll always be my Mari," he whispered.

Stuart hated her. Milo remembered all the times he and Mari had met for lunch or gone to the movies, and Stuart hadn't known he'd been with his bestie. Had never suspected either. One or two cutting remarks about, "Your little phone-clerk friend," had made Milo simply... not involve Stuart in his life outside of Stuart. Thinking about it now, about how Stuart *hadn't* liked Mari, *hadn't* understood the two of them, their bond through high school and into college, through life changes and beyond—that should have clued him in, shouldn't it?

It wasn't even that Milo had lied, it was that Stuart had made him. Milo had *told* Stuart that he and Mari had come as a matched set, and Stuart had laughed and said sure, any friend of Milo's was a friend of his.

And then Stuart hadn't approved of her, had asked Milo to blow her off, had made whiny punkass bitch noises when Milo had said, "Okay, I'll hang out with her. You don't need to."

And Milo had found it very easy to not involve Stuart with this part of his life.

Which was ironic seeing that Milo's relationship with Mari had gotten so tight because that's exactly what Milo's parents had done to *Milo*. Just... just *not involved* themselves with Milo's life.

"We understand you feel compelled to live this lifestyle, Milo, but don't expect us to be involved in it."

So they hadn't met Stuart, hadn't approved of Mari either—something about her father working as a garage mechanic—and had mostly sent him birthday cards and invited him to Christmas dinners they'd been relieved he hadn't attended.

"Milo?" Mari said softly. "Why did Stuart leave? You never told me."

He sighed, remembering their last terrible fight when Stuart found out Milo had been giving money to help her keep her sister in a good care home for mentally ill adults since she'd first found the place.

"And I never will," he said now, holding her tighter. "It's not nearly as important as you coming here today."

She might have pressed the matter then—he knew it—but they both heard the noise at the same time.

"What the...?" Mari said, peering into the kitchen and frowning. "Julia, quit that with the dog bed. What are you...? Oh."

Milo looked too and was surprised.

"What does she have?"

Julia trotted back to the couch where they sat, very pleased with herself, and Mari started laughing.

"Oh," she said, clearly surprised. "It's... see, I got sort of a new-dog bundle? You've got a plastic container of food and a list of vet's appointments and a bed and blanket for her, and I put that cat toy she liked and a few other dog toys in the bed, and it was *under* some stuff, and she dug it out. Wow."

"Wow what?" he asked as Julia began to gnaw at the bright yellow, soft-plastic thing in her mouth, her movements getting more and more gleeful as it made more and more noise.

"I've never seen a dog that into the squeaky toy. I mean... *look* at her!"

Shake-shake-shake-shake-shake! She was growling and shaking, and then to Milo's delight, she rolled over to her back and pawed the air, the squeaky still squeaking as she indulged in an ecstasy of "kill the squeaky!"

"Julia," Milo said with authority. He'd never owned a dog, but he assumed they responded to their names. "Julia, come here. Give me the squeaky!"

She did.

Mari burst out laughing, holding her hand to her mouth. "Oh my God! Lookit her! Throw it!"

The living room had a little bit of length on it, but with a turn, he could get the thing down the hallway from where they were sitting. He put a bit of spin on the thing, and it bounced off the hardwood floor in erratic loops as Julia—

Vroom!

"Wow!" he laughed. "*Wow.* Julia, *wow!*"

She was *so* fast and muscular and happy and excited to chase that wobbly, oddly shaped squeaky piece of rubberized plastic. She brought it back to him, and he went to take it, but she growled playfully and shook her head. He tugged on it, and she tugged back, and in a moment they were wrestling over the squeaky toy like they'd been wrestling buddies their entire lives.

"C'mon," he begged. "C'mon, girl. Give it back. Give it—"

"Drop it!" Mari commanded with authority, and Julia let go immediately, then sat back on her haunches, gazing hungrily from the squeaky to Milo's face and back again.

Milo turned for the windup, Julia got into position like a race car, and he threw it again.

Their sad, tired conversation forgotten, Milo and Mari threw the squeaky toy to the joyful dog for the next hour, until she didn't bring the thing *back* but simply dropped it in the middle of the living room and stretched out at their feet.

"Wow," Milo said, staring at her.

"I'm saying," Mari echoed. "I-I mean, I had dogs all my life, but I've never seen one so... so *dedicated* to the squeaky toy."

Milo stared at her and smiled. "She's got a one-track mind," he admitted, but that was fine. He felt like he already knew this dog.

He felt like they could be friends.

MARI HAD to leave shortly thereafter, but not before they both ate leftovers and she wrote out a schedule for him so he could take care of the dog and then come back and work and then take care of the dog and himself some more.

"She's going to ruin your stuff," she warned. "She's going to chew on your coffee table, your shoes, your rugs, your furniture. You are going to have to figure out when to put her outside to poop in the backyard, but go out with her first or she might escape."

He held his hands to his heart. "Escape," he breathed. "But she just got here! I *want* her here. How do I stop that from happening?"

"Take her out on the leash at first," Mari said patiently, "then take her around and look for hazards. Where can she get out? Where's the dirt soft? Where are there gaps? She'll probably tell you where the worst ones are, but use your imagination. Pretend you're a dog whose sole obsession is a squeaky toy, and that uses up your walnut-sized brain."

"Oh...," he said uneasily. "Mari, my brain isn't much bigger."

She smacked him. "Oh my God, Milo. You are *so* much smarter than that. That's your problem. You could never *see* why you were better than Stuart on any given day. He never deserved you."

"He was rich, he was handsome, he was—"

"A fucking putz," she said viciously. "Stuart was a fucking putz. Screw him." She scowled. "He was your first big relationship postcollege, and I get it. He was your Calvin."

Milo scowled back. "I still maintain that man would have looked a lot better with a price on his head."

She nodded, her short black curls dancing around strong features and snapping brown eyes. "*Now* you're seeing my side of the Stuart equation." She stood on tiptoes to kiss him on the cheek, and because she was Mari, she didn't bother to wipe her lipstick. That was her claim to Milo right there. He was hers for life.

Then she was gone, leaving him alone with Julia, who stared at him with the same sort of interest he was showing her.

"You ready to explore the backyard?" he asked dubiously, but when he picked her leash up from the kitchen chair, she trotted right to his feet, ready to do just that. He grabbed a roll of poop bags and headed for the sliding glass door, ready to embark on his new adventure.

Stuart, he thought grimly, would have *hated* this dog.

He was pretty sure he loved her already.

A WEEK LATER, he knew he did—although he was also sure she was trying to kill him.

Following Mari's carefully made schedule, he'd been taking her walking at the nearby park in the morning. The first day he'd had to stop every ten feet because apparently your body didn't forgive you for going to bed for two months and not getting up. The second day he'd hurt even more, but by the third he'd figured out that Julia had a… glitch.

She was fine, sort of. She didn't mind the leash, but she didn't understand it. She'd race behind him to sniff from the retaining wall to the grass or to scope out what was on the side of the walkway that looped around the park. Once she'd almost castrated him when she'd been behind him—and he'd had his arm behind his shoulder to accommodate that—and she'd seen a squirrel cross his path on the walk.

And then right when he thought he had a handle on how to get her to walk by his side, the leash would fall gently across her posterior, and she'd stop. Just stop, like a game of freeze tag with rules only she knew.

Milo tripped on her once and went sprawling, and she'd huddled abjectly under the leash, looking like she expected him to *whip* her with it.

He'd sat in the middle of the sidewalk and pet her until she stopped shaking, and then, unmindful of the blood on his palms or the holes in his old high school sweats, he'd picked her up and carried her the rest of the way.

So he was a little desperate the next day. For one thing, he wouldn't be able to take her walking the day after. It was the in-house day at his ad firm, and while he'd bought a sort of dog box and put a dog bed in it, which she seemed to take comfort in when he was home and could leave the door open, he wasn't sure she'd be so comfortable locked in the thing for an eight-hour day. He was contemplating barricading her in the kitchen with the dog-box cage thingy so she could maybe do less damage to the couch and the coffee table, but he still didn't like the idea of leaving her alone. Should he maybe leave the television on?

So whatever he was going to do, he needed to make sure *today* was a good day. Which was why, as he walked around the completely empty park, he had an idea. He took her to the middle of one of the soccer fields first, hoping that if this went horribly wrong, he'd be able to get a head of steam on her and body tackle her if he needed to.

Then he unhooked her lead.

She sat there untroubled and gazed at him, waiting for further instructions.

Then he wandered down toward the walkway, and she… well, wandered with him. She was fine. She'd run up ahead a little, then stop and smell the flowers or the sticks or the other dog's pee, and then wait for him to catch up. It was… *pleasant*. It was *blissful*. She was *so good*.

And then the most magnificent thing happened. The park had several sections, all of which were looped by the walking/riding path. He and Julia wandered the whole of the loop, from a rise on which picnic tables and bathrooms and a child's play area were set up, down past the soccer field, around a little wooded area, and around and back up the rise. On the other side of the rise was another soccer field, bracketed by a tennis/pickleball area way down the parking lot.

On this day as the sun leveled itself on the misty October field, Milo topped the rise by the picnic area and was confronted with, of all things, *turkeys*. A good two dozen of them!

At first he was amused. Oh my God, lookit the lot of them! Then he was horrified. Oh no, Julia!

Frantically he grabbed for her collar as she buzzed past his shins and onto that calm, strangely bucolic field of oblivious wild birds.

"Julia!" he called frantically, charging after her. Oh no! She'd eat them! Or they'd eat her! Or—oh God, oh—

"Oh my stars," he breathed. "Lookit you *go*!"

She never caught one. She wasn't even trying. She just raced from turkey to turkey, barking until the birds scattered, running from one end of the field to the other. She was so *happy*!

Milo stood, helpless to stop her, and watched a creature absolutely in her element, and while he *should* have felt bad for the turkeys, all he could think was that his dog was happy. *So* happy.

Without warning, a laugh snuck up his body, shaking his stomach until it ached, and he *howled* with it, feeling as happy and as free as his idiot dog—and for all he knew, as the turkeys, who once they stopped running, didn't seem particularly bothered by her.

He laughed until she slowed down and trotted to his side, panting happily. He put the lead back on her, a day late and a dollar short, perhaps. But still….

He'd forgotten how drunk you could get, how intoxicated, how shitfaced silly and oblivious, all by another creature's joy.

The Chad

GARTH POTTER leaned against the front of his truck and used the scooper thingy of his Chuckit to pick up the ball at his feet.

"Alrighty, Chad," he told his giant furry friend, "You ready for one last chase?"

Chad gave the sad eyes—but then given his heritage, sad eyes were pretty much his specialty.

"Two?" Garth asked, winding up for the toss before letting loose with a good, long chuck. He could get some distance with the Chuckit, but then, Chad had a twelve-foot stride when he was running full out. Great Dane mixed with Rottweiler and some mastiff, Garth suspected, glad for the short hair and hybrid vigor. Pure bred dogs this big often ended up with hip problems and sore joints way too early, but Chad was six years old and going strong.

But part of that might have been that Chad lived a *very* active life, accompanying Garth in his landscaping business. Anybody who hired Garth had to hire Chad too. The big doofus traveled with him from job to job. In the summer Garth gave him his blanket and a bowl of water, tying him up in the shade if the job was in the front yard or letting him roam if it was an enclosed backyard. Chad was the mellowest dog Garth had ever met. He'd been assaulted by little tiny yappy things on nearly a daily basis, and mostly he just ambled away. When he was extremely irritated, he put his paw on top of the thing's head and let it go when it stopped making noise. Give Chad and nearly any dog a chance, and they could be friends.

Garth was a lot pickier about his friends, which was kind of why he was leaning against the truck's hood and pensively throwing his dog the ball in the cold of this frigidly gray October day.

What *was* it with this day anyway? He stared at the sky unhappily. Usually this part of California had brilliant hot and golden falls that didn't taper off into drizzle and sadness until November, if then. But not today. Today hadn't dawned, it had gray-scaled through the window of his house—his parents' old house—and his mood with it.

God, he needed to get laid.

Normally that wasn't a problem. He wasn't vain. He knew tanned muscles and sunbleached brown hair weren't exactly man-repellent, and he'd developed an easy way of talking to people since he'd taken over his father's landscaping business. And yes, he *had* enacted the famous porn scenario of "Hello, blue collar worker, would you like to come inside for a glass of lemonade?" more than once without... well, there had been a couple of regrets. He'd started to ask, for instance, if there was a husband or boyfriend lurking about when the initial seduction began, particularly one who paid the bills. He was trying to run a business, dammit, and trading a job for a blowjob did *not* help one damned bit.

Besides, it was sleazy.

He enjoyed a little bit of no-strings sex as much as the next guy, but being someone's sidepiece was... well, demeaning.

So he hadn't done it for a while, and while he'd felt better for it, particularly in the self-respect department, he'd also started to feel...

A little like this day. Depressed and gray scale and not at all like his usual warm October self.

Of course Chad did help warm him up. The big doofus's long-limbed lope gave him a grace that a dog as big as Chad didn't usually possess, and watching him chase after the ball was a joy. And it was always nice when the park was empty, the big soccer fields on either side of the picnic rise vacant and waiting for a dog to enjoy all that space.

Garth frowned when he heard the shrill barking of a smaller dog and wondered where it was. Poor Chad. Garth tried to shield his awkward friend from all those intrusive yappers, but some people... oh hell.

Up over the picnic rise, a small, muscular blond bullet of a dog was stretching out gracefully, charging toward Chad like she was a torpedo and he was an awkward submarine.

Chad kept loping, because hey, there was a *ball* involved, and suddenly the dog was upon him, bigger than a Chihuahua but smaller than a real dog, her bark hysterical and fierce, and Garth was worried that Chad might react—or get hurt.

Shit! Where was this dog's owner? What kind of asshole let his dog get loose in a park without a leash when—

"*Julia*!" came a frantic cry, and Garth's attention was jerked back to the crest of a hill where a thin, fey figure in faded pajama pants and an old high school sweatshirt was running, elbows flopping crazily, spider legs churning like a drunken cartoon character's as he spun down the hill heading for the snarling blond dog. "*Julia!*" he cried again. "You leave that good dog alone! He is *not* a turkey!"

Garth would have wondered at that, but Chad had actually stopped his run and was analyzing the idiot creature with a bewildered expression on his long-schnozzed, jowly face. Garth's urgency to defend his dog doubled when Chad put his paw on the smaller dog's head and pulled out his last resort.

He woofed.

As a rule of thumb, a 120-pound dog has a 360-pound woof.

The little blond bullet let out a shriek and a snarl and went running right back up the hill. With a whimper she bounded right into the arms of her fey owner, who was likely not expecting an armload of titanic small dog and got clocked in the chin, sat abruptly on his ass, and held on to her, shaking.

"Julia," he ordered, sounding more woebegone than he had a right to considering his stupid dog had attacked The Chad and was now snarling in his arms, trying to get back into the fray. "No!"

To Garth's immense relief, the ragamuffin elf produced a leash, which he latched on to his dog's collar, and then—almost instinctively—he cupped his hand over the dog's nape.

"*Julia*!" he snapped, his voice assuming an authority Garth hadn't seen before. "I said *leave it*!"

To Garth's surprise, the dog subsided, a low growling emanating from her throat but with no physical attempts to defy her person's command.

Once the dog was in control, the ragamuffin elf, still sitting on the ground, glanced up and took the situation in with a sort of despair that actually wrenched at Garth's heart.

"I'm sorry," he croaked. "I'm sorry. I'm so sorry. You were just doing your thing, and my stupid dog comes roaring down here. I'm sorry. I should have checked. See, last time it was turkeys, and she... and she went bowling for the dumb birds, and she was so happy, and they scattered, and she frolicked, and I hadn't seen anybody frolic for so long, and... and it was wrong, but she was *so happy*. And then I looked up, and...."

The elf did something surprising then that sort of made Garth forgive him on the spot. "Oh, you good big dog. I'm so sorry. She's small and afraid, and she's been abandoned, and I shouldn't have let her come bother you. You poor good boy. Don't be so sad. This was not your fault." At his monologue, Julia-the-blond-bullet had calmed down enough to *glare* at Chad, and Chad contented himself with searching for the ball, which had been the object of this whole encounter in the first place.

Garth had to shake himself to answer. "Don't worry about it," he said, striding forward to offer his hand to the man—who at second glance was not as young as he'd first appeared. "He always looks sad. I think it's a breed specialty."

The elf squinted up at him through a truly stunning pair of brown eyes set in a delicate face with wide cheekbones and a point of a chin. "What breed is he?" he asked, blinking rapidly when he realized Garth was offering him a hand up. "And thank you, but I don't want Julia to growl at you. She…." He frowned at her. "She gets weirdly protective."

Garth laughed a little and stepped back, giving them room so the elf could scramble to his feet, the dog at his heels.

"You haven't had her long," he said, and it wasn't a guess. Everything about this encounter indicated a new pet/owner relationship.

"No." The elf stood up and dusted fruitlessly at his ass, turning around in a circle, the dog following curiously, as he tried to get a gander at his own bum.

"It's wet," Garth confirmed. "The grass was pretty dewy this morning."

The elf's sigh was heartfelt. "Figures," his new friend grumbled. He glanced back up at Garth. "I'm sorry," he said again. "I'm really sorry. I've imposed on your time too much."

But Garth was reluctant to let this new, interesting friend go. While the day remained cloudy, there seemed to be a bright spot of sunshine right over the rather fragile, spider-legged creature who, while not *great* at pet ownership, appeared to want to improve.

"Wait," he said. "What did you mean by 'bowling for turkeys'?"

The other man blinked. "Uhm… well, see, I'd never walked a dog before," he confessed rather nakedly. "And our first times out, she'd stop every time the leash fell across her butt. It was…." He swallowed and gazed at Garth beseechingly. "She almost killed me at least thirteen times, you understand. And I knew she knew her name—she comes in when I call her from the backyard. But… you saw her run." He gave a wistful smile. "She's so fast. She *really* loves to run fast. So there wasn't anybody here, and I let her off the lead, and she came over the hill, and there were all these… you know. Turkeys. Wild turkeys."

Garth could see it. The turkeys were a neighborhood hazard… erm, feature. They nested in parks and vacant lots and then wandered around neighborhoods crapping on rooftops and driveways and front lawns. He looked at Julia, who contrary to her early aggressiveness, was sticking to her person's heels with a rather touching display of solidarity.

"She chased them," Garth said, laughing a little.

"*Nyeeeeerrrrrrrrrrrrow boom!*" Julia's owner held out his arms and did an impressive impersonation of a dive bomber taking out feathered enemies. "It was *so* exciting. I mean, I was terrified, because, you know. If she was any smaller, they'd be velociraptors, and any bigger, they'd be lunch. But all she did was chase them and watch them scatter and…." He smiled wistfully, as though he would never capture this moment again. "Went bowling, like she was the ball and they were the pins. She was so happy," he said apologetically. "I'm sorry. That's probably terrible of me. I just…." He swallowed. "I guess I needed to see somebody happy, you know? But not if she's going to come after your dog. I'll keep her on the leash from now on."

Garth's smile twisted. "But won't she kill you?" he teased softly.

There was a delicate, heartbreaking shrug. "At least it will look like an accident," Julia's owner said.

And now it was Garth's *heart* that twisted. He stuck out his hand and said, "I'm Garth Potter. And—" He indicated his dog, who with impeccable timing had brought him the ball. "—this is Chad. Sometimes *The* Chad, mostly just Chad. Would you like us to walk you around the loop again, and maybe we can see if we can get Julia used to the leash… and other dogs."

"But what if she snarls?" the other man said, and then belatedly he took Garth's hand and shook, his grip firmer than Garth expected. "Milo. Milo Tanaka. I'm sorry. She sounded so terrifying. I was so afraid she'd hurt your dog, and then your dog would defend himself and…." He grimaced. "I mean, he could, uhm, snort her like a bump of coke."

Garth snickered at the image and batted Chad away as he nuzzled Garth's hand with the ball. "He doesn't do Chihuahua anymore," he said with a straight face. "The high doesn't last that long, and the comedown is awful."

Milo—and it was such an appropriate name—laughed softly back. "Terrible analogy, I know," he conceded. "I'm just saying, the heart attack I had when she was going after him…." He shook his head. "I have so much to learn."

"Well, come on," Garth said, reaching to the top of his truck where Chad's lead sat. "Chad's had enough excitement for one day, and I've got half an hour before my next appointment. That's fifteen minutes to walk with you and ten minutes to get there."

"What about the other five?" Milo asked.

"Coffee and a Pup Cup," Garth said seriously "What else?"

"What's a Pup Cup?" Milo asked, and Garth felt his chuckle come from deep in his belly.

"Oh boy, do you have some things to learn."

Milo blinked at him, looking dismayed again, and Garth gentled his expression, not wanting to scare his fey, elfin little friend away.

"Don't worry, Milo. Most of it is good. You've learned the hard stuff—use a lead unless you're at a small dog play park, no more bowling for turkeys, and no bowling for Chads either—it freaks him out."

"Small dog play park?" Milo asked, sounding bewildered. "Are there, like, swings and stuff?"

Garth hooked Chad's lead and then gently took Milo's elbow. "Come along, Milo. We've got fifteen minutes for you to ask me all the questions you want."

As he steered his new friend up the grassy rise to the walkway that looped around the park, he thought he could see the barest hint of sun peeking out.

BY THE time they'd walked half the loop—because Julia *did* stop every time the leash even touched her backside, and they had to work at making the leash shorter so she stuck directly to Milo's heels—Garth almost wouldn't have enough time to stop for coffee, but being late would have been worth it.

Milo was every bit as shy as he'd appeared at first glance, but he was also every bit as funny. In addition to "bowling for turkeys" and the drug of choice for giant dogs, Milo also talked about how dogs checked up on the pee wall—erm, the *retaining wall* that most of the dogs used as a urinal—to see how their friends were doing.

"That spot right there," he'd say seriously. "There is a *very* popular dog who pees right there under the rose bush."

"Lots of comments?" Garth asked, smiling. Chad was taking advantage of Julia's fixation with that spot to huff the same area, and Julia gave him nervous side-eye while they enjoyed the nuanced bouquet of some strange dog's pee.

"That dog's *been* places," Milo confirmed before giving Julia's lead a gentle tug. "Come *on*," he ordered. "We can't take forever here."

"So are you walking her before work? After work? During lunch?" Garth asked, none too subtly.

"I work from home four days a week," Milo said. "This is our midmorning break. Or at least that's what I'm trying to make it." He shook his head. "I need to get some of her energy out or she'll break me by bringing me the squeaky."

"Have you tried throwing the squeaky to her on the soccer field?" Garth asked. It seemed like that would have been the perfect solution.

But Milo's face got this bewildered, irritated expression, and he shook his head. "She… she *refuses* to fetch the squeaky in the park," he said.

"How dare she!" Garth replied, and Milo nodded his head without the slightest bit of play.

"It's *infuriating*. In the house she'll chase the ball until my arms fall off, and I'm ambidextrous. I'm throwing with both hands for a good half hour, and she's still ready to go. But outside, when I can *really* wind up?"

"No dice?" Garth asked.

"Apparently she only likes clean balls," Milo said with a completely straight face—and a fair amount of indignation.

Garth didn't have such luck. "Well, she's a very wise woman," he chortled and saw when Milo got the joke as a flush washed from his neck to the roots of his hair.

"Oh God," he murmured faintly. "I said that. I actually said she won't lick dirty balls."

Garth laughed some more. "That's not what you said at *first*, but not what you just said *now*!"

Milo moaned faintly, covered his eyes with his hand, and in doing so, inadvertently laid the leash gently across Julia's backside. She stopped, and he tripped on her and almost went sprawling, and if Garth hadn't saved him with a hand under his elbow, the damned dog *might* have succeeded in killing Milo and making it look like an accident.

"Easy there," Garth murmured, pleased when Milo didn't jerk away. While Garth didn't usually succumb to stereotypes, his onboard gaydar was gleefully broadcasting that Milo was very much his type.

But his other instincts, which were usually as finely honed as Chad's gentle-giant techniques for deescalating conflict, also told him that Milo was wounded—had been wounded for quite some time—and like Chad, Garth knew that you had to treat wounded creatures with care.

"God, I'm a mess," Milo muttered. He'd taken his hand from his eyes and was adjusting the leash again so Julia could trot at his side in rhythm. "I usually deal very well with my fellow humans, I swear."

"No worries," Garth told him, and then, surveying his outfit again, said, "I take it you don't get out much these days?"

Milo groaned. "No... no. I mean, my once-a-week staff meeting in person, but yeah. Until last week I was ordering my groceries in, and DoorDash was my friend, and...." He shook his head. "This is week one of plan 'get Milo out of the house and make him take care of something so he will take care of himself' month. I owe my bestie a full report on Friday, so when I was getting lost in work and Julia was worrying my pantleg, I sort of gave a squawk and grabbed my wallet, keys, phone and the leash and ran out of the house." He shook his leash handle, which had an attachment to hold his poop bags as well as some hand sanitizer and even a little bowl for water. "It's a good thing my bestie set me up for emergency exits, or I would have committed one more dog sin about five minutes before Julia rounded that hill."

"That's a bestie," Garth said. He pulled out some of the mailing wraps he'd saved, which had thicker plastic and holes big enough to fit his own massive, battered paws. "I'm afraid The Chad needs a bigger receptable."

"Yikes!" Milo squeaked. "Your dog pretty much craps bigger than my entire dog."

"Yeah," Garth agreed, "but he's big in spirit too, so that's okay."

While Milo was struggling with Julia and the leash—and Julia's desire to go places *other* than right next to Milo's left foot—Chad stayed on his eight-foot leash with a stately, measured pace that gave Garth lots of room to maneuver.

And lots of room to short leash his dog if Chad got crazy for some reason and decided to chase squirrels, which he'd never ever done before. But given the dog weighed almost as much as Milo, Garth was prepared for any eventuality.

"So," Garth continued, when it looked like Milo might not trip and die in the next few feet, "you weren't getting out of the house?" It was the most delicate way he could phrase it. Obviously this kid wasn't getting out of the house. He was pretty much a menace to himself.

"Bad breakup," Milo said miserably. Garth caught his little side-eye, like he was expecting some sort of blowback from that.

But Garth felt that one in his gut. "Ugh. I had one of those once," he confessed. "Right out of college. My dad took me for a drive, and I ended up working on one of his landscaping jobs." He shook his head. "Spent four years in school trying to be an engineer. Lost weight, drank way too much, got my BS, got dumped, and the happiest I ever was, I was shifting rock next to my father in one-hundred-degree heat." He shrugged. "Took over the business, and when my folks retired, I took over their house."

"Still happy?" Milo asked, and his voice sounded tremulous, like he was reaching for hope.

"So far," Garth told him, that morning's grayness forgotten.

"Win," Milo said, and now *he* sounded happy. "Oops!" Julia had stopped again but with a little hop and some flailing, Milo jumped over the leash and landed on his feet.

When he was stable, he let out a laugh and threw Garth a smile over his shoulder that melted Garth's soul into a golden puddle that surrounded his heart and seeped through his skin while a perfect chord vibrated through the heavens.

Garth swallowed.

Oh.

GARTH HAD his equilibrium back—mostly—by the time they'd finished the loop, and Garth watched as Milo opened the door of his small royal-blue Toyota and told Julia to hop in the car, which she did.

"Thank you for walking with me," Milo said, but his eyes still held some of the anxiety that had flooded them right after Julia had gone bowling for turkeys and had bowled into Chad instead. "I'm still so sorry about my dog—"

"Not at all," Garth said, mind scrambling for ways to make sure they met up again. "I'm here a lot in the morning. There's practically nobody here around this time."

Milo nodded. "Maybe I'll see you—"

Oh no. Not maybe. "Here," Garth said. "Give me your phone."

Milo pulled it out of his pocket—he had a *Bloodborne* phone cover, which made Garth smile because *of course* he was a gamer—and handed it over, blinking as if completely surprised to be doing such a thing.

"Okay," Garth said, typing in his number and then calling himself, "I will text you tomorrow right before I leave and meet you back here. Right here. Maybe we can see if Julia and Chad chill with more familiarity."

"You mean if Julia chills," Milo said, and Garth held the phone up for a selfie and grinned while he clicked it.

"How long have you had her?" he asked, to clarify as he gave the phone back.

"Two weeks," Milo said.

"And when did your boyfriend leave?" Garth asked, taking a risk.

"Beginning of August?" Milo answered, staring at him in surprise. "How did you know that?"

Garth winked, although his heart broke a little, because he knew that wasn't quite long enough. That's okay. Garth could wait for it to be long enough. He was patient like that.

"Because hurt and heartbreak take time to overcome," he said gently. "She lost her family and then found herself at your place. Let her get comfortable."

"But... but... but... the boyfriend?" Milo asked, his ears turning red.

Garth couldn't help it. He reached out and brushed the top of one of the ears protruding a bit from the straight, raggedly-cut dark brown hair.

"I know the signs," he said, remembering his own woebegone face in the mirror the summer after he graduated. "Take care of your dog, Milo. Take care of yourself." He gave a gentle smile. "I'll text you tomorrow."

And with that he whistled for Chad. Now that Julia was safely stowed in the little-mobile Milo drove, Chad was safe to amble on the soccer field, whuffling the dewy grass until they came to the truck with the Chuckit and the ball on the hood.

Chad didn't whimper, but his eyes went to the Chuckit as though he hadn't spent an entire half hour out there chasing the damned thing before Julia arrived.

Garth took in that look and checked his phone. Skip coffee or.... Quickly he texted his new client, asking if he could bring some coffee to make up for being five minutes late. He got a heart-eye emoji in return and figured since his phone showed Mrs. Parcival, he would *not* be obligated to do anything untoward to repay the client's graciousness.

"Okay," he said to Chad. "One more time."

Recovering Zombie

"OH GOD, Mari," Milo moaned over the phone. "It was so embarrassing!"

"Which part?" Mari asked, obviously amused. "The part where your small idiot dog tried to *eat* his giant Daniff, or the part where you had to confess you had her bowling for turkeys all last week?"

"I didn't tell him I did it for a week," Milo mumbled. "It was bad enough she *attacked another dog*, and I was the idiot who let her off lead! And she sounded *ferocious*—I wanted to check the other dog over for, like, giant rips in his skin, and all I could think about was how I'd fucked up *again*!" His voice rose in a wail, and he wanted to lash out at something, but Julia was sitting at his feet, the squeaky in her mouth, waiting for him to do his job.

He threw the squeaky, and she was happy.

"Did you know dogs were a paradox when you brought her to me?" he asked Mari suspiciously, and Mari's grunt indicated she, too, was invested in animal maintenance on her end of the line.

"No," Mariana said thoughtfully. "But listening to your stories is almost as good as being there. How did you fuck up?"

"I just told you," he muttered. "Julia, bring the ball *to me*. No, no, do *not* drop it halfway down the hall and then come stare at me. It's not… okay. Fine. I'll go get it. God."

He threw the ball—because she'd apparently misplaced her last rubber squeaky toy so there were only these fuzzy pretend tennis balls that also squeaked—out his office door, ricocheting it off the wall so it would go farther down the hall.

He was getting pretty good at that, but he was also wondering how to get rid of the scuff mark left on the paint from the many, many times he'd already done it.

"You shouldn't have let her chase turkeys," Mariana confirmed, "but your motives were pure. And now you know what can happen if there are *no* turkeys on the turkey field and other dogs instead. I mean, she's going to have to learn how to follow the lead sometime, Milo. This is not a tragedy."

"No," he admitted. "But I'm trying to get my shit together, and I was just letting my dog run wild, and now——"

"Honey," she said in that voice that had gotten him to chill for the last fifteen years, "lookit you. You are getting up, eating, going to the store, taking the dog for walks. You're making all these strides into being a real boy. You screwed up. We all do. Keep your dog on a leash, be glad she didn't attack a dog who would rip her face off, and let it go."

"Why do you think she was so mad at him?" he asked miserably.

"I got no idea," Mari told him. "It's weird. But maybe she hasn't been well socialized. She gets weird in your living room when it's clean. Maybe we should buy her a crate——"

"Like a milk crate?" he asked, confused.

"No, like a dog crate. It's basically a box that dogs sleep in. Where's she been sleeping so far?"

"My bed," he said, fondling her ears as she sniffed about his feet for another lost toy. "Under the covers. She likes it there. But we already have one of those dog boxes. We keep it in the kitchen. She likes it. She goes in when the door is open and mulls. It's her thinking place."

Mari snorted.

"What?" he asked defensively.

"You're just really attached to that dog."

"She seems to like me," he told Mari. "I… you know. Besides you, there's not a lot of that going around."

"Oh, baby," Mari said gently. "You absolutely can*not* use Stuart *or* your parents as an example. You realize that, right?"

"I'm not so good at making friends," Milo told her, as though this was a confession of huge proportions.

"Milo…." She sounded pained. "What part of that is supposed to surprise me?"

He sighed. He'd been shy in high school, huddling deep in the fallacy that he was a lone wolf purely through his own devices until Mari had tumbled into his life—and his locker—with her usual force.

As in she'd plowed her way through the hallway at passing period to glare at him.

"*You*," she'd accused, as he carefully put his English notebook *in* his locker and pulled out his math textbook and the notebook that went with it, "don't have a locker buddy."

He'd stared at her, a diminutive powerhouse with a strong chin, a bold nose, and a lot of dyed blond hair piled high on top of her black roots in a fashionable messy bun. He had her in homeroom and art but couldn't remember her name. "Nobody wanted me," he blurted, not realizing how pathetic that sounded until it cleared his lips and settled in the air.

She'd stared back. "Your locker is pristine. I've seen messier libraries," she told him. "Scooch over. I'm taking bottom bunk."

"But—"

She'd glared *up* at him with snapping black eyes, because she had already reached her full growth at five feet four inches, and he'd already been on his way to five foot ten. "Milo Tanaka," she said, and she'd won the battle right then—they both knew it. "You are honestly going to tell me that having no friends at all is better than having me as your locker buddy?"

"No," he said in a small voice. "No, I'm just... you know. Surprised."

She'd nodded sagely. "I was too when I saw that sketch you did of the fountain in front of the school, with all the students' faces in it and the branches overhead. It was fucking haunting. I've been trying to write a story for it for a week. You're going to help me, right?"

He'd smiled a little. "Here," he said. "Put your big binders on the bottom with mine and your books flat on the top, here, and the notebooks will fit in the side."

"We," she said distinctly, "are going to be *fabulous*."

And they had been, pretty much from that moment on.

"I mean," he said, back in the present, "I thought, you know, I would have grown into more friends by now."

She laughed and then coughed, and Milo's antennae went waving in overtime.

"Are you okay? Are you sick? Are you getting sick?"

"Oh my God!" She coughed again. "No! I'm fine! I mean, a little under the weather—"

"Soup," he said, plonking onto the stool at his standing desk with sudden panic. "You can't get sick, Mari. You—"

He heard a sudden gulping sound, probably as she downed water like an Olympic sprinter after a dash, and then a deep breath. "Calm. Down. Milo. No. I'm fine. I'm not dying right now, I swear."

He let out a breath. "Sorry," he said, although he wasn't really. Mari had given him so much as a friend, but she'd also given him some big scares. Her breakup from Calvin had resulted in the drinking and the trip to the women's health clinic and the accidental overdose and the trip to rehab and the subsequent trip to the mental health facility until Mari had, in her words, gotten over herself and gotten her shit together.

She'd had to. Milo had sobbed on her after the overdose. He'd been the one to find her, seizing in her bedroom, and he'd been the one to call 911, and then when she'd been in the hospital, he'd been the only one to visit, because her sister hadn't been able to deal, and their parents had pretty much checked out of their lives when they'd been in high school.

He and Serena depended on her, dammit. She *had* to get her shit together. There was no functioning without her.

And she had. And while their friendship had been set in stone before then, now they were part of each other's molecular DNA. If she so much as had a hangnail, he was suddenly transported to those terrible months in college when he was at her dorm every day, and if he got a call from her number, he was never sure if it was because she wanted pizza after class or if her roommate needed his help getting her to crawl out from under her bed.

After Stuart left, he'd had nightmares that she'd been grievously ill and at the far end of a long tunnel, and he couldn't get to her.

There were only certain people in your life who could show up at your house with a dog and say, "Get the fuck out of bed and live, asshole," and Mari was one of them, but that kind of friendship didn't come without its price, and Mari and Milo's price was that if she so much as choked on her water, Milo was pretty sure she was dying.

"No worries," she answered dryly. "But it's my turn to freak out over you. Are you going to see the handsome Daniff owner again, or was this a one-time magical encounter at the park?"

"Why do you keep calling Chad a Daniff?" he asked, not wanting to answer her question.

"Because that's what you *call* a Great Dane/mastiff mix," she said. "That is, if it doesn't eat your city and establish a name for itself on the monster circuit."

"But he said Chad was also part Rottweiler," Milo told her conscientiously. "So that would make him—"

"A RottDaneroff?" she quipped, using a *bad* German accent so it sounded like *Götterdämmerung* except in dog breeds.

He gaped for a moment, tempted to hang up on her on general principle. "That's terrible," he choked finally. "That's a terrible pun, and you're going to writer hell for that!"

"Oh no," she said. "I'm going to writer hell for the *Twilight* fanfic I wrote in high school, but *that* pun is gonna get five to ten off my sentence!"

"You never let me read your *Twilight* fanfic," he complained, stung. "Was it Jacob/Edward?"

"Yes," she told him. "And I didn't show it to you because I didn't want you to feel fetishized."

Milo snorted. "You didn't want me to read it because you didn't know what an actual penis was until college, and you didn't want me to give you notes."

She howled in outrage, and he laughed, delighted because he couldn't usually score points on her like that.

And then she returned to her original topic and he was stuck having to give an honest answer.

"Well, he's going to text me in the morning," he admitted.

"Like, before twelve?" she asked, and he could hear the horrified fascination in her voice—and he approved. Unless it was his on-campus-meeting day, he usually didn't clear the bedroom until eleven at the earliest.

"Julia needs me to let her out by eight," he admitted. The first two days he hadn't known this, and his reward had been a rather pungent reminder left in front of the sliding glass door to the backyard—and Julia's flat-eyed reproach. Apparently pooping in the house offended her dignity, and he'd responded to *that* more than the cleanup, because he felt like she was sort of a dignified creature for all her weird size and her elongated nipples, and he felt deeply that *all* creatures should have their dignity.

"Ooh…," Mari replied. "So you're going to start living human hours and not vampire hours. *Fascinating*."

"Listen," he said firmly, "I don't know anything about dogs, and he seems to be able to control one who weighs more than you do. He has things to teach me, that's all."

"Really," she replied, and he sensed another barb coming on. "A man who has had two adult relationships in his entire life needs to learn things?"

Ouch. "I don't count whatshisface as an adult relationship," he muttered, talking about his first boyfriend in college, who pretty much held Milo's head on his cock until he came and then went ghost.

"I didn't either," Mari scoffed. "I'm talking me, Milo. You've had Stuart and you've had me. No, we're not a couple, but I'm pretty much the only other adult you know."

Milo let out a breath. "How am I supposed to know the people at my office?" he whined. "I only see them once a week."

"Then ask them out to lunch once a week," she chided. Her voice softened. "Come on, Milo. Look at what you've done with Julia in two weeks. You've taken her outside, you've made mistakes, you've met a cute guy who hit on you—"

"He said I wasn't ready," Milo told her, trying not to nurse the hurt.

"Oh my God—you found a *perfect* guy who hit on you and then wants to be your friend. Think about what you could do in the world of adult relationships if you set your mind to it."

"I'm fine," he said.

"No, you're not," she badgered. "Milo, come on. For me?"

"But what if all the other people become noise?" he asked, feeling a little desperate, "and I can't hear you if you need me?"

He heard her suck in a breath and wondered if he'd just made her mad. "Oh, Milo," she said after a moment. "My God. You must be raw. That's... that's some honesty right there."

Milo tried not to whimper. "It's been a rough couple of months," he admitted. Julia must have heard something in his voice, because she glanced up from the pink-and-violet dog bed he'd bought for her in that first week. She had several beds—one for each room where he went, including the one in the crate that he kept in the kitchen—and she would follow him from room to room. Should he decide to stay in one, she would curl up, often worrying a squeaky, and watch him warily, as though trying to determine if he could be trusted.

He had to go into the office in two days, and he was starting to think he might have to take her with him.

"SO WHAT would happen if you did?" Garth asked the next morning, his long-boned, athletic body uncoiling as he let loose another ball for Chad.

Julia sat at Milo's feet, keeping up a perpetual low growl that Garth insisted was good for her. It would wear her out, he said, and she'd eventually get used to Chad's company. All Milo had to do was keep a good hold on her leash and let her know he wouldn't tolerate any funny business.

Milo watched Garth's body move again under a hooded sweatshirt and battered jeans, enjoyed the way his tanned face seemed to glow as he smiled at his giant dog in action, heard his *very* deep voice as he urged Chad on, and had a passing thought that there was some funny business Milo wouldn't mind in the least.

Then he drew his attention back to the matter at hand.

"I don't know," he said nervously. "I mean, she seems to have the sense to pee outside." In fact, he'd taken her on a couple of errands that week, because he didn't fancy leaving her at home, not when she was so new and seemed so devoted to being near him. She'd hit the shrubbery or the planting boxes in *front* of the PetSmart, but hadn't gone inside. (Although there were stations there with spray bottles and plastic bags that assured him that if she *did* hit the floor in the PetSmart, she wouldn't be the first.)

"What did you do the last time?" Garth asked.

Milo grunted because he wasn't particularly proud of his final solution to this. "Called in sick," he said apologetically.

"Aw, Milo," Garth said, giving him an expression of pure pity. "You said she was fine with the crate—"

"I just… she gets this look of, you know, reproach?" He dropped his voice to as close to Helen Mirren's as he could figure. "Far be it from me, old chum, to tell you how to live your life, but do remember, *you* brought me here."

Garth chuckled. "Didn't you say your friend brought her to you?"

"Mari, yes," Milo said. "My only friend and the sister of my heart."

Garth's good humor seemed to fade. "Not your *only* friend, Milo," he said firmly, and Milo smiled.

It did seem like Garth had decided they would be dog-park friends, and he treasured that.

"No," he said, nodding toward Garth. "You and Chad are friends now too. But me and Mari have been friends since high school. There's history. You don't fuck with history."

Garth nodded, and threw the ball again. "No, sir," he said. "You don't. Why would anyone want to?"

Milo *hmm*ed and shrugged and bent down to fondle Julia's horizontal bat ears. She tended to keep her head tilted, so her bat ears looked like an airplane coming in for a forty-five-degree landing, particularly when she was fetching the squeaky. Milo was pretty sure that was magic and no other dog in the world did that, but he wasn't willing to risk ridicule by asserting that to anybody but Mari.

"You ready to walk?" Garth asked.

"Sure." Milo smiled brightly. "But only if Chad's done."

Garth and Chad looked at each other like longtime coconspirators. "Oh yeah," Garth said. "Me and Chad have a big yard for him to wander today. Lots of places for our boy here to stretch his legs." He hooked his lead—a thick rope-like thing—to Chad's collar, and together the two of them wandered up the soccer field, which was slick with dew, to the walkway. "Easy there," Garth murmured, sticking a hand under Milo's elbow when he slipped. "Maybe we should go through the parking lot instead."

Oh, how embarrassing. Milo resisted the urge to cup his elbow, though, where the warmth from Garth's hand was buzzing like the touch of a heated wand.

"No—it's good for me to climb the steeper incline," Milo told him. "I'm just getting my wind back."

"From what?" Garth asked.

"Just, you know, forgot to exercise for a while. Do you see any other dogs?"

While Milo's and Garth's vehicles were the only ones in the parking lot, Milo had started to wonder if people didn't come in from the neighborhood around the other side of the park.

"Usually not this early," Garth reassured him. "But yeah—this park gets used a *lot*. It's a good thing you didn't have Julia off lead any later in the day."

Milo sighed. "I need to take her to that park you told me about where she can run. Maybe in the afternoon before it gets too dark."

"She'd like that," Garth rumbled. "But how about Saturday morning? I'll meet you there, and Chad can run around his side of the park and Julia can run around hers, and then we can go get breakfast or something."

Milo brightened. "Waffles," he said happily. "You can't get waffles from DoorDash, and I don't have a waffle maker."

"I have just the place in mind," Garth said. "My treat. But first you have to tell me why anybody would want to get in the middle of you and your sister."

"Of the heart," Milo said. "We're not blood related, but—"

"No, no—sister. I get it. I mean, I *have* a sister, and we're okay, but she's not my best friend."

"Who is your best friend?" Milo asked. "Besides Chad?"

Garth laughed a little. "My old college roommate, Doug. He's using *his* engineering degree as a well-paid handyman, and he lives up in Folsom, but we get together once a week or so, grill some burgers, let his kids play with Chad. Love that guy. Would die for him. He's my brother. So she's your *sister*. You'd die for her. I get it. Why would anybody try to get in the way of that?"

Milo grunted. "You don't want to hear about my ex," he said uncomfortably. "That's... you know. Not dog-walking conversation material."

"Sure it's not. Tell me anyway."

Milo heard the implicit command there and thought about disobeying it. The image of Julia, disregarding feelings and stampeding boundaries, came to his mind, and he realized that he could be the turkey or he could be the dog.

Garth had done nothing to deserve Milo disregarding his feelings.

"I don't know," he said, as honest as he had been on this subject. Suddenly he *yearned* to tell *somebody*. He *couldn't* tell Mari. She'd feel terrible. Or she'd take out a contract on Stuart like he'd threatened to do on Calvin the creep. Either way, she didn't need that sort of emotional overload. "He just—he said he was fine with it," he tried to explain. "Me and Mari, it's… it's *not negotiable*. It's a no-brainer. There's no Milo without Mari and no Mari without Milo. Not since we shared a locker in high school."

"What's she like?" Garth asked, and he sounded genuinely interested.

"Short," Milo said, nodding, because that had been the first thing he'd noticed. "Blunt. Abso-fucking-lutely honest about everything. Mari doesn't bullshit. She notices *everything*. She has *eight cats*, even though she's only supposed to have five. Her newest boyfriend gave her three of them, because I guess she finally met somebody who sees that she's *meant* to love *the whole world*. She's been trying to find the whole world to love since we met, and…." His voice wobbled.

"The world can be stupid and blind about that," Garth said perceptively.

"High school sucks," Milo told him with feeling. "Unless you've got that best friend who gets you and cheers you on and tells you your art is good and warns you when you've got bats in the cave, high school can be a wrist-slitting catastrophe."

"Oh, Milo," Garth said, voice soft.

"I never tried it," Milo assured him. "But… but I think I might have. If Mari hadn't just thrust herself into my life. Into my *locker*. And when we got to college, we were there for everything. First kisses, first sex." He sighed. "First breakups. First sleazy ex-boyfriends who go ghost, first drink…." He wondered how much more he should say.

"First trip to rehab?" Garth asked softly.

"Yeah," Milo conceded. "Yeah. She used to drag me out of bed for high school. It was my turn for college. You don't… don't let go of that friend, do you understand?"

"Of course I do," Garth said, sounding surprised. "Why would your ex ask you to?"

Milo let out a frustrated groan. "Jealousy?" he said, as puzzled now as he had been then. "Control? I… don't know."

"Did you stop seeing your friend?" Garth asked.

"No," Milo said promptly. "I just… pretended like I didn't. In a way I guess it was like cheating on Stuart with Mariana, but, you know, no sex. But I couldn't see what he was weird about. I'd *told* him we were inseparable. Nonnegotiable. And he was horrible about her when I even mentioned her name, so I just…." He shrugged. "Pretended it wasn't happening. Went out to lunch with her anyway. Went to movies with her and told him I was going with friends from work."

"How'd he find out?" Garth didn't sound judgy, which was a relief, because Milo was starting to judge himself.

Which was why the next thing slipped out. "He went through my finances," Milo said, disbelief coloring his voice.

"He what?" Garth asked, surprised.

"It's… see, Stuart was a lawyer, the lawsuit kind. He made a lot of money, wore the sharp clothes, drove the fancy car. And I'd just bought the duplex when we met—I rent out the other half to a retiree who likes to sit on his porch and do the crossword—but he moved into my half. He kept asking why we couldn't move someplace, you know, better." Milo sighed. "I got it at the time. He works down in Sacramento, and he had to commute. But then, I didn't make as much money as he did, so the one-day-a-week commute helped me pay my mortgage, and the renter next door is an investment, and I like having a neighbor I can talk to. So I told Stuart I didn't make as much as he did, and he'd have to make the down payment and put his name on the deed."

"He didn't want to do that because…?" Garth asked, and Milo shrugged.

"I don't know. At this point I'm starting to suspect second family, or he's about to be arrested for embezzlement, or he was planning to kill me and inherit. I have no idea. But it was a big deal to him that I be the one who took the financial risk and bought a better house. I didn't wanna. I told him I didn't wanna. I said I had my finances to my liking and the duplex to my liking and…." Milo gnawed his lip. "He said he was pawing through my finances to find a way to make it work, which is stupid because I didn't look through any of *his* financial papers. And he found a big monthly bill for…." This was embarrassing. Not even Mari knew this part. "Well, Mari's sister. Mari was at her wit's end trying to find a place for Serena that… didn't *suck*, you know? Adult care homes—it's a crap shoot. So I found one that wasn't awful, but the bill was six hundred dollars more than Mari could afford, but *I* could, so…."

Garth actually stopped. "Milo," he said softly. "That's…."

"Stupid?" Milo supplied bitterly. "Irresponsible? Shows my shitty priorities?"

"No," Garth said. "No. Did he say that? Because seriously, I'll take out a contract—and I bet Mari will help. No, I was going to say kind. I'm… it's like you've got a cape now. Like Superman. People talk about being friends all the time, but that's… that's being a friend."

Milo was *really* embarrassed now. "It's nothing," he insisted. "I just… you know. Couldn't let her… you know. Suffer. And she would have, knowing her sister was someplace she was unhappy. It's like…." He gave Julia's leash a gentle yank so it would clear her backside and she would get a move on. "C'mon, baby," he muttered. "I know you can do this."

"Like how Mari showed up at your door with a dog?" Garth asked.

"Part of that was that Stuart took the cat when he left," Milo admitted.

"Oh my God!" Garth exclaimed. "This guy keeps getting worse!"

"Time doesn't always heal all gaping assholes," Milo said shortly.

"So how'd he take your beautiful act of philanthropy?" Garth asked, and Milo had to work to not blush.

"He called me stupid," Milo told him, remembering being shocked at the word. Milo had always been smart—he'd been tested a million times, and his IQ was off the charts. His parents had despaired of the graphic-arts thing until it had started making money, because they'd felt it was "beneath his potential." Of all the names Milo had been called— and there were a lot—"stupid" had not been among them.

"That's obviously projection," Garth said.

Milo felt a tiny part of him—maybe his toes?—that he hadn't realized had been cold suddenly warm up.

"Well, he was the one who didn't understand. He was, like, 'I thought you weren't hanging out with that bitch anymore.'"

"Oh my God," Garth muttered.

"Yeah—he said that. And I…." Milo glanced around the park mournfully, noting the sky was gray again today and grateful it hadn't opened up to rain. Yet. "I sort of told him off."

"Yeah?" Garth asked, and he sounded… brighter. Like this was something good. "What did you say?"

"I told him he was jealous," Milo said. "And controlling. And cheap."

"What did he say?" They were rounding the final corner of the loop now, with only a long straightaway shaded by trees until they took the turn to the picnic rise.

"I don't want to talk about what he said," Milo murmured, because it was still a knife in his chest.

"Aw, Milo," Garth replied. "How bad was it?"

Milo shook his head. "He gutted me," he admitted, and saying the words felt like picking the scab off an infection. "Just… can you imagine all the things you're most afraid of as an adult?"

Garth let out a sigh. "Yeah. But mine might be different than yours."

Milo wanted to ask what Garth's fears were—with all his heart he did. But then he knew he'd have to confess his own. "Stuart knew mine. He used every one of them, and then told me I was a coward and a terrible lover and a parasite to boot. And when I was standing there, my mouth open, and I knew I was going to sob but it hadn't hit me yet, just how awful it all was, he told me he'd take it all back if I stopped paying Mari's sister's bill."

"Oh my God," Garth said, and Milo heard a note of boiling fury that was oddly satisfying. "What did you say?"

Milo shook his head because although that moment had been nearly three months ago, he could still remember it so clearly. It had felt as though he was floating outside himself, watching his mouth gape, his eyes welling with tears, his hands clasped around his middle as though Stuart had used his actual fists. And that floaty person, watching Milo, was remembering all those great movies and TV shows with heroes in them. Neo, Indiana Jones, John Wick, Tony Stark, Captain America, Bucky Barnes—they all floated through his head, and he watched his mouth open and thought, *Please, Milo, be heroic, just this once.*

"What?" Garth prodded, and Milo shrugged.

"Did you ever see *My Fair Lady*?" he asked.

"No…." There was an expression on Garth's face as though everything in his life hinged on what Milo said next.

"There's this song at the end about how the whole world would be standing without the manipulative asshole who told her he made her," Milo explained. He and Mari had memorized that song in their senior year in high school. Whenever their peers got nasty—and high school had been a cesspool of misery on its best day for the two of them— they'd sung it. "Mari and I… we sang that song at the top of our lungs every day for a year. It was our fuck-you song for anybody who tried to make us feel small. And suddenly I'm standing in my kitchen, knowing my life has just ended, and I open my mouth and… and that song comes out. I… I never thought, in my entire life, I could be brave like that."

"That's amazing," Garth said, and Milo glanced at him quickly to see if he meant that or if it was sarcastic and, well, mean. But Garth was grinning at him, open admiration written in his eyes, and Milo felt his cheeks heating against the cold.

"I was still singing it when he left," Milo said and then shrugged. "The next day I had lunch with Mari, and I went and… well, didn't tell her about the fight because I didn't know what to say. And when I got home…."

"All his stuff was gone?" Garth surmised—correctly, in fact.

"Yeah." Milo's shoulders hunched, and he almost tripped over Julia for the nine-hundred-and-twelfth time, and for a moment, he wanted to stop on the path and shrink into himself like a slug. "Including the cat."

Suddenly there was a warm weight over his shoulders, and Garth said, "I'm so sorry about the cat." Milo allowed himself to be comforted.

"Stuart hated that cat," he said in a small voice. "I… I spent a week checking the shelters in the area to make sure she hadn't been turned in." It had actually been Stuart's sister coming over to get Chrysanthemum's collar collection that had sent Milo into the depression Mari had interrupted. Because that meant Stuart meant to keep him. He'd *never* get him back.

"I'm so sorry," Garth said, and God, hearing that—it made a difference. "You know, I've never heard that song. Sing it for me."

"Seriously?" Milo asked. "It's pretty bitchy." That lovely warmth suffused him, and he wanted to melt into Garth's protection. But nothing was ever that easy, was it?

"Naw—look around us, Milo. It's sort of a dismal day, and I have to go work outside when the whole world would rather be drinking hot chocolate and watching old movies. You said the song made you brave. Let's hear something brave."

Milo was shorter than Garth, but their strides still seemed to match, and it was almost like they were keeping time with the music.

In his head, he could hear Audrey Hepburn singing as Eliza Dolittle, complaining bitterly about being a fool on a puppeteer's string, and his mouth opened, and there it was. He felt it in his chest.

Milo sang, the words coming back to him automatically, much as they had done with Stuart, except with Stuart his voice had been choked, he'd been sobbing, and he'd snorted his way through the end. This was different. This time, singing the song was redemption, and as his voice grew stronger, he raised his head, belting out the final words.

Of course when he was done with the final words, he was left with the look of disgust, of superiority, on Stuart's face, and his voice dwindled into nothing as he remembered that, in the movie, Henry Higgins had used that lovely, perfect, dignified "Fuck you!" to claim credit for Eliza Doolittle's personhood.

For a moment, the grayness of the day had faded, and Milo was left with that same feeling Julia must have had, chasing the turkeys in the dawning sunshine, but as usual it was a feeling destined to fade.

Except Garth's arm was still around his shoulders, and Julia, perhaps encouraged by their beat-keeping lockstep, had managed to stay, trotting at the same speed, a couple of steps ahead of them, not letting her leash go slack enough to touch her bottom and make her stop in her tracks.

The warmth that suffused Milo's belly then was better than soup *or* coffee.

"That was a *great* song," Garth told him, not dropping that lovely living security blanket. "That song was everything you should have told that guy for trying to control your heart."

Milo sighed and relaxed a smidge. "I haven't told Mari," he confessed. "She'll feel like it was her fault, or she will take out a contract on him, and either one of those things would be bad."

Garth's chuckle seemed to warm him from the toes up.

"I'll take your word for it on the second one," Garth told him, "but you're right about the first, and we don't want her to feel bad. It's not her fault Stuart was a terrible person."

"Is it bad that I'm willing to let it stand there?" Milo asked. "That you think he was a terrible person? I keep thinking I should try to balance it out. Say, 'Well, he did this bad, but he did other things good.' But I don't think I'm that nice."

"Good," Garth said simply. "You are under no obligation to both-sides a controlling asshole who asked you to do the unthinkable, Milo.

You and your friend have a right to *be* friends. As long as you're not dragging each other to opium dens and bank robberies, Stuart, God rot his soul, has no place to complain."

Milo nodded and took a glance at Julia, who finally seemed to be okay with this trot around the park. No tugs on the leash to chase after the turkeys—who were just as insolent as they had been earlier—and she seemed to have found a sort of rhythm to get them down the path.

"Mari put cat ears on her," he admitted. Milo had replaced the cat ears with a pumpkin sweater, via Amazon. "I think she'd chase cats—that was probably an affront to her dignity."

"We won't tell her what it meant," Garth admitted. Chad shifted in his grip, and Garth had to drop his arm. Milo resisted the urge to give him a shy smile—partly because he was afraid Julia would stop again and they'd go sprawling if he looked away, and partly because... well, because.

"She's probably better off not knowing," Milo figured. They were drawing around the corner to Milo's little sedan, and Garth and Chad walked him to his door.

"So," Garth said, "what are you doing with her tomorrow?"

Milo gazed down at his protective little dog, who gazed back up at him with zero expectations. "I think I'll take her with me," he said thoughtfully. "If she behaves, my boss might not even notice. If she doesn't, I'll look up a dog walker or something." Julia reached up and put both her paws on Milo's knee. "It'll be fine."

Garth's warm chuckle made him think it would be.

"Well, Saturday's the day I take Chad here to the dog playground. Does your girl have all her shots?"

Milo recalled the long, detailed explanation of Julia's healthcare plan that Mari had walked him through. "Yes!" he said excitedly. "Should I bring her paperwork?"

"Just her little tag that says she's had rabies vaccinations," Garth said. "Otherwise the rest is for her protection. Anyway—Julia and Chad will be in different enclosures, but maybe afterward we can take a loop around the park, okay?"

Milo paused enough to *really* smile this time. "Yeah," he said. "I'd... gee, I'd like that."

Garth's tanned face was such a thing of beauty. Milo practically lost time when he smiled.

"So," Garth rumbled, his voice cutting into Milo's dreams, "I'll see you the day after tomorrow, here, and at C-Bar-C Park on Saturday."

Milo nodded, then bit his lip. "Would you like me to… uhm, bring coffee?" he asked shyly.

"Sure," Garth said. "I'll text you with my order."

Milo wondered if he glowed on the way to his car. He certainly *felt* like he glowed. Was it possible to glow, like a radiated bauble?

It must have been. He didn't trip on Julia *once*.

Nosy Clients

MISTY PARCIVAL was bored. So bored. Garth almost felt bad for taking advantage of her boredom to landscape the acre behind her nearly palatial home *again*. It was the second time in the last three years, and Garth was pretty proud of the *first* time he'd been there. He'd managed to utilize the clusters of granite boulders present on her property to create organic-looking flowerbeds of native flora. He built rock fountains near the property boundaries that were amazing, with the waist-high brick fencing she'd insisted upon, even knowing that California's unstable ground often tried to shake off brick walls like a dog shook off mud clumps.

He even "decorated" her oak trees, creating a light-spun fairyland that could be changed on a seasonal basis with a few deft button pushes on the battery pack.

Right now, the three trees were set to showcase a rather spooky combination of orange and purple, with a blackout relief of jack-o'-lantern faces in the foliage as it was aimed at the house.

Her entire backyard had taken him—with help from his dad and a few part-time workers he used—a month and a half, and a lot of that was shifting rock from the back of his truck to the rock fountains, which were specially placed to help drain water into the flower beds. The whole layout was very drought resistant without looking "cactusy" as Misty called it.

Garth couldn't figure out why Misty would want to mess with a good thing by putting vegetable boxes on the far end of the property, replacing half of the flowerbeds with raised wooden boxes full of rich soil meant for nutritious tomatoes, with no walkways in sight.

He'd spent the last two days changing out the tree decorations—adding the relief jack-o'-lantern faces had taken him a day of programming, but it had also given him a day to work on Misty to get her to change her mind.

He honestly didn't think she *wanted* to vegetable garden. He'd watched her spend an hour deciding what to wear to sun herself for fifteen minutes before the sun got "too sunny" and, in spite of the very mild morning, the air got "too scorching."

The thing was, Misty wasn't really a spoiled heiress. She *had* been a very busy mother of three, and the backyard had been her first project after the youngest had gone off to college. Her husband made a mint and continued to make a mint, and she was left to her own devices.

She just hadn't figured out what her devices *were*, Garth firmly believed, so she had called him to redo her backyard because it had worked so well the first time.

Oddly enough, as he pulled up to Misty's lush front yard—which was decorated to *Jonathan* Parcival's specs, which were, in turn, derived from Jonathan's late mother, and were not, thank fuck, open to changes or redecorating schemes—Garth was thinking about Milo, and how his best friend had shown up at his house with a dog wearing cat ears in an attempt to drag Milo out of what even a stranger could see had been a devastating depression.

It took a good friend to show up at your house with a dog and say, "Look, it's this or I have you committed."

Garth wasn't a good enough friend to this nice middle-aged woman to actually *bring* her a dog, but suddenly, as Chad gave a hopeful woof upon seeing what he knew to be one of his favorite yards, Garth was beset by another idea.

"C'mon, big fella," he said as he let Chad out of the driver's side. "Let's see if we can get Michael to watch you for a bit. I've got a plan."

MICHAEL WAS Misty's sixtysomething assistant/majordomo, and he had a soft spot for Chad. Maybe it was the big dog's playfulness—Garth traveled with a bucket of toys, and Michael and Chad had played tug-o-war and kill-the-squeaky for hours when Garth had been here last time. Michael's husband was deathly allergic to animals, and Garth could tell big good dogs were a thing that had been missing from his life.

He was at the door to greet Garth and escort Chad around to the back while Garth consulted with the mistress of the house, and Garth pulled a battered twenty out of his wallet and had a murmured conversation with Michael.

Michael made him put the twenty back in his wallet and said, "It's brilliant. I wish I'd thought of it. Do you think you could make it happen today?"

"Would you like me to text you before we come back?" Garth asked. "In case we're bringing a friend with us?"

"Definitely," Michael said. "I could send Sandy to the store for a bed and some food and such. Let us know."

Garth nodded, although he knew that if this worked like he planned, Misty might very well be the one to go shopping. This was going to be *her* dog, after all.

So Michael took Chad to the back to play fetch, and Garth went to talk to Misty in her study. The study—another leftover from the former Mrs. Parcival—was a fussy, ornate sort of place that seemed to oppress its current owner with an overabundance of clutter, complete with curl-embellished bookshelves in dark red cherrywood, and red velvet drapes.

It was a shame Misty couldn't convince her husband to let her decorate other parts of the house besides the backyard, but they had to work with what they had.

"Garth," she said, her face lighting up when she saw him. She was a pretty woman in her early fifties, with hair kept a rich chestnut brown by her hairdresser and a body that showed a devotion to tennis courts and gym memberships and a secret addiction to the rich coffee drinks that were *not* forgiven by a waistline. She was fit, but round and soft, and her smile was genuine.

"Misty," he said fondly. "How you doing?"

"Are you ready to build my—" She was betrayed by a softly bitten lip and a slight hesitation. "—garden boxes?"

Garth sighed. "Misty," he said, "you hate dirt. You hate the out-of-doors."

"I don't *always* hate it," she protested. "I used to love taking my children to the park or watching them play sports." That last was said so wistfully, Garth suddenly knew he had to follow through with this idea or die trying.

"Which is what we're doing today," he said with grim determination. "We're going to find a reason for you to go out and play in your backyard that doesn't involve trying to raise prize tomatoes."

She bit her brightly painted lower lip again—but this time in what looked like hope. "What did you have in mind?" she asked.

WELL, FIRST she had to change. One didn't go to the animal shelter on Bradshaw in a pink twinset and white slacks. Garth told her jeans and a sweatshirt; she used to take her children camping in an RV, surely she had *that* wardrobe leftover.

She did, in fact, and when she'd pulled her hair back in a ponytail and put on jeans and Keds, she looked ten years younger.

"We don't have to do anything permanent here, do we?" she asked nervously as they drove.

"We're only going to look," he soothed. "Think of this as research for maybe why you don't want to grow tomatoes."

She let out a disconsolate sigh. "I don't even like marinara," she admitted. "Whenever we go Italian, I get pesto."

Garth tried not to laugh, but he knew the corners of his mouth quirked up a bit. "Then maybe this could be a solution. It's worth checking, isn't it?"

"I was supposed to be working on my book today," she said.

"You're writing a book?" That was something he hadn't known. Misty liked to dress and behave as, Garth assumed, the previous Mrs. Parcival had, but he knew from earlier conversations that she had a degree in history and librarianship, and she'd had a career and goals and everything before being whisked away to the big mansion to be a wife and a mother.

"It's romance," she said, peeking around like she was afraid somebody would bug Garth's bruiser of an extra cab truck to listen in on Misty Parcival's most profound and shameful secret.

"Why's that bad?" he asked, flummoxed.

"Jonathan thinks all romance is trash," she mumbled, and Garth snorted.

"Yeah, straight white men often say that," he commented. "They're sort of… you know. Assured in the pecking order. If they see a pretty girl, they're absolutely positive they can have a pretty girl. Women and people who *aren't* straight and white, they don't always get what they want. Having a happy ever after is a lot harder when you're making sure everybody gets one."

Misty made a suspicious sound, and Garth finished making a very tricky left-hand turn off the freeway before glancing over at her.

"Misty?" he asked. "Honey, what's wrong?"

"It's just... you get it!" She sniffled. "Jon doesn't get it, and it hurts explaining it to him and... how is it you *get* it?"

Garth sighed. "I... well, earlier this morning a new friend—" He smiled a little. "A new *doggy* friend, told me that his boyfriend broke up with him because he was helping his bestie pay for her sister's hospital *bills.*" He felt only a little guilty talking about Milo's problems. He was dying to tell somebody about them, because it *wasn't* his imagination. Milo was a *really awesome guy* who just needed a little help with his dog. And, well, his life. And his self-esteem. But that morning, Garth had seen the *awesome* come alive in his new "doggy" friend. Everything from helping his best friend with her sister to that amazing breakup song, sung defiantly when the relationship was obviously over, made the slender, elfin adopter of difficult dogs more and more interesting.

"What's that got to do with writing romance?" she asked, sounding bewildered.

Garth tried to put that conversation with Milo into perspective.

"Milo," he said, thinking about it hard, "wasn't asking for a lot outside his relationship. He'd started out with this one person—this family—and he asked that his boyfriend respect that, even the financial part. And his boyfriend couldn't. He felt *entitled* to all of Milo's attention, all his respect, all his affection, and that's not fair, is it?"

"No," she said, and he liked that she sounded definitive and the slightest bit pissed off. It wasn't only him and his fascination with Milo—Milo's ex had been totally out of line.

"No," he agreed. "When people feel *entitled* to happiness, they don't know how to work for it. Milo's ex wasn't recognizing that Milo got his own say in how he spent his money. He felt like all of Milo belonged to him. It's like sometimes people need a road map for how a partnership works. And sometimes they need a promise that it *can.* That's, you know, what romance books or movies are all about, right?"

Misty gave a soggy little laugh. "Do you like them?"

Garth figured that they'd gone beyond client/service provider by now. "If I let you in on a little secret, do you promise not to tell?"

"Okay," she said, and she sounded breathless, like a teenager. "Tell me."

"My buddy Doug and I were supposed to have a guys' weekend, right? His wife and kids were off at her parents for a week, and neither of us had any jobs. We were going to play poker with our friends and go fishing and watch sports." He negotiated Bradshaw Road with one hand and pounded his chest with the other. "We were men! Rawr!"

She giggled like a teenager, and he found himself liking her even more. "Did you kill and eat your own food?"

"Yup. Not a pizza was safe for a ten-mile radius. We were ruthless."

More laughter, so he went on.

"See, our poker friends all ended up with the flu, which sucked, and it was just us. And it was raining, and while we *could* have gone fishing in the rain—we have before—we were both feeling... I don't know. A little blue. We ended up shotgunning *all* the romantic movies. All of them. From the ones that were big when we were in high school, our parents' favorites, even Katharine Hepburn and Cary Grant."

"He was gay, you know," she said like she was offering him a chocolate.

"Mm-hmm," he said, nodding because what boy didn't appreciate himself a little Archie Leach? "I am aware. Anyway, we spent three days watching romance movies and listening to the rain. The rain finally stopped, and we both went running—we were *so* bloated after all the pizza—and when we got back, my buddy was like, 'Man, I gotta tell you. I watch postapocalyptic sci-fi all the time, and it leaves me depressed about life. That shit was *fun*. I want to watch that with my *wife*. No offense.'"

He laughed a little because the "No offense" had been such a dude-bro thing to say.

"That's lovely," she told him.

"It is." And there was their turnoff. "It was. And we haven't stopped watching them since. I've actually gone over to their house to watch romance movies at least once a month. It's cute. He and his wife laugh and make snarky comments, and then they try to figure out how

I'll meet the man of my dreams. It's a good time. But it's important too. Because it's hard to have a relationship, and it lets my friend and his wife know that it's possible, and that sometimes people communicate like they do."

"And it lets *you* know that it can happen," Misty said, sounding happy and validated and all the things Garth had planned.

"Yup. Hope all around. You keep writing—and you tell your husband that if he doesn't get that it's important to you, he's missed something sort of amazing about you."

"Well, your friend's ex missed out on a gem there, that's for certain," she said, and Garth felt his chest warm with a compliment aimed at Milo. "That sort of dedication, of loyalty—it doesn't happen all the time. People get so hung up on what they deserve, on their own piece of the pie or their own recognition... they literally sell their souls, or their hearts, and they positively devour anybody who offers them kindness. I've seen it happen."

"Me too," Garth said softly. He didn't want to think about that, though—that memory was painful, but it was also faded. The sunshine of too much living had blurred the edges, made it something from youth and not an adult debacle. Not a toxic nightmare. He only had Milo's relationship to look at to know that a love affair ending when college ended was not the worst thing that could have happened to him. "Here we are, Misty. You ready?"

"I'm just here to look," she said, but she already sounded more sure of herself. She was *definitely* more excited about this than she was about tomatoes.

"Of course," he told her. He was pretty sure they were going home with a dog.

WHEN GARTH walked Misty around the big-dog enclosure at the animal shelter, she did not, as he suspected she would, go immediately for the puppies. Instead, she found two dogs, four and six years old respectively, middle-aged dogs, as she said. Old enough to know better. They were pit bull mixes—although what they were mixed with only their mother knew for sure—and they didn't look at all like a matched set, but after Garth and Misty spent an hour with the two dogs in the shelter's outside enclosure, it appeared as though the dogs could play together happily, and Garth got to use his finely honed ball-throwing muscles for a whole new appreciative audience.

The dogs were named Butch and Daisy, and Daisy might have been the ugliest, most brutish-looking dog Garth had ever seen. But the moment she was brought into the greeting room, both Misty and Garth were subjected to the sweetest, most thorough slobbery tongue bath in the history of big derpy dogs, and the first thing Butch did when he met Daisy was start to clean her ears.

It was kismet for dogs—or two supersweet animals who were absurdly happy for a friend.

Misty was half an hour into their playtime when Garth realized she was wiping away tears.

"Misty?" he asked hesitantly as he threw the ball for the umpteenth time. "I'm sorry. I didn't mean to take you to a bad place."

She shook her head. "Look at them," she said, choked. "They need me. They... they really love me. I can't leave them here, can I?"

"We have plenty of room in the extra cab," Garth told her, pleased. "And if we called Michael, he could have Sandy get a head start on supplies."

She sniffled and wiped her eyes on the inside of her sweatshirt before she rubbed Daisy behind the ears some more. Daisy was apparently a shameless attention whore, because she gazed adoringly at her new mistress and slobbered some more.

"I think if everything's in order," Misty said, continuing to rub Daisy's floppy ears and big, blocky triangle head, "we should stop on our way home. I want to pick out the dog beds—I think Daisy needs something pink and frilly, don't you?"

Daisy's enormous jowls sagged as she gave Garth a doggy grin.

"Oh absolutely," he said. "She's a pretty girl." He sank to his haunches and scrubbed at her back end until her wrist-thick tail practically vibrated. After she flopped to the ground, a quaking blob of canine Jell-O, he turned to Butch, who shyly thrust his head under Garth's armpit in an attempt at a full-body hug. "And you're a good boy," he crooned. "Such a good boy."

Butch moved his head to Garth's shoulder and whuffled, and Garth figured they should get out of there before *he* ended up bringing home another big good dog. He was starting to see how they could be addictive.

"So," Garth said as Misty practiced throwing for the dogs in the backyard, "you should probably practice walking the both of them on leads back here before you take them somewhere."

Misty nodded and looked beseechingly to Michael. "Would you be willing to help me, uhm...." She paused when she saw Michael on his haunches, petting Butch's stomach and wiping his eyes on his shoulder. "Would you need an increase in...? Michael, are you okay?"

"I'm so happy," he said, wiping his eyes again. "They're perfect."

"Oh," she said, and then peered at her employee—and friend—in surprise. "Michael, why didn't you tell me you wanted a dog?"

He gave her a droll glance, which was quite an accomplishment given the red-rimmed eyes. "I don't live here, Misty. It's not my place. But you know Andrew's deathly allergic. We can't have pets. He'd wake up one night and forget to breathe. But... but if *you* have dogs...." He gave her a winsome smile.

"Well, it's like *we* have dogs, isn't it?" she asked happily. "And we can learn how to walk them, and we can take them places...." She turned to Garth. "Where do dogs go?"

He laughed a little. "To the park. To the lake. To dog parks." He gestured toward the acres of land he'd landscaped as organically as possible. "To their own amazing backyard. I mean, hang a platform swing under that oak tree, Misty, and attach some ropes to it, and I'll bet they invent their own games. Big rubber trash cans—as long as you don't let them fill with water. And like I said, I could set you up with a small pond with a filter and recycled water so they can swim in the summer."

She glanced around. "Anything else?" she asked.

He pointed to their back porch, which was shaded by an overhang from the house but was just big enough for a soda refrigerator and to house the lawn furniture.

"Do you want an apron there?" he asked. "It would take me about three days, but a concrete apron, with an awning from the house, would give you a place to eat lunch or dinner alfresco on good days. Think about it—bring out the right furniture and you could eat out here if you wanted, and the dogs wouldn't be cooped up in the house. Or, if you want, I could call Doug, my contractor friend—"

"The one who likes romances?" she asked hopefully.

Garth grinned, pleased she'd remembered. "Yup, that's the one. We both got our degrees in engineering and then went on to do nothing with our degrees. But if you like, and you get permission from Mr. Parcival, we could convert the small porch into an office with a wraparound window, and lay an apron for an adjoining porch with an awning and some lawn furniture. So, you know—"

Now *Misty* was, well, misty. "I could have a place to write that doesn't smell like dead mother-in-law?" she asked pitifully and then clapped her hand over her mouth. "I'm sorry. Mrs. Parcival was a wonderful woman who—"

"Wasn't you," Garth told her firmly. "I'll give you Doug's number, and the three of us can have a sit-down. In the meantime, if you like, instead of the whole garden reorganization we had planned, let me start on the dog pond. Think about some requirements if you like."

"Can the grandchildren wade in it?" she asked hopefully.

"Steps and a slip-proof bottom," he ticked off.

"Can we have places for toys?" she asked.

"Shelves," he said.

"What about their hair—"

"Superintensive pool filters," he said, holding up three fingers.

She paused and stared at both the dogs in a semihorrified way. "What about the dogs'…." She waved her hands. "I should have thought of this before, but what about their…." Her voice dropped to a whisper. "Their dookie."

Michael and Garth shared sympathetic gazes as they both tried not to burst out laughing.

"I can dig a pit," Garth said, "with a pipe that comes out. You deposit the, erm, dookie in the pipe and add enzymes every so often to turn the waste into fertilized dirt. Good for the environment. We'll make sure it's far away from the pool, with a completely independent water filtration system. How's that?"

Misty brightened so much Garth almost had to shade his eyes. "And that way," she said, her voice trembling, "I wouldn't have to feel bad about having you map out a month of your time for tomato boxes that"—her voice caught happily—"I don't have to make you build!"

Garth managed a chuckle. "Nope. Absolutely no tomato boxes in this contract, Misty."

She gave a happy little squeak and threw her arms around Garth's neck. "You're a really good friend," she sobbed. "Thank you."

THAT NIGHT, Garth left Misty and her new friends to their own devices, knowing Michael would help with any problems she might have. On his way home, he tagged Doug about the back porch, and he had a vision he wanted to share with his friend, so they talked long past the time Garth pulled into his own driveway and parked. Chad had run around the backyard and sniffed all the flowers (and given Garth even more matter to put in Garth's own poo pit) by the time that conversation was done, and Garth was left in the heavy, humid air of a mid-October night, staring at the orange moon over his backyard.

He felt… well, a lot of things.

Pleased at how well his experiment with Misty had worked, happy for the new dog adoptions, and hopeful that Misty's husband would see that his smart, savvy wife needed more in her life now that the children had flown.

But there was more. He'd outlined the specs of the job with Doug and explained how it had come about. Doug had his own dogs—a couple of Labrador retrievers, one black and one yellow—who were sweeter than pie and loved Doug's little girls like their own puppies. Doug had been all for the "dog-and-office porch," as they'd phrased it, as well as the shaded concrete area for picnics and alfresco dining. They'd worked together before—they were good at it—and Garth looked forward to the project.

But that still wasn't the conversation he wanted. He stood under that orange moon, sweating a little now that the breeze from the morning had died down, leaving the earth blanketed by the thin clouds that had once been fog, and remembered Milo that morning.

God, he was cute. The almost pointy ears, the almond eyes, the hard little apples of his cheeks. But he was also so vulnerable—any fool could see that. Garth couldn't make a move on him *now*, not just after Milo pulled his britches on and found his inner dog man. That would be... well, it felt predatory.

But Garth had loved their connection so far. Maybe... maybe just a little text?

Before the thought had even cleared his brain, he had the phone in hand, pulling up Milo's number to text, along with pictures of the two dogs.

You should tell your friend she inspired me, he texted. *I helped my client adopt these two beauties today because she needed the dogs more than the garden boxes. I thought if you could take on Julia, she could deal with these bruisers.*

He grimaced after he sent that. Ooh... way to imply that Milo was incompetent. But that's not how he meant it. Julia was a *challenge*. Lots of energy, lots of quirks, and she was behaving for Milo around Chad, but Garth was so worried about her for Milo's work situation. She had a shrill sort of bark; he wasn't even sure she was that vicious, but her *bark* sounded savage, and other dogs reacted to that sound. If Chad hadn't been such a... a.... *Chad*, Julia might have gotten a rise out of him, but Chad would literally let a small dog gnaw on his leg and stare at it before he so much as *woofed* to protest his abuse.

Shit! Did he need to explain all that to Milo, or—

You're such a good guy!

Garth stared at the phone hungrily, because another bubble was working.

And Julia IS a challenge. God, she snarled at the neighbor today, and it's a good thing Jerry's a good guy because he yelped and scared her back. I picked her up and held her, and she whimpered in my neck, and I'm starting to think her bark is the most vicious thing about her.

Maybe the neighbor snarled first, Garth texted loyally.

He seems sweet, Milo returned, *but we don't talk that much.*

Well, maybe Julia is also shy. Perhaps give your neighbor some treats and have him greet Julia with them.

Bribes—good idea. But back to your day. You helped a woman adopt two giant dogs instead of going for the big job. I think you got it backwards. You're the one with the cape.

Garth swallowed, suddenly hungry for the praise. Milo wouldn't know what that meant to him—not after what happened with Garth's own ex, who had given up their relationship for the big job out of state.

You're the one being a good guy. But you do need to tell your friend. Sometimes we need to know our risks pay off.

I'll text her. She'll be insufferable. It'll be great.

Garth chuckled to himself, thinking about the kind of friendship a sentence like that implied.

Have you decided what you're doing tomorrow? he asked.

Yeah. Julia's coming with me. I'm bringing a travel crate so she can be safe. Cross your fingers—I hear consulting work is where it's at these days, but I don't want to find out the hard way.

Garth laughed some more. Maybe it was because Milo wasn't tripping over his dog's leash every ten steps, but the pixilated, almost dark humor that he'd seen in the other man before was even more apparent in text.

Let me know how it goes. I can commiserate with pizza.

Ooh—Mari always brings ice cream and vodka. It'll be good to add protein.

Sausage and pepperoni?

There is no bad pizza. Even the kind with fish, which I understand some people think is an abomination. I just think it's for a refined palate. It makes my oatmeal and my fruit and cottage cheese all worth it.

Garth shuddered and gave Chad a short whistle to get them back inside the house. *Cottage cheese is the abomination. Even with fruit.*

But it's so slimming!

Garth didn't even have to hear the tone of voice to know that had been sarcastic.

I'll take my love handles, thank you, he replied, and he busied himself locking up the back and getting Chad set up with food and water for a minute so he didn't see Milo's reply.

The GIF with the cartoon character rolling its eyes did *not* disappoint.

And it didn't hurt his ego any either.

They continued texting while Garth stripped off his work clothes in the mudroom and clunked his boots out on the back porch to shake off some of the extra dirt from the tread.

Finally he texted, *Must shower and eat now. Let me know how it goes tomorrow. Will see you Friday, NMW.*

NMW?

No Matter What. Good luck.

Thanks. And thanks for the nice thing to tell Mari. She said you're making her blush. If you knew her, you'd know how unlikely that is.

Garth smiled and shivered a little as he stood in his mudroom in his briefs. *I'll have to meet her sometime.*

I'd love that. Get fed!

Will do. Night.

Night.

As Garth trotted to the shower and then started the spray, he thought about the conversation and let it keep him warm. Yeah, so maybe Milo wasn't in a place for romance right now, but a friendship—*everybody* needed a friend.

They could discuss what kind of friend later. Maybe naked. Maybe not, but… well, maybe.

That kind of friend could be *very* awesome at this stage in Garth's life. A friend who loved dogs. And Garth's love handles. And sarcasm.

And maybe, hopefully, nakedness.

He tried not to hope too hard.

Friends With Dogs

MILO HAD found an ingenious soft-sided crate that folded up into his briefcase/satchel, along with Julia's favorite blanket and a couple of her most comforting soft squeaky toys. He even had treats *and* poop bags in his pocket, and he'd mentally rehearsed a day with a break every two hours so they could *both* visit the restroom, so to speak. The campus of the ad firm he worked for was actually lovely, with a nicely landscaped lawn, complete with picnic benches and a little walk through the modest hedges in the back. Not that he'd let Julia loose there, but they could have a periodic stroll when they needed one, and hopefully this whole endeavor might not end with embarrassment, tears, and the circulating of his admittedly impressive resume for consultant jobs.

He actually *liked* working for H<3Art of U Inc. They were sort of a boutique company that catered to small businesses with limited budgets, and they tended to hire some of the best and brightest copywriters, artists, and PR people in the area. It wasn't a bad place to hang out, all in all, with one or two possible exceptions.

"Milo!" cried one of the two exceptions as Milo and Julia walked gamely up the paved path to the front office. "Is that you? I didn't recognize you with your hair, uhm, brushed."

Milo regarded Rick Kasich unhappily as he stood blocking the entrance. Rick liked to talk. Loudly. And usually he reserved his garrulousness for people who returned it, but sometimes he liked to get in Milo's face to "bring the little guy out of his shell."

"Yeah. I got it trimmed," he said, referring to his hair, although "trimmed" meant Mari had come over two nights before with a pair of scissors, and they'd sacrificed a garbage bag. The good news was, Mari knew how to hack beyond the standard bowl cut—she was good at layering the top and using clippers on the sides and back so it appeared as though Milo actually *cared* about his appearance when that was just what his hair *did*. Next to him, Julia let out a kind of hamster-using-a-chainsaw sound, and Milo tightened her leash.

"Julia," he warned. "Leave it."

"And who do we have here?" Rick Kasich liked to work out, and he did all sorts of grooming things to his hair and his skin and his nose hair, and the result was he looked *really good* and he *knew* he looked *really good* in a sort of blond, European perfection way. He was unafraid to push his presence, his person, into any space, whether he was wanted or unwanted.

Milo had a sudden panic about how much Julia did *not* seem to want Rick Kasich in her space.

"Julia, leave it!" he snapped, tugging on her leash and squatting to put his hand on the back of her neck. "Rick, I'm sorry," he said, trying for diplomacy as Julia's hamster ramped up the chainsaw. "She's in an unfamiliar place, and she's not up for meet and greet right now. I'm trying to introduce her slowly so she can sit at my desk while I work on meeting days."

"But I'm not a threat!" Rick laughed loudly and thrust his hand into Julia's face.

Milo yanked on her lead before her teeth clicked together, his heart hammering in his ears.

"She doesn't know that!" he cried. "Rick, please. Give her some space. If she bites you, I have to take her back to the shelter, and they'll put her down, and it will be *your fault* because I'm *begging* you to back off."

"Okay, okay!" Rick said, taking three steps back and regarding Milo with an absolute mask of hurt. "I'm sorry, I'm sorry. I was trying to be friends!"

Belatedly Milo recognized that Rick had probably been trying to be his friend for the last three years, but Milo hadn't responded.

Oh. Would he forever be knocking down turkeys who didn't deserve it?

"I know," Milo said, tempering his voice. "And I appreciate it. Hold on a sec." He rummaged in his pocket for a treat and handed it to Rick. "Here. Stand back about three feet and hold this out to her. Don't talk loud—sort of be soft. Hold your hand out flat and make sure she sees it."

"What do I do if she takes it?" Rick asked, sounding almost awestruck, like Julia was a capybara or an anteater or something that didn't normally crap on every sidewalk in America.

"Tell her she's a good girl," Milo said. "But if she doesn't, simply back away. We can try during lunch."

Rick gave him a quick smile over Julia's head, and Milo realized the hamster chainsaw had subsided somewhat. "Yeah? You don't usually talk to people during lunch."

Milo gave his own small smile. "I'll probably have to," he conceded. "I thought I could slip inside and have a dog at work, but look at me. I couldn't even get through the front door."

Rick kept his voice pitched low as he continued to offer the treat. "I was worried," he said. "You didn't show up last week. You've been looking sort of, you know. Rough. I was afraid we'd have to call the police or something to do a wellness check."

Milo's stomach sank. "I'm sorry," he murmured as Julia stretched out her neck and lipped the treat off Rick's hand. "Good girl," he crooned, and Rick said the same thing.

She ate the treat and gave Rick a glare of contempt that stated patently that she thought he was a sucker, and suckers gave out more treats. Milo shook his head and tugged at her leash, and Rick stepped aside to accompany them in.

"My friend brought me the dog for the same reason," he admitted. He hadn't realized his breakup had been so apparent. "I didn't want to leave her home alone last week, so I kept her home until I could figure out an alternative. I called in to Angela. She knew I was fine."

Angela was the other reason Milo hadn't wanted to come into work today. She was his team leader, fiftyish, fit, and tanned from a "hobby" job of teaching aqua aerobics in the mornings and on weekends, she tended to hover over any of her team members if they weren't fit and chipper.

He'd been avoiding the hover for the last two months, but he'd just shown up with a hamster-chainsaw mammal, and he knew there would be some explaining to do.

"She may not have sent the fire department," Rick said, pushing the door open for them, "but she really doesn't think it's all fine. She's going to want to talk to you." Julia had apparently decided that being able to take a deep breath between her and this new person made him tolerable, because she kept her basic leash plot going. As long as Milo kept the lead adjusted so it didn't fall across the back of her ass, she kept trucking.

"Well, that's why I'm here," Milo said, although his heart wasn't in it. "I guess it's to talk to people."

"Yeah, sure," Rick muttered. "That's why you brought an attack Chihuahua... sort of. A giant attack Chihuahua? An attack capybara?" He paused to stare at Julia, whose ears had gone flat and straight out to the sides in what Milo thought of as "airplane mode." "No, seriously, Milo, what kind of dog is she?"

Milo, who had spent twenty minutes that morning rubbing her tummy while her head flopped to the side and she drooled slightly, gave a small smile. "She's an Attention Hound," he said soberly, and felt a small shaft of pride when Rick laughed. He didn't make jokes often—he should use that one on Garth.

He'd already heard Garth laugh. It was pretty impressive, rumbling out from his stomach, echoing up from his chest. It had made Milo warm all over. Rick's laugh didn't do that so much, but Milo was surprised to realize that he could make somebody besides Mari and, well, Garth laugh.

As he continued to walk through the office building, giving shy smiles and waves to his other coworkers, all of whom regarded Julia with interest, he wondered why he couldn't remember making Stuart laugh.

"Good one, Milo," Rick said as they were walking. "See, I knew you were funny."

"My drawings are funny," Milo said in surprise.

"Well, yes, but you don't ever... you know, say these things."

Milo blinked. It was true. Before the breakup with Stuart he'd been working on a series of humble animal comics, thinking about putting them up as a web series. He'd run them by his crew and had gotten laughs—and some tears—and had generally been confident that his sense of humor wasn't completely alien to humans, but that had been before he'd dropped off the map.

But he didn't talk about those drawings, or the moment they occurred to him, except to Mari.

Stuart used to say he should keep that stuff to himself.

He wondered if he should pull those comics up and start it again. Maybe it would make him feel more... more *connected* if he used his art for fun again as well as for work.

"I think they have to percolate," Milo said, and some of Julia's airplane-eared dignity seemed to stiffen his spine. "But I'll try to share them more often."

Rick shook his head. "I'm really glad you're back," he said after a moment. "Last week we had a strategy meeting for the new account—"

"Organic baby products," Milo said promptly.

"Yeah, that was the one. And the six of us were all spitballing and spinning off into the stratosphere—"

"You do that every strategy meeting," Milo told him, surprised. Rick was upfront and in your face, but he was also, like most of the people in their specific marketing group, creative and enthusiastic about his job. It helped that Angela tried to orient the company to healthy, environmentally friendly products, and her staff had an age range. She had recent college grads and a couple of people she called out of retirement to show everybody how it was done. She liked to shuffle the groups now and then, which was a nice way of letting grudges fade and old acquaintances seem new and vibrant again—or that's what Milo heard.

He generally sort of spaced out on the task and came back with some ideas.

"Yeah, we do," Rick agreed. "But generally you're there with a couple of sketches to pull us back down to earth. We look at the sketches, and even if we don't agree on them, you're like our 'Runners take your mark!' call when we've been wandering around the track doing stretches and shaking out our muscles. We didn't notice it until last week when we realized we'd spent the entire session off in outer space, and you weren't there to pull us back." He let out a burst of air. "And then we all started talking about how you'd gotten even quieter in the last two months, and how the week before you'd shown up in your pajamas with some sort of gum in your hair."

Milo grimaced. He'd hacked that out before Mari had arrived at his place with intervention on her mind. "I don't remember how that happened," he said truthfully. He was half afraid it was toothpaste and he'd fallen asleep on the toilet while brushing his teeth.

"Well you had us worried," Rick told him. "So what are you going to tell Angela?"

Milo swallowed. "My boyfriend moved out in August," he said baldly. "I was... not prepared."

Rick stared at him. "I had no idea you were even in a long-term relationship," he said, shaking his head. "We're not real to you at all, are we?"

Turkeys squawking! Feathers everywhere!

"It's hard," he said, his voice so quiet he was surprised when Rick turned to meet his eyes. "To talk."

Rick blew out a breath. "Yeah," he said, taking in Milo's appearance once again. "Is that what the dog is for?"

Milo peered down at Julia, who regarded him with that baffled sort of dignity that seemed to envelop her. "The dog was to get me out of bed," he admitted, still gazing at her. Out of nowhere, she took two quick steps in his direction and bounded into his arms. He caught her, startled, and she resumed her stare of baffled dignity, but this time she touched her nose to his.

"Hello, Julia," he said, and she snuggled in a little closer.

"Wow," Rick said, watching the two of them. "Would you like a room?"

"She's not my type," Milo told him. "I'm a great believer that interspecies relationships should remain fully platonic."

Rick chuckled. "See? Funny. Can I grab your satchel?"

Milo realized that the thing had slid down his shoulder when he'd caught his dog.

"Yeah. Let's get her crate set up by my desk so she's got a home," he said, carting her awkward twenty-pound-dog body toward the back of the offices where his own workspace sat.

"Where did you learn all this stuff about dogs?" Rick asked, doing exactly what Milo asked.

Milo paused. "The internet," he said. "My friend who brought me the dog. People at PetSmart." There were some super-hot young men at the one by his house who were always sweet and ready to help, and normally this would have had him all flustered, but it helped that he was pretty sure none of them would even look twice at him, and, well... there was Garth. "The guy who was walking his Daniffweiler in the park when Julia decided to go all commando on his ass."

"Was walking his *what*?"

Milo set Julia down and patted her head in reassurance. "Here," he said absently. "Hold her leash so she can't go walkabout. It's a Great Dane, mastiff, Rottweiler mix, and me and Mari—my friend—decided it was a Daniffweiler."

"Wow," Rick said, holding on to the leash like he'd been given the Ark of the Covenant. "What's *that* dog look like?"

Milo blinked at him. "Like it could eat your car," he said, nodding. "But he *didn't* eat Julia, so right now he's sort of a golden dog god in my eyes." Milo *should* have been thinking about Chad, and how the dog came to his waist and had feet almost as big as Milo's own and who probably outweighed Milo by about twenty, thirty pounds. But instead he was picturing... well, Garth, six feet plus, tan, brown hair streaked gold by the sun, hazel eyes crinkled at the corners, and the level patience in his eyes as Milo tripped on Julia's leash for the fifty-dozenth time.

In fact when Milo thought about the two of them, he wasn't sure which one conveyed the most forbearance—the giant handsome dog or the big handsome man.

But he wasn't going to tell Rick that.

"I'd like to see that," Rick said, smiling slightly. "Where do you walk her?"

"Garth, the big dog's owner, is sort of giving me dog walking lessons," Milo said hastily as he pulled the crate assembly out of his knapsack. "It's probably best we go alone."

"Oh," Rick said glumly. "Sorry. Didn't mean to intrude on your space." His shoulders drooped, and Milo gazed at him in consternation while he shook the crate's frame out.

"We're going to a dog park—sort of an enclosed space for them to play, but Julia's on the small dog side and Chad is on the big dog side. If that's not a total and complete disaster on Saturday, maybe you can come one day." While he spoke he tucked the blanket into the big fabric box and then added a couple of toys.

Rick looked at him oddly. "Why can't I come help it not be a total disaster?"

Milo stared at him. "I don't know how to manage more than one other friend and my dog," he said, thinking this should be self-evident. "I'm not quiet because I hate people, Rick. I'm quiet because I'm a class five introvert. I *like* people, but I also like ducks, and I don't know how to talk to them either."

Then he stared at Julia who, upon seeing the crate and all the comforts of home, wandered inside, curled up on the blanket, and began chewing fitfully at the squeaky.

Rick's puzzled expression relaxed some as they both stared at the contented dog. "You do fine, Milo. But I get it. Too many stressors in one place. Just...." His face did something complicated then. "Just give other people a chance, would you? I'm not even trying to hit on you when I tell you this. You're funny. You're *interesting*. Don't assume we wouldn't miss you if you crawled into your home and stayed there forever, okay?"

Milo nodded. "Thank you," he said, meaning it. "That's kind." He glanced at his desk and pulled his laptop out. "I'm going to clear out some of my paperwork before the meeting," he said apologetically. "I'll see you there."

"What are you doing for lunch?" Rick asked.

Milo pointed to a foam lunch container. "Casserole," he said. Mari had brought it over when she'd cut his hair.

"Eat it for dinner," Rick said. "Angela and I will take you out. Don't worry, just us. I'll get some sandwiches, and we can eat by the picnic tables with the dog. It'll be fun."

Milo glanced at Julia, who was still chewing her squeaky. "We'll be there," he promised. Julia didn't seem to object, so he left it at that.

MILO WASN'T sure how Julia did it—mostly she hung out in her crate and chewed her squeaky, with occasional forays outside to water the flowers—but she seemed to have a fan club by the time she was done with her first day at work.

And Milo was surprised at how productive he was, even with her next to him. Maybe *especially* with her next to him. He couldn't woolgather as much because he had to have his tasks done before he took her on her little walks, and when he *did* woolgather, it had to be the planned kind that would result in those wandering sketches he did that pulled a concept together. By the time the last hour rolled around, he was waiting on responses from the rest of his team, so he spent a few minutes with his tablet and stylus and drew… well, Julia.

His first sketch featured his Attention Hound with slightly crooked airplane wings for ears. She was in mid leap, soaring above the clouds, her head at that odd, downward tilt as she searched the earth below her for squeakies.

Milo put little labels on the sketch—her paws were "landing gear," her eyes were "squeaky identifiers," and her ears were "fondling platforms," and, well, her back end was the "unpleasant biscuit manufacturing plant." He chuckled a little to himself as he wrote *that* label and then started working on her background.

The result was an almost WWII era comic, with his "Biscuit Bomber" searching for Target Squeaky. He grinned when he was done and saved the thing, and over his shoulder his boss said, "I love it. Send it to the group, Milo. She's become our mascot."

Milo smiled at her, not able to hide his happiness. "She was *so* good today," he said. He'd been pleased and surprised. "I'm so glad. I didn't want to leave her alone, and finding a dog sitter sort of freaks me out."

"So I gathered," Angela said dryly. "Why didn't you call me and ask me, Milo? If she's your emotional support animal, we could have figured this out last week."

Milo gave her a fleeting smile but didn't meet her eyes. "She's not officially my emotional support animal," he said. "My friend brought her to my house to get me out of bed."

There was a speaking silence over his shoulder, and while his mom hadn't been great at the job, he did seem to remember that sort of silence had strings attached. With a sigh he swung his chair around to face his boss.

"I was going to talk to you during lunch," she said, pulling up a spare chair from the back of his cubicle. Their floor plan was semi-open—they were given partitions if they wanted, but nobody was allowed to wall up in isolation. He liked to keep a partition behind him and to his left, which was the main passage through the office space itself. That way he could turn inward and ask his colleagues questions or hear their off-the-cuff creative chatter if it pertained to him, but he wasn't constantly distracted by traffic through the office.

For the most part, it worked. As introverted as Milo was (he didn't deny it), the compromise kept him engaged with his team but not freaked out by all the people. In this instance, because many of his colleagues were off on the yoga mats in the far corner of the office doing some afternoon stretches, her move gave them privacy.

"Sorry," he said automatically, and she grimaced.

"I didn't because Rick was there, and you like to stay private, but we've been worried about you these past months. When you took last week off...."

He let out a breath. "Yeah, I know. You thought you'd never see me again. I didn't know what to do with the dog." He gave her a hesitant smile, hoping that would be it, but she shook her head.

"That's last week—"

"I got promoted!" he protested, suddenly super embarrassed. "I mean, I couldn't have been *that* depressed, right?"

The look she leveled him was as sober and as tragic as he'd ever seen. "Tell that to my sister," she said softly. "The one with the scars on her wrist and the 4.0 college GPA. Don't joke about this, Milo. We were worried."

Milo sighed. "My... my boyfriend moved out in August," he said. "After a super heinous fight. I... well, I didn't deal with it well."

"Aw, Milo," she said. "Why didn't you say anything?"

Milo considered that seriously. It wasn't like he'd thought of work as the enemy, was it? Suddenly he heard his mother's voice in his head. *Nobody wants to hear about your stomachache, Milo. Why didn't you do the dishes? Who cares about the flu, Milo. B's aren't acceptable. It's an enlarged spleen, not congestive heart failure.*

Oh God, he'd almost forgotten about getting mono in high school. Mariana had gotten it from her sister, and it wasn't like Milo and Mari had ever drunk their own soda after that first meeting at Milo's locker.

"Programming," he said now, faintly. "Not supposed to let outside problems interfere with your performance, right?"

Angela's expression grew soft. "Yeah, I've heard that, but mostly from people my age." She gave an almost manic pixie grin. "Don't mess with Gen X, Milo. I played softball finals with a burst appendix and spent half my senior year with a shunt coming out of my stomach. We're hard-core."

He laughed a little. "Yeah, well, Millennials have their moments."

"And we all have our damage," Angela said softly. "But... but Milo, if you're sad, or struggling with work, you should come to one of us. I mean, I've never let you think you're not wanted, have I?"

Milo shook his head. "I love working here," he said, surprised to find it was true. "I'm proud of the work I do." This was also true. "I just... you know. Was sad."

"What was the argument about?" she prodded. "I hope you don't mind me asking. Some breakups can be worse than others."

"He... he wanted me to break up with my best friend," he said. "I... I think he was threatened? I don't know. And then he wanted to tell me how to spend my money. And then he said I wasn't worth his time if I didn't listen to his advice. And then he said...." He shook his head, not wanting to go there, just like he hadn't wanted to go there when talking to Garth. It was so pathetic. "Anyway, I should have seen him for what he was a long time ago, but—"

"Nobody likes to be alone," she murmured.

"He took my cat," he blurted, because those moments when he'd realized that Chrysanthemum was gone had been some of the worst, the lowest and darkest, of the breakup.

"Oh my God. Did he like the cat?"

"No!" Milo said, and while he heard his voice pitch, he couldn't stop himself this time. "He just… his sister came by for the cat's stuff and said he'd brought the cat to her, and she couldn't give him back or her brother would get mad, and… and he took my cat to be an asshole." The wonder of it would not leave him alone. "Who does that?"

God, he still missed his Mumsy. Chrysanthemum had rich chestnut fur and was one of those flat-faced Persian cats with the enormous feet and lack of motivation to go anywhere besides the food bowl. Sort of the anti-Julia in the four-legged pet department. He'd groomed the cat and fed the cat and trimmed his nails and had fallen asleep to the cat purring when Stuart was out late with his friends or staying up late to work on stuff he'd brought home. Milo had *loved* the dumb cat, and Stuart had felt entitled to walk away with him.

"People who are angry and hurt about something else often feel entitled to hurt you," Angela said staunchly. "Jeez, Milo, I'm so angry *for* you! Is that why you got Julia?"

Milo glanced down at the dog, who was lying in an awkwardly stiff position, legs straight out and poking at the soft sides of the crate. She appeared to be asleep; she just didn't appear to be relaxed.

"My friend—"

"The one you wouldn't give up for your controlling asshole boyfriend?"

He smiled. It did feel nice to have a consensus among his friends that *this* had been the problem, not the things Stuart had said on his way out about how awkward Milo was, how underdeveloped, how incapable of talking to other humans without being an asshole. "That's the one. Mari showed up at my house two weeks ago with her." He laughed a little. "She was wearing cat ears. You know, to make up for the fact that Chrysanthemum was gone."

"The friend or the dog?" Angela asked, but her eyebrow was arched, so she was obviously teasing.

"The dog," he said, pleased that he could tell this story and make it funny. "She looked adorable." He gazed down at her some more. "She's very sweet," he said. "But, you know, even though she's young, she was abandoned for some reason. She's got damage. She wants to kill all the squirrels. She thinks other dogs are assholes. I thought she was going to *eat* Rick when we first got here."

Angela laughed into her hand.

"It's not funny!" Milo protested. "I mean...." He gave her a pleading look. "He's got that note in his voice...."

"The one that seems like it should be making all the windows vibrate?" she said. "Yeah, I know. Some people are just... vibrant. Rick's vibrant. We like him that way, but it's like Tajín in lemonade—it's an acquired taste."

"They have that?" he asked, baffled.

"Yeah, not as bad as it sounds. Anyway, so Rick came on a little too strong, and Julia almost ate him—"

"I would have had to have her put down!" he squeaked.

Angela grimaced. "Well, I would have thought twice about letting her come to work, but if you're taking steps to modify her behavior—and given that she was taking treats from Rick all through lunch, I'm going to assume you are—"

He nodded. "Oh yes. I *like* her. I just...." He glanced at her again. "I worry."

"Good," Angela said. "It sounds like your friend knew what she was doing when she brought Julia over. If you can be proactive for your dog, you can be proactive for yourself. I'll put in the paperwork to call her an emotional support animal, so if she, you know, loses her mind and piddles on the carpet, we can get the carpet changed." She grimaced. "It's sort of an ugly purple beige anyway. I almost wouldn't mind." Then she sobered. "But seriously, Milo, you were in a dark place, and you didn't come to anybody here. We were worried. We try to respect your boundaries, but I don't know if we can do that if you drop off the map again. I'm going to be calling you on off days from now on, to make sure you're still functioning, okay?"

Milo knew his ears turned pink. "Honestly," he said, "you don't have to do that, Angela. I'm better now."

"Yeah, but I like talking to you." She glanced around. "I mean, I like talking to my whole team. On the one hand, I'm blessed because you all work so well on your own, we only have to meet once a week, and you all produce wonderfully. But on the other hand, one of the best things about a five-day-a-week office was that everybody got to *communicate.* Don't make me bring everybody back for another day a week—I'll be *despised.*"

Milo gave her a small smile. "I wouldn't despise you," he said loyally. Angela had hired him, had looked at his drawings, had laughed at his jokes. He did love working for her. "Especially not if you let me bring Julia."

She laughed loud enough to make the dog snort and half struggle to her feet before collapsing back in her stiff-legged, dead-dog posture.

"As long as you can keep her from eating Rick, that's fine," she said. "Maybe we can get her to fetch the—"

Milo flailed, holding his finger to his lips. "No!" he whispered harshly. "Don't mention fetching the s-q-u-e-a-k-y. She'll drive us all batshit. I swear!"

Angela gave him an evil smile. "Julia," she sang. "Get the squeaky!"

At the word "squeaky," Julia scrambled to her feet and grabbed hold of one of her favorite toys. Happily, she stuck her face out of the crate and gnawed on the squeaky, making the noise and begging Milo with her eyes. Before Milo could grab the toy, Angela—moving slowly and talking in her most soothing tone—urged, "C'mon, girl, give me the squeaky. I'll throw it for you. Let's fetch the squeaky!"

Julia gazed at this new friend with worship in her eyes, and in short order Angela was throwing the squeaky down various corridors of the enclosed office space, and Julia was scrambling over empty chairs and under empty desks and around partitions to get to the toy of her dreams. Angela was laughing so hard she almost couldn't throw, and still Julia ran, as enchanted with this game and this new player as she had been with Mari and Milo.

Milo watched them play and laughed and thought that maybe bringing her to work was genius, and he couldn't *wait* to tell Garth.

And Mari, of course, but also he couldn't wait to tell Garth.

My Fair Milo

GARTH COULDN'T help it. He took one glance at Milo's beaming face as he waited in the upper parking lot for Garth and Chad to top the rise to the walking loop, and his heart leapt.

He's got a lot of rebounding to do, Garth warned himself. *So much healing. He may not even like you that way.*

But Milo's apple-cheeked face, his slightly prominent ears—highlighted, of course, by a spiffy new haircut—and his sweet, sunny, open-faced grin, and it all... all *buzzed* every one of Garth's favorite places.

Just *look* at him, leaning on a parking post, Julia gazing at him besottedly. He was so damned heart-stoppingly cute.

"So," Garth said as he and Chad neared their meeting spot, "I take it things worked well?"

The day was going to be a bit warm, so Garth was wearing a T-shirt and cargo shorts along with his comfy work boots, and as he drew near, he saw that Milo was wearing skinny jeans and a pale pink T-shirt that was... well, tight. *Very* tight. It revealed slender muscles, a concave tummy, and tiny pebbled nipples.

"Also," Garth said, staring at that almost delicate chest, "somebody seems to have stolen your wardrobe?"

Milo blinked and then grimaced. "Yes, yesterday went really well," he said in response to the first thing. "And... you know, I don't know why this shirt was on top. It's weird. It was like only my old clothes were out today. I haven't worn these jeans in years, but I couldn't find the new ones Mari bought for me last week."

Garth blinked. "That doesn't seem, I don't know, strange to you?"

"It does," Milo said, nodding. "It's... well, before I cleaned up, the place was like a hazardous waste dump hit by a tornado. But it's been clean for the last two weeks, and this morning it was looking... I don't have a word for it. Rifled. Weird."

Garth felt prickles along the back of his neck. "Yes," he said, thinking of the unlamented Stuart. "Weird. Anyway, tell me about yesterday."

"Oh my God!" Milo's initial excitement was back, and Garth was glad. "Oh, hello, Chad." Milo patted the dog's neck as Chad buried his face against Milo's hip. "Yes, big guy, I missed you—wow."

Chad was snuffling the skinny jeans, and now he dragged his tongue along the outside seam as though there was something glorious on them. He went to do that again, and Garth gave him a playful cuff on the neck. "Come on, Chad. What's the deal here?"

Milo shook his head. "I have no idea, but Julia went a little nuts over my socks this morning too." He wrinkled his nose. "They were sort of oily. I think there was something in the wash." He shook himself. "Whatever. Can I tell you about my day?"

He launched into a description of his day with his work people, and it was the first time Garth had heard him talk about a world bigger than Milo and Mari. Garth listened, enchanted as always, because Milo's point of view was as fey as Milo himself.

"So after Julia tried to *eat* Rick, he spent the day giving her treats, and now she thinks he's peachy, don't you, baby?"

Julia glanced up at him, and then driven by some irresistible force, she wandered back to nuzzle his socks as he walked.

"Knock that off," Milo muttered, and Garth wondered at the dogs' reactions even as he heard Milo's story of the dog cartoon and his boss, who'd been worried about him.

Well, good on that. Garth suspected Milo had *needed* to be worried about, and he was only sorry he hadn't known Milo at the time, because he thought he might be happy to spend lots of energy worrying about Milo. But beyond that, there was a… a thing. An aura about Milo that Garth was struggling to identify as they walked.

"So," he said, that part of his brain busy while he engaged Milo in their usual conversation, "do *I* get a picture of Julia? Can I see that?"

"Yes!" Milo all but chirped. "But first I'm working on a picture of Chad, because when I got home I was so excited about drawing Julia in a cartoon I wanted to show them both meeting, and *I* thought it was hilarious, so I wanted to show it to you."

"But the first thing—"

"But I want you to see it all together!" Milo insisted. "And, you know, cleaned up. And perfect." He paused, and Garth sensed his gaze on Garth's face. He glanced over at Milo and gave a gentle smile. "You've been so kind," Milo said softly. "I want you to see it good."

Garth winked at him and kept walking. "I can't wait," he said, although he thought he would love to be in on the work in progress. Artists didn't always work like that, he knew. You had to be in on someone's innermost circle of trust to see the half-finished product. He wondered if Mari had seen it, and then before he could make an ass of himself and ask that, he reminded himself that Mari and Milo had collectively saved each other's lives in innumerable large and small ways.

It was like dating a cop, he thought. A person's partner or bestie was always going to have a part of them that the romantic partner didn't. Just because Garth was sort of hoping for romance didn't mean that he got to jump spots in Milo's line.

"I can't wait," Garth murmured again softly. In the ensuing moment of quiet, Garth smelled it, and then he suddenly *got* it.

"Milo?" he asked. "Did you wash your clothes with a peanut butter sandwich?"

Milo gaped at him. "No," he said. "I actually *hate* peanut butter. My mom used to use it as punishment if I didn't like what was for dinner the night before. But…." He sniffed and wrinkled his nose. "But you're right!" He lifted his arm and gave a big whiff into his own armpit. "That's *so weird*. It's like my clothes—God, everything that was on top of the pile smells like *peanut butter*." He sounded horrified. "Isn't that like a dog aphrodisiac?"

"Sort of," Garth said darkly, his suspicions confirmed. "You're not allergic to peanut butter, are you?"

"No," Milo muttered. "I just don't like it. Why?"

"Who knows about the peanut butter thing? Your mom of course—"

"She doesn't," Milo said. "I mean, she didn't know it stuck and traumatized me." He grunted. "Not that she would care, I think. But Mari knows."

"Anybody you work with?"

Milo shook his head. "No, I mean, other than in passing. When we order sandwiches, I beg for anything *but* peanut butter, but other than that, I'm not picky. Tuna, Italian, barbecue—I'm easy to please."

Garth couldn't help the sideways look he slid toward Milo's puzzled face. God, he hoped so, he thought with some serious sexual hunger. "Good to know," he said. Then he did the hard thing. "Does, uhm, Stuart know?"

Milo grunted. "Well, yeah. He'd buy it anyway. I mean, I did all the shopping, and then he'd go buy peanut butter and jelly to have it in the fridge."

"Did he like peanut butter and jelly?" Garth asked.

"No," Milo said. "He never used it. I think he just liked it when I went 'Ew.'"

"What. A. Dick." Garth couldn't help it. After all of Milo's other stories—and what Garth suspected had happened *this* time—it absolutely had to be said. "Does Stuart still have the key to your house?"

"Yes," Milo said. "I mean, I never got it back." He paused. "You... you don't think...."

"Your horrible ex-boyfriend broke into your house and washed all your old clothes with peanut butter?" Garth asked, fury rising in his gullet. "Yes. Yes I do, Milo. I think he definitely did that."

Milo stopped abruptly in the shady part of the path. "But... but *why?*" he asked. "It's been two and a half months! I-I mean, right when he left, I could see it, but now? Shouldn't we be moving on? I mean, I am."

"Yeah, you are," Garth said, proud of him even though Garth himself had nothing to do with it. "But I suspect *he* hasn't. I bet he's been watching you."

Milo shuddered, looking absolutely like a light-struck deer. "But... *why?*" There was a note in his voice, a sort of hurt panic, that absolutely broke Garth's heart.

"To see if you moved on," Garth explained patiently. "And then to creep into your life and make sure you couldn't."

Milo blinked at him. "That's *so weird.* Would he really do that?"

Garth sighed, not wanting to break his heart further but thinking Milo probably deserved to hear the truth. "Baby, if any ex-boyfriend was going to turn into a stalker, it was going to be the guy who stole your cat and went through your finances and expected you to buy a new house just to accommodate his life. I hate to say this, but he sounds sort of like a controlling bastard from beginning to end, and this little bit of creepiness is par for the course."

"But... but what should I do?" Milo's frown of baffled hurt got a little sharper. "What would I have done if you hadn't pointed it out? I mean, I could have gone on for a month and not figured out why Julia was so in love with my socks. And I never pay attention to what I'm wearing. What a weird thing to do, right? I mean, creepy and controlling, but… but I might not have noticed."

In spite of his sudden worry, Garth found himself chuckling. "No," he said. "You might not have. Listen, what are you doing today?"

"Going home and taking a shower and putting some sort of degreaser in the washer and rewashing all my clothes," he said promptly. Then he shuddered. "Or maybe rewashing my favorite clothes and ordering new ones." He glanced down at what he was wearing again. "I probably could have ditched this outfit right out of high school and the world would have been a better place."

Garth's absolute delight with him could not be contained. "Milo, did Stuart tell you what to wear a lot?"

Milo wrinkled his nose. "He tried," he said. "I would come home and find big bags of stuff going to the Goodwill on the porch, and I'd look in them, and it would be all my stuff. I'd hide them in the garage and then put them back in my drawers when Stuart wasn't there to see. 'Did those bags get picked up, Milo?' 'Yes, Stuart—they're gone now.'" Milo shrugged and, to Garth's relief, continued to walk. "And then I'd wear something he didn't like again, and he'd ask me where it came from, and I'd forget."

Garth raised his eyebrows. "You'd forget?"

"Well, yes. I mean, the thing with the bags would happen and the clothes wouldn't resurface for another month, and I'd, you know, forget." Milo blinked a couple of times, leaped nimbly over Julia, who had stopped again, and then tugged on her leash. "He'd… he'd get sulky after that, but he'd never tell me what was wrong."

Garth had never felt so much like crowing before. "What was wrong," he said, "is that he was trying to control the wind. *Stuart* was engaged in psychological warfare, and you were engaged in passive resistance. It's like swinging a tennis racket at what you think is a ball and hitting Jell-O. It's brilliant."

Milo blinked. "Well, when I talk about it, it sounds like he was a real prick!"

"He was," Garth said gently.

"But how could I be living with a real prick for over a year and not know it until he tried to divorce me from my best friend?"

Garth knew he'd regret it—knew he'd smell like peanut butter for the rest of the day—but he didn't care. He draped his arm around Milo's shoulders like he had the day before and pulled him close. "Because you are so sweet," he said softly. "You are so sweet, it didn't faze you. You just sort of... bobbed and weaved whenever he tried to control you. And then you broke up with him, and he thought it would break you. And it didn't." Garth sighed.

"That's bad?" Milo asked, still baffled and confused.

"Only because that's when guys like this get dangerous," Garth said. "Look, I'm going to call my client and postpone my work today, and then you and I are going to take a peek around your house to see what we can do to prevent this from happening again."

"You can't do that," Milo said. "Your job is important!"

Garth grunted. He couldn't really argue with that. A bunch of supplies were supposed to get delivered that morning, and Doug was coming over so they could solidify work on the porch. But Garth didn't want Milo in his house if Stuart had been there. He just didn't. He wanted security and a cleaning service and—

"Okay," he said. "You're right. Okay, can you bring your computer over to my client's house? She's got a big place. You and Julia could hang out there and get some work done—"

"You can't just drag me into this woman's house!" Milo protested, sounding horrified.

Garth shook his head. "I'll ask first," he said. "And you'll bring Julia's crate. We're adapting her house to hold two big dogs, which was supposed to be my big news, but I'll fill you in later. Don't worry. You and me can make this work, but in the meantime, I don't want you home without a security system, okay? Your house needs to be your house, Milo. Let's get you in charge of your own destiny, okay?"

Milo was staring at him with an uncomfortable amount of worship in his eyes. "You're like Superman," he breathed.

"I'm a guy with a dog," Garth told him, but inside he was warmed from his toes on out.

Okay, he thought. Let's make some empowerment!

MISTY WAS fine with Milo coming over for the day, and Julia?

Well, she might have spent the entire day in her crate, Milo nervously fretting about her reaction to Daisy and Butch and Chad all at once, but things went so fast! Garth—after a quick phone consultation—

followed Milo to his sweet little duplex and, after waiting in the truck with Chad, took Milo and Julia to Misty's house. Julia and Chad, after exchanging a brief growly greeting, backed off immediately when Garth and Milo both barked, "Leave it!"

Julia turned toward her corner and Chad to his in the back of the extra cab, and they both sniffed and ignored each other after that.

"Wow," Milo muttered. "I must really be off my game to not think that they'd have problems. She does make everything more challenging."

"Well, she also makes you more aware of your surroundings," Garth said. "Did you notice anything when you went back inside?"

"Yeah," Milo said glumly. "I could smell peanut butter *everywhere*. I rifled through my drawers and realized that one of my old shirts was smeared in it, like it had been washed that way. I did laundry the day before yesterday—there was a load on top of the drier waiting to be folded. Stuart put the load of all the clothes I wore as a last resort in the washer and *then* the drier with a peanut butter sandwich." Milo shook his head. "Which I would not have known, but I got home and the drier door was open, so I thought I'd spaced out in mid-laundry, because I've done that, you know?"

Garth suppressed a smile. He could not imagine spacing out in the middle of laundry, but it was nice to know Milo's quirks.

"Of course," he said.

"Stuart used to yell at me about it," Milo went on guilelessly. "Milo, you fucking space cadet, take care of your shit!"

Garth had to keep himself from braking mid traffic. It wasn't just the words, which were pretty harsh, but the *tone*, which Garth had never heard Milo use, not even when Julia was being her most intractable.

"Milo," he said, keeping his voice soft. "Is that how he spoke *to you*?"

Milo nodded, seemingly unperturbed. "I mean, that's how people talk to you when you space out, right?"

"Who else talks to you like that?" Garth asked, almost afraid of the answer.

Milo shrugged. "Mom, stepdad, my college roommate. Not Mari, though. Or, come to think about it, the people at work. I-I mean, even Rick, who can be *loud*—he doesn't talk like that." Milo snorted. "He's just loud."

Garth drove to Misty's house on autopilot. "Milo?"

"Yeah?"

"I will *never* speak to you like that. Please, *please*, don't hang out with anybody who speaks to you like that."

"Oh, it's okay," Milo explained. "That's how people who love you talk when they lose patience because you fuck up."

Garth's heart was starting to hammer in his ears. "Baby," he said, knowing it was the second time he'd used the endearment that day but not sure that Milo had caught it, "that's how people who love you talk to you if you're about to run into traffic, or if you're standing next to a bomb. Anything less dire needs a better tone of voice. Please, *please* believe me on this. Stuart had no business saying those things to you, I don't care *how* many loads of laundry you left in the drier."

"Oh," Milo said softly.

"Oh, what?"

"Just… just I had no idea how much I needed to know that, that's all. Is that why your dog is so sweet? Nobody spoke to *him* like that?"

Garth's heartbeat eased up. "It could be. You don't speak to Julia like that," he said. "I mean, you call her idiot dog, but your voice is affectionate."

"Well, yeah," Milo responded. "She's like Mari. She trusts me. You… you don't abuse somebody's trust when they think you're a safe person." He let out a breath. "Like, you know, letting Julia chase turkeys when they thought they were okay to walk in the park. I shouldn't have let her do that."

Garth agreed, but he also understood a little better now. "Yeah, but sometimes when you've been pecked to bleeding by the other turkeys in your life, you end up lashing out at the innocent birds who were in the way."

"You just need someone to teach you better," Milo said. "Like I'm trying to teach Julia. And you're trying to teach me."

"Yeah," Garth said and felt like he needed to add, "but I'm not entirely altruistic." He pulled into Misty's driveway and proceeded to follow the paved track that swung around to the back, relieved to see that his friend Doug was there already with his pickup and that the supply people were *not*.

"You're not?" Milo said, and he sounded puzzled. "Why… why would you be my friend like this? What on earth could *I* give you?"

Garth chuckled, but it wasn't his happiest laugh. "Milo, don't panic. I like you. I think you're cute as hell. Someday, when Stuart is not your go-to, when you think about a boyfriend, I hope you might consider me for the job. And if you consider me, and it's a no, I hope you'll be honest and tell me we can be friends. But not now. I get it. You're a mess. But someday. Is that okay?"

Milo blinked at him, and for a moment Garth's heart absolutely wilted under the weight of his bafflement. Then a look of shyness passed over Milo's face—a sort of bashful recognition.

"You *like* putting your arm around my shoulders," he said, looking sideways out of those remarkably fey eyes.

"Yeah," Garth admitted, knowing his ears were turning red, "I really do."

"You can keep doing that," Milo said, a smug, self-important little smile on his face.

Garth's own smile was much bigger than that, but he didn't care. "Good," he said.

And that's where they were when Doug came and opened Garth's door, saying, "C'mon, man, we got shit to do!" and all hell broke loose.

First Chad scrabbled out of the truck from behind Garth's seat, Garth hollering—but not meanly—at the dog the entire time. Then while Chad was woofing at the fence to go visit his friends, Daisy and Butch, who were woofing at the gate as well, Julia pulled a spectacularly awkward, splang-legged leap from the back of the truck on Chad's heels. Before he could register the change of circumstance, Michael, who had been standing by the gate, opened it up to let Chad—and presumably the other humans—inside, and Chad zoomed in to play with his old friends, Julia following hard after.

"Julia!" Milo cried, and scrambled out of the truck on behind Garth as they raced toward the backyard to hopefully allay a bloodbath.

They both petered to a halt right inside the gate, and Garth put his hand on Milo's shoulder to make sure he could breathe.

The dogs—all four of them—were performing magnificent happy zoomie loops in the vast backyard, legs pumping, tongues lolling as each dog took turns being in front. For a few moments after Michael clanged the gate closed behind them, they watched in breathless wonder at the sheer spectacle of dogs playing.

Then—oh no!—Daisy got a little too close to Julia. Julia turned on her and snarled, and Garth's heart stuttered in his chest, but before he could run in to stop an out-and-out brawl, Chad turned around and head-butted Julia, sending her sprawling but completely unhurt.

She lay on the ground, stunned, before picking herself up and trotting back into the fray.

"Oh God," Milo said.

"Yeah—I thought that was it," Garth muttered. "God, I'm sorry, Milo. I'd had plans to do that slowly, maybe play with the ball a little, have some supervised introduction time."

"I'm so sorry," Doug said, coming up alongside them. "That was a *perfect storm, wasn't it?*"

"Wow," Milo murmured. "Maybe they can tire her out, you think? She... wow. She's really athletic."

"I think you need to stay in her sights the whole time," Garth told him. He nudged Milo toward the lawn furniture on a temporary pallet porch that he and Doug had set up the day before. "You and Misty can sit there and oversee the dogs while Doug and I get the supplies in. Michael's going to make sure they don't escape, and then after some consultation, I'll go over to your place and oversee your security."

"Are you sure your friend won't mind me and—"

"Oh my God!" Misty approached, wearing the same sort of clothes she'd worn when going to pick out Daisy and Butch. "You must be Garth's friend, Milo!"

Milo turned toward her, surprised, and Garth's favorite client met Garth's new favorite dog walker. "Hi, uhm, yes. It's nice to meet you—"

"Misty. Misty Parcival. Come sit with me and let the boys do their thing," she said, waving her hand. "I understand you work from home, doing something creative. I want to pick your brains for a minute about how you make that work."

Milo blinked at her, and Garth could almost *hear* his surprise that he had an unusual and marketable job skill that wasn't his art.

"O-okay," Milo said. "I'd love to. But I swear I'm sort of a space cowboy."

"Show her some of your commercial work," Garth told him, because Milo had told him where to look. Milo's logo work and with his advertising firm was *so* striking—clean but creative, with smooth, organic lines. Garth thought Misty would be as impressed as Garth had been, but that didn't mean Garth wouldn't like to see more of Milo's personal work.

He *so* wanted to see Julia as a comic-dog superhero. He couldn't help it. He thought that those weird airplane ears could do *great things* if only somebody with Milo's sense of whimsy could draw them.

But that's not what Milo was doing now. "Okay," he said, casting Garth a hopeful look over his shoulder before following Misty to their improvised outdoor office.

Garth let out a sigh of relief and turned toward the dogs, who were taking turns chasing each other. Chad tended to stick to a steady lope by Julia's side, sort of a proprietary "if she screws up I'll take care of it" posture, and Garth crossed his fingers. Julia might not be fully socialized, and everybody would have to be alert, but for a moment he could focus on his actual job.

Of course Doug wasn't going to let that slide.

"So you're doing what, now, while I'm digging out the area for the apron?" he asked, as both he and Garth helped the delivery guys shift supplies into the backyard. The dogs, for the most part, were staying away from all the commotion, and it had helped that Garth and Doug marked an improvised "fence" using yellow tape and stakes to ward them off.

"I'm going to his house to install some security," Garth told him. "His ex-boyfriend still has keys to his house and apparently snuck in to do some creepy shit yesterday."

"Like…?" Together they lowered their load carefully to the ground, making sure to lift with their thighs and calves and not with their backs.

"Like rearranged his laundry and washed all his old clothes with a peanut butter sandwich because apparently he hates the stuff."

Doug stood up. "Holy crap! I mean… what a creeper!"

"You can call him an abusive motherfucker," Garth growled. "I'm starting to think of him like that."

"Aw, man—for real?" Doug was six feet two inches and two hundred and thirty pounds of gruff muscle, but that included his heart, which he exercised frequently on his two daughters, who adored him. "Like, you know, physically?"

"No," Garth told him as they made their way back to the truck for more bags of cement. "Like, intimidation. Calling him names. Trying to control his life. Milo drew the line at buying a new house and breaking up with his best friend to make the guy happy, and the guy lost his shit and left. And stole Milo's cat. Anyway, this weird stalking thing is new, and I think it should be stopped immediately, don't you?"

"God yes. In fact, how about you and me both go check out his house. My wife's got a friend in the police department who can help us set him up with a porch camera and a security system and maybe a heads-up with the cops. Guys like this usually—"

"Escalate," Garth said grimly. "Yeah, I know. I'm hoping that maybe knowing Milo has a dog might put the guy off, but—"

"You never know." Doug and Garth had roomed together, and they'd been pretty tight even before their romance-movie weekend. Garth *deeply* understood Milo's attachment to Mari, because he wouldn't trade Doug in for any money.

"Let's get this unloaded," Doug said, "and I'll come with you. Maggie had one of these when I met her in college. You remember?"

"Sugar-in-the-gas-tank Bill?" Garth said grimly. "Yeah. I seem to recall we had to go to some extreme means to get the guy to back off."

They'd filed a restraining order, of course, but when Bill had shown up on campus, shadowing Maggie's movements within visual distance of her as she went from class to class, they'd taken some… unusual measures. Almost *stalker*-like measures, if Garth had to be truthful about it. When they'd realized Bill was shadowing Maggie on campus, they'd superglued his car locks. While he was trying to get into his car, they'd visited his parents' house and shown them pictures of Bill violating the restraining order.

Then they'd taken turns, all four of their friend group, escorting her from place to place while the rest of the group took photos of the ex-boyfriend and texted them, one after another, to the local police *and* the campus police *and* social media.

By the time they were done with him, he was the most hated man on campus, and he'd had to replace all the door locks on his car *and* his apartment because this went on for a week.

And finally they were able to get him arrested.

But Maggie had been looking over her shoulder for a long time. She and Doug had almost moved out of state when they'd gotten together, but Bill had managed to get himself thrown in prison for armed robbery before that happened.

"Yeah," Doug said grimly, and it was clear they were on the same page. "I do not like the idea of that guy on his own with a Bill on his tail. Here, let's go talk to Misty about taking a powder. You think she'll mind?"

Garth glanced over to the little pavilion Misty had set up under the porch overhang and was forced to smile. Julia had run herself out and was flopped under Milo's chair, panting happily while Misty poured Milo tea and was talking his ear off. Milo's expression was attentive and quite cheerful.

And Misty seemed enchanted.

Garth knew how she felt.

"I think they'll be okay," he said.

"Yeah, she's a good dame," Doug told him. "I really like your ideas for the porch and the pond—and the dogs—better than the other stuff you told me you'd be doing. This feels like it'll make it a place for her, you know? The inside of that house…." He shook his head. "That feels like a movie set."

Misty deserved a home, Garth thought, not for the first time.

"Look at us," he said with a grin. "We may seem like humble working stiffs, but in truth we fix people's lives."

Doug cackled, obviously pleased, and they went after the last load of concrete and wood so they could close the gate.

TWO HOURS later, standing in the shade of Milo's porch, they were not nearly so jubilant.

Are you sure you don't have a security system? he texted Milo for the second time, looking directly at the *security system camera* next to Milo's doorbell.

Yes. I asked Stuart if we should get one, and he said my house was a shithole with nothing worth stealing.

DIDN'T HE LIVE WITH YOU? God, Garth wanted two minutes with this guy.

Yes, but remember, I'm a slob.

You have a busy mind, Garth told him staunchly. Yeah, he and Doug had been inside, smelled the peanut butter, and spent an hour taking apart and bleaching the inside of the washing machine. Doug had needed to do this before—for exactly the same thing—when his preschool-aged daughter had washed her own peanut butter sandwich in a front-loader.

Milo was not a neat freak. In fact, Garth could trace multiple paths through the house. From the study, where Milo would bring a stylus from his tablet, to the kitchen where he'd set the stylus down to get a soda, to the living room where he set the soda down to throw the dog toy for Julia, to the back door where he'd let Julia out to run around. Or from the bedroom where he grabbed a sweater and set down his portable-phone charger, to the den where he set down the sweater and rifled through his desk—probably looking for the phone charger—and back to the kitchen where a drawer was open, full of styluses for his tablet.

It wasn't mass destruction; it was… well, wandering clutter.

I'm a slob, Milo returned, and Garth didn't lose it because he could hear that secret little smile Milo wore sometimes when he was tweaking somebody.

It's charming, Garth assured him. *But about the security system that Stuart didn't tell you he installed—do you have his phone number?*

Why?

Because Doug and I have a plan. Don't worry, I promise I won't call him.

No, but Stuart might wish he had.

Doug was looking over his shoulder, nose wrinkled because after cleaning the washing machine they both smelled like peanut butter. Garth was pretty sure they were going to have to do the same thing to the drier.

Milo texted the number, along with, *But I really don't think I have a system. Stuart assured me we didn't need one.*

Baby, I need you to, from now on, think very hard about everything Stuart told you and regard it as a lie. So if he said anything bad, like you being a slob? That was a BIG FAT LIE. And so was not installing a security system. I'll explain when I get there. In the meantime, can I pack a bag for you? You can stay at Mari's house tonight, or mine. I promise you I'll explain.

Okay. I'll text Mari, but she's got eight cats—Julia might be a bit much.

Mine, then. I've got a guest bedroom. No arguments.

Okay. You've seen what I wear. But, you know, something that fits and doesn't smell like peanut butter.

Understood.

And with that Garth pocketed his phone and turned to Doug.

"Did you get the number?"

"Yup," Doug said, and indicating the logo wrapped around the three tiny cameras they'd found on the porch, in the foyer, and—worst of all—in the bedroom, he grunted. "So my cop friend has the security system on the line. She gave them Stuart's number, and they're pulling up all the feed to his phone in the past two and a half months."

"Since the breakup," Garth growled.

"God, what a douche." Doug shook his head. "Why do guys gotta be like this? I mean, I *get* it. Why women can hate us. And you don't think of them doing it to other guys but... but your guy, he's sweet as a kitten!"

Garth thought about Milo cheering Julia on as she chased turkeys with abandon. "Kittens can lash out," he said. "We need to take care of this problem before this guy really hurts him."

"Wait," Doug said, "here we go. He had everything set up for motion detectors. Hunh."

"What?" Garth asked, peering over his shoulder.

"It doesn't seem like Milo did a lot of moving there for a while."

"Well, breakups," Garth said, but his heart ached. Stuart hadn't deserved that sort of devotion. Together they watched as Milo lay facedown on his bed for hours at a time. He'd wake up, work frantically at the computer, and then fall asleep again. Garth was on the verge of telling Doug to forget it, this was intrusive and heartbreaking, when a movement on the porch caught the camera.

It was Stuart, peering in through the window. Milo had just departed for work, looking... well, much like Garth had first seen him, which was not put together at all, and suddenly Stuart was showing up on his porch.

Rifling through his mail.

He put it all back but—oh. He stole an envelope. And another.

"Can you fast forward that camera?" Garth asked.

"Yup," Doug said grimly. A few days later, Stuart came by and did it again.

"What mail is he stealing?" Garth asked.

"I don't know," Doug said. "But tampering with mail is a crime. I'm sending this to my friend in the department. Is his name on the deed?"

"Nope," Garth said grimly. Because that had been the beginning of the end, hadn't it? Stuart wanted Milo to move so he could put his name on the deed. Milo had wanted to keep the duplex, because he was making money from the neighbor next door and he liked his little living space. Garth had to admit, although cluttered, he kept it cleaned and vacuumed, and the space was airy and white, with bright little accents—trim painted blue or red or yellow in most of the rooms, or faux gates with the same colors. The kitchen tile was mostly white, with the occasional primary colored tile thrown in, and the bathroom did the same thing. The floors were blond hardwood laminate, and the bedding and towels were those same bright, whimsical, comic-book colors. The place was... happy. And whether or not Milo and Stuart had been happy inside it, Garth had gotten the feeling Milo, at least, was trying.

That much effort deserved some real happiness, Garth thought with determination. The least he could do was try as hard as Milo.

So they forwarded their info to the police and finished the repairs on the washer and dryer, and then feeling like intrusive perverts, they sorted the wash that had been contaminated to send it through again.

"Okay," Doug said, holding up a rumpled, now-brownish rainbow-colored T-shirt that announced Pride Spirit Week on it. "This is obviously from high school. Does he really want this washed? Or should we maybe throw it out."

Garth grimaced. "I suspect," he muttered, taking a look at the affected load of laundry, "that this entire exercise was an attempt to get Milo to throw out his old stuff—his Mari stuff—so Stuart could maybe drive a wedge between Milo and his friend." He snorted. "The truly ironic thing here is I don't think Milo noticed. Having seen him dressing for the past week and a half, I think this shit was on the bottom of his drawers. But now that Stuart tried to *make* him throw it away...."

"We'd better leave the choice to Milo," Doug said. "I get it. God, how insecure is this asshole anyway?"

"I am at a complete loss," Garth said, shaking his head. "So do we want to install the real security system and then rip this shit out, or rip this shit out and let him guess?"

Doug was unbuckling his pants, and for a moment Garth stared, but then Doug turned around and glanced over his shoulder.

"Dude," he said, "you gonna leave my ham swinging in the wind here? I'm trying to make a statement for your boy!"

"Oh! Yeah. Sorry." Garth did the same, and in a moment, the two of them were serving up a double order of pressed ham.

And *then* Doug drove a ball-peen hammer into the fisheye lens, and they bid Stuart and his creepy, controlling security system that Milo did *not* know about adieu.

Then they did the same for the back door, and then for the bedroom.

And then they got to work.

What Bites You in the Ass

MILO ENJOYED Misty Parcival so much.

She was smart and funny, and she loved Julia almost as much as she loved Daisy and Butch, and she thought Milo was *brilliant*, which Milo loved hearing even if he knew it wasn't true.

They talked creativity and schedules and how sometimes you had to let your dragon ride you; for instance, when you had an idea for something that had *nothing* to do with your deadlines or your plans and just insisted on being heard. And how sometimes you had to ride your dragon, like when your boss said, "Milo, I need this in a week. For God's sake could you get your head out of the clouds and help us out here?" (That last one had only happened once or twice, and since it had turned out that Milo's wandering off usually helped him create *really amazing* art for the thing he needed to do, Angela had learned to trust his dragon as much as he did.)

And then Misty fed him cookies.

The day, spent under a temporary awning and a sunny October sky, would have been nearly perfect if it hadn't been for what Garth and his friend Doug were doing while they sat and chatted, sometimes worked, and chatted some more.

The second time Garth asked Milo if he was *sure* he didn't have a security system, Milo got a little chill. If he didn't have one, but Garth thought he had one, did that mean....

No. Stuart wouldn't do that, would he?

Would he?

Milo resisted the temptation to text Stuart and ask him, mostly because the only texts he could wrap his head around to post read something like *Stuart you controlling bastard, did you bug my house?*

He wasn't sure he was ready for that confrontation—or even if it was healthy. At this point, Stuart was already doing things like washing Milo's old clothes with peanut butter—probably to make Milo throw them away. Milo was suddenly wondering if, in his rather dreamy approach to the world, he hadn't missed some *other* things Stuart had done that he didn't know about.

Unexpectedly he got a frisson of fear up his spine, and he thought of Mari.

Mari he could text.

Guess what?

Chicken butts.

He smiled at her usual return, because it was such a high school thing to say.

Also, I think Stuart washed my old shirts with peanut butter to make me throw them away while I was gone from the house yesterday.

His phone buzzed in his hand, and Misty Parcival glanced up at him from her computer.

"My friend," he said, standing up to take the conversation to the middle of the yard. Julia followed him, her squeaky in her mouth indicating that any motion in this direction should be accompanied by throwing, and Misty waved him on with a smile.

"What in the hell?" Mari asked as he accepted the call.

"Well, I showed up to walk Julia wearing my old art-club shirt—"

"The one you wore before your growth spurt?" she asked.

Milo grunted and looked happily at the long-sleeved blue henley he'd thrown on when he'd gone inside to change. "Yeah. What can I say? It was on top."

"But *why*? You haven't worn that thing since—"

"Yeah, I know, but you and I designed them, so I kept it. But it was on top, and so were these skinny jeans from our first year of college, and I put them on, and they smelled like peanut butter."

"You hate peanut butter," she said blankly.

"Yeah. I didn't put it together until Garth and I were walking, but… well, there's no reason for these clothes to be on top. I didn't even wear them when I sort of boycotted laundry for a month, but suddenly they're on top of my folded clothes, and they smell like peanut butter, and—"

"Stuart."

Yeah, Mari always *had* been quicker on the uptake than Milo.

"So, my friend Garth—"

"Hot guy, giant dog," she said to prove she'd been listening.

"Yeah. He took me to his client's house. She's nice. She has dogs. Julia and her dogs get along. Anyway, he and his buddy went back to check my house out and…." He didn't know how to say this. "He's asked me twice if I have a security system. And the only reason he would ask me that is—"

"If you have a security system you don't know about," she muttered. "Oh God, *Milo*. What are you going to do?"

Milo grunted. "Well, I'm going to wait until Garth comes back and gives me the whole damage report, and then I'm going to *plan*."

"What's your plan?" she asked.

"I have no idea," he said. "But there will be one by the time we leave Misty's house tonight." He swallowed. "I'd come to your house, but I can't bring Julia. Honey, you just have too many—"

"Cats," she replied glumly. "Although this last week I've had a guy too, so that might be awkward."

"Georgie?" he asked, hoping.

"Yeah." She sighed happily. "He's…. God, Milo. He's as dumb as I am, but he helps with all the cats, and at night when we're watching TV, he's surrounded by them. They all sit on the two of us and…." She grunted. "It's weird. I never put that as a thing I should want in a guy, but it should have been the *one* thing I put on the list. Forget handsome, forget rich—does he love my cats like I do. It's the only requirement necessary."

"But he can't be a freeloader," Milo said, in case she had forgotten.

Mari made a protesting sound in her throat. "He lives with his parents," she admitted. "Mostly because they're all trying to afford his sister's upkeep in the place. I guess I got a better deal than they did—or maybe Serena's Medicare pays more." She grunted. "Which reminds me, I got a letter from that place I should look at."

Milo's little frisson of fear—which he'd forgotten in the happy chatter about Georgie the great—suddenly hit him a little harder.

"Mari," he said, suddenly concerned, "I've got to make another phone call. I just wanted to keep you updated and let you know that I'm working on a plan, okay?"

"Yeah, sure," she said. "You'll text me when you have it in hand, won't you?"

"Of course," he said.

He rang off and then pulled up the number of Mari's sister's care home, his heart hammering in his chest at a thousand beats per minute. Oh shit. Oh hell. He'd sat at his kitchen table while she'd been right there, and he'd done bills, and he hadn't seen one bill from the place that had started this whole cascade of consequences in the first place, and he'd been *such* a dreamy, stupid little freak the obvious hadn't occurred to him.

"Sunshine Adult Care Facility," came the chirpy voice on the other end of the phone. "What can I do for you?"

By the time the conversation was over, Milo was one harsh, hyperventilated breath away from falling down and weeping on a stranger's lawn.

"MILO," GARTH was saying, and Milo realized Misty must have set him back down in her shaded porch. "Milo, c'mon, buddy, you here with me?"

"I… I owe them *money*," he said, trying not to pass out over the amount. "I… they raised the price, and he's been hiding it for three months and… oh my God, Garth, I could get her sister kicked out because my ex-boyfriend is a douchey creep, and *I had no idea*!"

Garth nodded, seeming, oddly enough, relieved. "And that answers whether or not you figured that out yet," he said, and Milo stared at him helplessly.

"He was watching you," Garth said. He was… he was *kneeling* at Milo's feet, holding Milo's hands, and Milo could only grip them as spots swam in front of his eyes. "He put security cameras around your house, and he caught himself taking mail out of the mailbox."

Milo let out a small moan, but Garth shook his hands and pulled his attention back.

"Stay with me here, baby. I need to know if he had residence in your house. Cohabitation is one thing, but did he have bills or correspondence or—"

Milo frowned. "No," he said, this much clear. "His sister sublet his apartment in Sac. He stayed there sometimes when work went late, but all his bills and his correspondence went there."

"So he had no reason to be checking your mailbox," Garth said.

"Only to steal my bills from Serena's care home," Milo told him bitterly. "I just called them up. I-I had this weird feeling. When Mari came over with Julia, she had all my mail. I sat down and started going through it, and none of those bills were in the pile. They should have been. I should have been a little late on the last one. But Stuart's been taking *all* of them. The last *three*. It's the only bill I pay by check, you know? Everything else is direct deposit. But there are fees, and she's about to get evicted, and they need another chunk of money to keep her spot, and I could have it in a *month*, but I don't have all of it *now*, and—"

His voice was rising with panic, and only the warmth of Garth's hands on his kept him sane.

"Okay. Okay, it's good that we know this. Look, Milo, you're sounding a little unhinged right now. Do you mind if I call up the care home? Maybe if somebody explained the situation to them who *isn't* losing his shit, they'll be more receptive to a month's grace."

Milo gulped and choked, and then Garth was standing enough to wrap his arm around Milo's shoulders and pat his back.

"We got you, baby," he said softly. "I promise. Don't panic."

Milo nodded and handed his phone to Garth, who took his turn in the middle of the yard, absently throwing a giant rope to the three big dogs.

"Can I ask?" Misty said from his side. "I hate to be nosy, but you've been such a good friend today. I was so excited Garth brought you to me, I didn't even ask you why you're here."

Milo was usually *such* a private person. Later he would reflect on how raw he must have been, how vulnerable, in these past months, to open himself up to Garth, to Misty, with so little length of acquaintanceship.

The story came pouring out—Mari, Stuart, even Julia and then Garth. He cried a little, while watching Garth talk on his phone, and Misty passed him a tissue.

He turned his head and said, "Thank you. I'm sorry. I'm... I mean, I'm usually sort of a space cowboy, but I'm not usually this much of a mess."

She gave him a soft smile. "Oh, honey, I've got kids your age. You're fine. Not every relationship is a home run right out of the box. I'm sorry you ended up with *this* nightmare, but you've got to know it's not your fault, right?"

"Isn't it, though?" Milo asked. "He... he asked me to ditch my best friend, and I stayed with him."

She patted his hand, a simple gesture of human contact that made him want to hold on to her hand like he would with Mari. "But you *didn't* ditch your friend. And you didn't incite a confrontation. I know you're a man, but women have known these things for years, Milo. Abusers start out by isolating their victims so they have nowhere to turn. You never let him do that. In fact you put your foot down when he tried to isolate you further. You didn't know he was spying on you—why would you think he would? You did nothing more or less than take a person at face value when they said they cared for you. All the bad things that followed are on *him*, not on you."

Milo nodded and wiped his face on his T-shirt. "You're really nice," he said. "But so is Garth. I guess I've got certain expectations, now, that Garth's friends aren't going to suck."

She laughed a little. "Garth was supposed to come and fix my back fence for me," she said. "Three years ago. That was the job. My friend Margie said he was great, and even when he seduced her grandson, he still finished the job."

Milo sputtered. "Seduced her...."

Misty waved her hand. "The boy was older than Garth, but I gather he was as surprised as Margie to learn he was gay. And Garth hasn't done anything like that for a while." Misty gave Milo a conspiratorial look. "He grew up, and he always did have a core of sweetness in him. But see? When you're young, that's when you make your heartbreak mistakes. It wasn't your fault your mistake had a core of rot in him. But don't worry. You've got friends besides your beloved Mari. We'll sort this out. Mari's sister won't suffer. I promise."

Milo smiled at this sweet woman who had only met him today and tried not to cry some more. "I-I promised Mari it would be all right," he said on a hiccup. "See, I had money from my family. They suck, but I had their money, and the least I could do was help. But...." He swallowed. "I'm going to have to tell her. I didn't want her to know. People get weird about money—look at Stuart."

She snorted. "Honey, I think Stuart was weird to begin with. It's your money. You get to say what it's for."

At that moment Garth stalked over, Milo's phone in hand. "Okay," he said, brow furrowed. "I think we've reached an understanding. The problem is they need the papers re-signed, which means...." He looked at Milo meaningfully.

"Oh God," Milo muttered. "I have to tell Mari."

Garth nodded. Milo took the phone and stood to head for the middle of the yard again, but Misty put her hand on his arm to stop him.

"Honey, you can do this one inside," she said, and he nodded.

In his head he saw a cartoon, a sweet woman in a flowered sweatshirt and denim leggings, but with a gauzy cape. Cape of Human Kindness, he labeled, and the cartoon got him through her guided tour into her official office, which was so baroque and stilted that he suddenly understood why Doug and Garth were working to transform her porch overhang into an office that the dogs could have access to.

The superhero in his imagination didn't belong in here, and he hoped she wrote thousands of words so she could be a mild-mannered romance novelist by day and a superhero by night.

And his imagination got him about to there when he sank into the office chair, pulled out his phone, and called.

MARI WAS... well, puzzled.

"You... you've been paying part of Serena's bill?" she asked for the fifth time.

"Well, yes. It's what I spent my trust dividends on. Or part of them. You know, most of them are being reinvested, and I live on my salary. But, you know, I had the money, and I spent it."

"But... but Milo. That money was for *you*," she said, her voice wobbling.

"But this was for me," he tried to explain. "You were so worried—it was eating you alive. And you love your sister so much, and you needed her to be someplace safe. I was worried about you, so, well...."

"You made it better," she said, like that was what she was having problems with.

"I'm sorry," he said, meaning it.

"No. No. Don't be sorry you were being kind," she said firmly. "I'm just—you said she might be evicted because you stopped paying?"

"Oh! No, I didn't stop paying," he said. "Not on purpose. Stuart stole my mail."

"He did *what*!"

After that the conversation felt much more normal, and Milo explained about getting pictures of his ex going through the mailbox and stealing stuff, and how he'd been so out of it for a couple of months that it hadn't occurred to him that he *hadn't* paid something he normally paid. "They don't have a mechanism for automatic deposit," he said plaintively. "They still don't. I know. I've asked."

"But… but you have to pay three months in a lump sum *plus* re-enrollment fees—"

"And the cost has gone up because we had to re-enroll her," he said glumly. "So yeah. I… well, Garth and Misty said they could front me the big chunk of change while I withdraw some more dividends from my investments."

"But, Milo, that's *your money*!"

"But it's just, you know, sitting in the money place, procreating. We were planning on taking a vacation when we were thirty, remember? And I said I had it covered. How did you think I had it covered? I just need to… I mean, I have an accountant, but I usually only see him once a year."

"Oh my God," Mari said, and he could hear the headache in her voice. "*Milo*. If you do this, I'll never speak to you again."

"You will too," he told her sharply, because the threat was terrifying. "You show up at my apartment with a dog and literally wade through my trash, and you don't think that matters to me? Money is… I don't know. Imaginary. You're real. And you need your sister to be okay. So I'm sorry this came up. I'm sorry we have to sign papers again. And I'm sorry it makes you squidgy to think of all the money. But I also don't care." He paused. "Oh God. Wow. That's bad. I'm a bad person. I'm a *horrible* person. Which is why you've got to stay my friend. It's in the bylaws. It came with the dog. You have to stay my friend even if it makes you squidgy, and I'm sorry, but I can't take it back."

When she spoke again, she was in tears—he could hear it, and he couldn't stop it. "But Milo, why wouldn't you tell me?"

His throat was thick, and he knew he was crying too. "Because I didn't want to have this stupid conversation! We're crying. I hate crying!"

She laugh/cried then, and the sound was disturbingly like a goose honking and then getting it's bill stoppered. "I hate it too! But… but…." He heard the horror dawning in her voice, and he knew. Knew what was coming next and couldn't stop it.

"Don't go there," he begged, still crying.

"Is this why Stuart left?" she asked.

He managed to make a snorting snot sound—not his finest moment. "It was more... nuanced than that," he said, and he glanced down at his feet and saw Julia practically nodding at him as though yes, this was how you did something with dignity. It was like she was there to show him how it was done.

"Milo, get it out. Get it all out now, and then I can cry and rage and be pissed and get over it. All at the same time."

He grunted. "He... he wanted me to not be friends with you," he said. "From the beginning. He... he said horrible things about you, and I just... I ignored him. I was your friend anyway. I lied to him about where I was going when we met." He let out a little laugh. "Remember when we drove to the coast and stayed in a hotel for three days?" It had been one of the best times of his life.

"Yes," she said. "I had to get someone to watch my cats."

"I told him it was a work conference." He'd come home and found PrEP in his medicine cabinet and knew why Stuart hadn't been mad about the sudden notice, but he'd kept quiet about *that* too. In fact he'd gone on his own prescription, in case Stuart forgot his, but Milo kept *his* hidden in his briefcase with his tablet.

"Why would you do that?" she asked.

"Because I couldn't live without you," he said miserably. "And I couldn't figure out why he'd hate you so much. You're perfect. I figured he'd come around—how could he not? I didn't realize he was a controlling bastard who didn't like that I had someone else in my life that I loved."

"An *abusive* controlling bastard," she said, her voice low and venomous.

"He cheated on me all the time," he admitted. "He went on PrEP and didn't even care that I knew, and then I went on it and hid it from him because I knew I couldn't trust him."

"Oh God," she muttered. "Milo, it's impossible to be mad at you for this, but do you see that it was wrong?"

"Not really," he said, "but I will believe you when you say so and try to do better."

"Augh!"

They were silent for a moment, both of them breathing hard on their end of the telephone line. When she spoke, she kept her voice modulated and calm.

"Okay, so we're both having amazingly bad days," she said.

"You have no idea," he muttered. "Peanut butter, Mari. *Peanut butter.*"

"Yeah, baby," she soothed. "It was bad. And the stalking and the cameras in your bedroom—"

He moaned a little because that one hadn't set in yet.

"So yeah," she said. "And you will never *not* be my Milo, and I will never *not* be your Mari. You believe me, right?"

"Yes," he said miserably, because he knew a "but" was coming.

"So I'm going to hang up and call Serena's home, because you're right, we've got to do some paperwork. And you're going to—oh Lord—try to find a place to live while your new dog-walking buddy is trying to stalk-proof your house. You *do* have someplace to stay, don't you?"

"His house," Milo muttered. "He's got a guest room."

"Well, that's kind," she said, letting out a breath. "So we're going to talk in two days. Put it in your phone, Milo. Right now. Two days."

"Why am I doing this?" he asked while he was doing this.

"Because I'm mad and I'm frustrated and I'm working out all my feels, but I don't want us to stop talking to each other because it's awkward now. And I know you. You will let this slide if nobody makes you face it."

"Sorry," he mumbled.

"Yeah, no, don't be sorry," she told him. "You… you spend too much time being sorry for shit that's not yours. And technically you were trying to do a nice thing, even though you were being sneaky because of the unbelievably low threshold you have for emotional discomfort."

"I'm literally queasy," he told her, although part of that might have been that he hadn't eaten. Peanut butter. Blargh.

"So am I," she said. "So we're going to talk in two days. And then we're going to talk in another two. And maybe eventually you'll see why you should have told me, and I will eventually forgive you for not. But in the meantime, we're still Milo and Mari, we just gotta be careful of each other, okay?"

"Okay," he said in a small voice. "Thank you, Mari. For planning to forgive me."

She sighed. "Thank *you*, Milo, for trying to take care of me. As mad as I am, I *do* recognize that this was a very generous thing you did, okay?"

"You needed to know your sister was okay," he said humbly.

"Yeah. Yeah, I did. Just... remember how Stuart made you feel powerless? How he tried to control you and tell you what you could and could not do?"

"Yeah," he said.

"Not knowing what you were doing—it makes me feel the same way."

"Oh, Mari...."

Her voice got thick again. "Don't worry. Two days. We'll talk. Love you always."

"Love you back."

And then she hung up, and he was left, huddling miserably on the giant modern office chair, which was still the most comfortable thing in the entire formal nightmare of a room.

Mitbewohner

GARTH FOUND him, knees drawn up to his chest, head resting against the back of the office chair, almost asleep.

"Milo?" he said softly.

"I'm a mess," Milo muttered.

"Well, it's been a shitty day."

"I mean before that," Milo told him. "My life—me. I'm not suitable for human company. You should lock me in a room until I chew my way out."

"She can't be that mad at you," Garth said reasonably, although he knew that there was an enormity to what Milo had done that might piss somebody off.

"She needs time to breathe," Milo mumbled. "We're talking in two days. She made me put it in my phone."

Garth smiled to himself. If nothing else, the way Milo and Mari seemed to interact would have attracted Garth to him. It was like nothing he'd ever seen.

"That's very promising," he soothed. "Misty is serving us lunch on the porch, and she wants you to be there. She said you looked peaked."

Milo lifted his head from its lifeless droop on the back of the chair. "What's she serving?"

"Wonton soup and walnut shrimp on noodles. Her cook is *amazing*. It's better than a restaurant."

"And it's *not* peanut butter and jelly," Milo said, perking up.

"No, it is not. Come on out, Milo. Let's have some lunch and discuss your security system and enjoy the sunshine. You can fret about the state of the world later, but now it's going to be okay."

"Okay," Milo said, and no sooner had he swung his legs down to the ground than Julia leaped into his lap and rested her head on his shoulder. He wrapped his arms around her and held her for a second. When he spoke, his voice was muffled. "This is why people have dogs, isn't it?"

"Yeah," Garth told him. He and Chad had their own private hugs to not tell anybody about. "It's one of the best reasons in the world."

Milo nodded. "Now I know," he whispered, and then he stood up, Julia still in his arms, and followed Garth back through the house.

He seemed to be okay during lunch, and while Misty, Garth, and Doug kept up most of the conversation, almost all of it focused on the work to be done in her yard, as well as the newly installed security system at Milo's duplex and how they should put it on the other side of the house and show the tenant how to use it, Garth kept careful note of Milo's expressions as he followed the conversation.

He wasn't there for all of it, Garth noted. There were moments when his eyes unfocused and he was obviously somewhere else, and Garth could read an entire adventure in his expressions as he wandered. Then he came back to what they were talking about, and his gaze sharpened, and he seemed to be taking notes.

And then, after an *outstanding* meal, which was reason enough to keep coming to Misty Parcival's house and doing work, he seemed to droop entirely.

Garth was going to suggest he take Milo home and then return to work, but Misty spoke up first.

"Milo," she said warmly, "I have a guest bedroom. You've had a day, and you need some alone time. How about you go inside and work or nap or navel gaze and leave the rest of us out here while the boys finish up."

And if Garth ever wanted the key to Milo Tanaka's heart, he saw it in the way Milo's face lit up at her words.

Introverts, he thought in wonder. Such simple needs, such amazing emotional dividends. Now he knew.

GARTH AND Doug worked until the light failed and planned to come back for a half day after a stop at Milo's place, as long as it was okay with Misty.

"But it's Saturday!" she said, surprised.

"We spent half of today somewhere else," Doug told her. "Let's get as much done as we can so you've got your closed-in porch when it gets too cold for office alfresco. My wife and the girls are out of town at a trick-or-treat thing in Jackson, so I've got time."

"Chad's happy, I'm happy," Garth said easily, but inside he was thinking that one more day here, in Misty Parcival's yard, watching the dogs play, could not possibly do Milo any harm and might certainly do some good.

He drove them to his house in the early evening when the last fingers of sunshine seemed to have stirred up the scent of a golden day. He cracked his window so he could smell woodsmoke and cut grass and earth, which were atmospheric things a person overlooked when they were younger but that seeped into the muscles and sinews when they approached thirty.

"It was such a pretty day," Milo remarked, seeming to read his thoughts. "I mean, it was unexpected, but last week was so gray. I'm glad we've got some more autumn."

"My favorite time of year," Garth confessed. "But that might be because I look forward to it getting colder for work. The summers can suck here."

Milo chuckled. "Even before Julia I used to walk early in the morning. When I was a teenager, it was so I could go angst alone, but I think it… it gave my mind a chance to wander so I could focus when I need it."

"ADHD?" Garth asked, because it was a common enough difficulty.

"Who knows," Milo replied. "Not severe enough to diagnose, I guess. Just… wandering brain. It's funny, because I've gotten yelled at all my life for it, but I've never felt the urge to fix myself. I made my deadlines at school, and now I make them at work. I pay my bills and manage my finances. Until recently I cleaned the house on my own schedule. I mean, it wasn't to *Stuart's* specs, but I didn't think it was bad."

"Seemed okay to *me*," Garth said. "And by the way, I'm sorry I had to see it for the first time without you there."

Milo glanced at him and shook his head. "You have friendly eyes," he said simply. "And I'm glad I got the artwork out of the garage. I swear, one of the best things Stuart did when he left was take his gawdawful art."

"What's gawdawful?" Garth asked. "I have no idea." Milo seemed to like the classics—Monet's *Water Lilies*, Manet's ballerinas, a few French wild-beasty type paintings, even that one poor soul with the psychedelic cats—all of it had added to that brightness in the pale white space.

"Pigs and penises," Milo said in disgust. "Contorted faces. Disjointed animals. I didn't recognize any of the artists, but Stuart was constantly saying that was because my tastes were plebian and uneducated." The insult rolled off Milo's tongue like he'd heard it too many times to dispute, but he followed it up with, "I don't know—considering my degree was in media communications with an emphasis on art and his was in political science, I think he was using the wrong words."

Garth had to bite his lip not to laugh. "Milo," he said when he could get control of himself, "I need you to remember what we talked about when it comes to what Stuart ever said to you."

"That it was a lie?" Milo clarified.

"Yeah, that."

"Okay, but what—"

"Your taste in art is fine," Garth told him. "It's your taste in men you need to work on."

Milo said, "I gotta say, I'm feeling sort of a soft spot for the guy who held my hand all day and is helping me get my ex-boyfriend out of my virtual house."

Garth chuckled softly. "Well, that's a start," he said. "But that guy thinks we need to wait until Stuart is all the way gone and you've got your feet under you before we jump into anything."

"Oh." Milo's voice held a wealth of disappointment.

"I used to take love and sex lightly," Garth told him, wanting him to understand. "I was, in fact, sort of a porn cliché."

"Ooh…." Milo's voice held no judgment. "Did you knock on doors and say 'I'm here to excavate' and—"

"And excavation meant something super dirty?" Garth said, laughing. "Yeah. I was that guy. And… I don't know. I got caught by one too many mothers, fathers, surprised and tragic wives. It… see, I started this job right out of school, and I'd sort of had my heart broken and I wasn't ready for something real. And suddenly I realized that it may not have been real to *me*, but what I was doing had consequences, and they were often painful, and—"

"Bowling for turkeys," Milo said, his voice throbbing with empathy. "Like… like when Julia was chasing the turkeys and I thought it was hilarious, but then suddenly she was chasing Chad, and I was horrified."

"Yeah," Garth said. "Exactly. It's all okay until you realize who you could hurt. So, you know, it's been a while since I've done that, but—"

"But you like me, and you don't want to knock me over," Milo murmured.

"Yeah," Garth said. He swallowed hard, suddenly wanting to touch that slight fey figure more than he could say. "Would hugs be okay? I mean, you know, after dinner or when we're watching TV or—"

He heard a sniffle, like a sob, and tried to backtrack.

"Or no hugs, zero hugs, no touching at—"

"It has been the *worst* day," Milo said through a voice made thick with pain and confusion. "I would *love* a hug."

Garth reached over and patted his knee. "A hug," he said. "And a snuggle on the couch. And some comfort. I think we can arrange that. It's a plan."

Milo laced his slender fingers over Garth's rough ones. "I like this plan," he said, and they were quiet for the rest of the way to the house.

UNLIKE MILO'S house, which was in Fair Oaks in a neighborhood of duplexes right next to a neighborhood of *really nice* houses built in the sixties and seventies—with appropriately bizarre rich people's floor plans—Garth's house was situated in Orangevale, in an old neighborhood of ranch-style homes that was one of the few places left in Orangevale still backed up with orchards.

Garth's parents had retired shortly after Garth came home from college, and had gone to live in a condo on the beach in San Diego, where Garth's mother constantly posted pictures of the beach, of the museums, and of food she didn't have to cook.

They'd left Garth the house and told him to do whatever he wanted to it, and he had. The house sat on a quarter of an acre— enough of a yard for Chad to wander, sniff, relieve himself, and roll around on his back, but not enough for him to chase Garth's farthest throw of the ball using the Chuckit. Garth had kept the dog-friendly landscaping, re-sided the ochre stucco with a cheery yellow paneling, and painted the walls a soft cream on the inside with accent walls, adding recesses that held family photos or tchotchkes—all of them well out of Chad's reach.

He'd opened up the living room/kitchen so the view one got from the entrance was of a brief foyer and a hall on the right leading to bedrooms, and a large living space on the left consisting of a great room with a television and leather couches opening to a kitchen Garth could knock around in. He did enjoy cooking once in a while—often making enough to last him part of the week and then treating himself to takeout for a night and a sandwich or soup when he really didn't feel like eating.

"So," Garth said as he walked in, swung his work belt from a peg in the foyer, and set his toolbox right underneath it. There was another pegboard for jackets and such, but Garth lived by himself and had no problem with his boots and tools tucked in their spot in the hallway. If they were dirty—if *he* was dirty—he went around back to the mudroom and cleaned up there. His mother had given him flack for this, but Milo wandered in and glanced around appreciatively.

"It's a home," he said, his face lighting up. "I love it!"

"Yeah?" Garth asked, suddenly hungry for more of that easy approval. It was funny because his parents had always been warm, and he'd had an easy time of it in high school and college—even coming out had been nontraumatic. But he hadn't realized how starved he was for praise from the man standing in his foyer, his blond dog at his heels, until Milo gave him words that were unforced and happy.

"Part of it is the size," Milo confessed. "My house is pretty small. But the open floor plan, the colors—it's happy and soothing at the same time."

Garth found himself smiling into Milo's eyes for a moment and had to shake himself to offer basic courtesy. "Well, there's two guest rooms, but one of them has my computer and work station in it, so take the second one on the right. Stow your stuff, set up Julia's crate, and when you come out, I should have some casserole and salad ready for us."

Milo brightened. "You have casserole? Comfort food! That's amazing! Pasta, cheese… tuna?"

"Chicken," Garth said.

"Oh yum." Milo's rather forced dreaminess faded, and the look he sent Garth next was a little naked and a little tired. "Seriously. You're… you're the one with the cape tonight, you know? So thank you."

Garth stepped close enough to lean down and kiss Milo's temple. "Go stow your stuff and wash up," he said. "And we can have that hug and that cuddle, and you can go to bed by yourself and know you're safe."

Milo nodded, his eyes getting a little shiny. "Okay," he said. He took a step back then and hurried to the bedroom, and Garth let him go.

HE WAS more composed when he came out for dinner, and Garth had some spare bowls for Julia, which he put on the other side of the kitchen from Chad's. Milo saw this, ran back to his room, and returned with a towel he'd brought in his briefcase.

"I used it for her food and water bowls at work," he said. "Hopefully she'll feel that it's, you know, hers."

"Good idea," Garth told him. "You're becoming quite the dog whisperer."

Milo sank to the floor and petted Julia as she approached the bowl of kibble and sniffed. "Stuart hates dogs," he confided. "He hated the cat too. I-I guess one of the reasons I love Mari so much is she sees me as somebody who needs a pet."

Garth nodded and continued to dish up their dinner. "Living room or dining room table?" he asked.

"Living room?" Milo asked, and Garth could see the bags under his eyes. Whatever he'd done in Misty's spare room, it hadn't been sleep.

"Sure," he said gently. "Come on up and get your plate, and we'll watch some TV. Any requests?"

"Old NCIS episodes," Milo said promptly. "But they do put me right out, so you may need to catch the plate."

Garth chuckled, and soon they were settled on the couch. When Garth saw Milo's plate sitting on his lap, some of the casserole eaten but not much, he told Milo to give it up, put the plate on the coffee table, and come lean on Garth and sleep.

"Hugs and cuddles," Milo said sleepily, and then he did exactly that.

Garth ended up watching three episodes, feeling Milo's limp weight against his body, Garth's arm wrapped around his shoulders. Finally, when his leg started tingling, he stood and urged Milo down the hallway to his bedroom.

"Not enough hugs," Milo murmured, so Garth wrapped his slender body up in his arms and held on.

For a moment, two, it was just that blissful contact, the warmth, the smell of cut grass, of Milo's hair and the lavender in his fabric softener.

"This is so good," Milo murmured. "It's so much better than sex."

Garth's chest constricted. He bent his head to Milo's ear and whispered, "I think, maybe, after some time, we need to go correct that impression you have about sex too."

"But not tonight?" He was practically begging, and Garth was only human.

He dipped his head and tasted, relieved when Milo parted his lips under Garth's and Garth could sweep his tongue in gently. Mmm.... Garth's body was tingling, and not because his leg had fallen asleep. One moment, two....

Garth pulled back. "Not tonight," he said, and then hugged Milo once, briefly, before stepping away. "By the way, I know you brought Julia's crate, but it's fine if she sleeps on your bed. I saw her use the pet door to do her business, so I'm going to leave the door open, okay?"

"Perfect guy," Milo mumbled, turning away. "Julia, I found the perfect guy because you tried to eat his dog. Life is so weird."

And then Garth fled down the hall, turning off the light as he went.

He could only resist so much temptation.

THE NEXT few days were rough, but they were also awesome.

Garth had to skip out on the promised big-dog park visit on Saturday while he and Doug made up work on Misty's place and then he went back to Milo's little duplex to double-check the new security system and see if there were any cameras he'd forgotten. He found one on the outside—which he replaced with one of his own—and helped Milo fill out the paperwork for a restraining order. Misty chimed in here unexpectedly—her oldest was an ADA and helped to fast-track the paperwork through. The footage of Stuart stealing Milo's mail was sent to the DA's office, and they were assured that, while charges may not be pressed because Stuart had been a cohabitant, Stuart would be approached at work to give a statement. For somebody as vain and self-conscious, the cops visiting would put a real crimp in Stuart's style, but Garth wasn't secure enough in Milo's safety to think that would be the end of it.

He asked Milo if he could stay at Garth's house until a week after the statement was taken, to make sure, and once Milo had retrieved his own vehicle—as small as it was—and could visit when he needed to for his own stuff, he agreed.

All told he spent three weeks with Garth—from mid-October to the first week in November—and it should have been... awkward. Uncomfortable. They weren't lovers yet; they were friends who cuddled. Garth was reasonably certain Milo got the same things from his relationship with Mari that he got with Garth, except Mari seemed to be more acerbic and comfortable enough to push Milo harder out of his comfort zone. But then, that probably came with time, and also with being Mari.

Garth's hope in the beginning, that after a couple of "dates" in which they scheduled a talk and then hashed out the hard stuff, proved well-founded. Mari and Milo's relationship went back to the comfort place of two people who couldn't live without each other—except not lovers.

And the longer Garth and Milo roomed together, Garth *really* yearned for that role.

Milo was so *kind*, and so *funny*, and so... marvelous. Unexpected. They walked their dogs every morning together, and Garth had gotten used to Milo talking to Julia like she was, well, Mari.

"No. I said no. We're not chasing the squeaky. Except this once, but you know it's addictive. Do you think there's a clinic? Squeaky addiction? And of course the squirrels hate you. Yes, they do. No, they *do*. Do you think they haven't realized yet that *they're the squeaky*? Yes they are. No, they *are*. The squirrels are the squeaky. So are the cats. The cats are the squeaky too. I am not the squeaky. No, you can't have it back. I'm gonna keep it. Because I'm mean like that. You want the squeaky? Get the squeaky back. C'mon. C'mon... nope. Nope, 'cause it's mine."

And then there would be the bounce and bumble of Julia's favorite rubber squeaky toy as it caromed off Garth's walls, followed by the scrabble of Julia's toenails on the hardwood as she frantically tried to get the toy midbounce.

Garth couldn't help contrast that conversation with Milo's conversation with Mari right before he was scheduled to move back to his duplex—after Milo had recovered some of his confidence and their relationship had settled in as well. "No, you've forgiven me. Of course you have. Listen, if you weren't going to forgive me, you would have blocked my number and Garth would have had to put me in a hospital. But you didn't, so stop pretending you haven't. You are too pretending. How do I know? Because you called me up to ask me for a recipe for cat treats. Cat treats, Mari. Who cooks for their cats, even the ones allergic to gluten? Yes, I *do* know it's expensive. What about Georgie—he's the one who gave you the cats allergic to life. What does *he* say? Yes, but I will. No, I will. I will *too* meet him, because you've been dating him for a month. You haven't dated *anybody* for a month. This guy is important. Because if he wasn't important he wouldn't get your need for cats in your life. *I get your need for cats,* Georgie does. Because *you* call him Georgie, Mari!" And then, "Oh. Well, how was I supposed to know his name was Alistair? You've only ever called him Georgie. Do you expect me to call him Alistair?" Another pause. "Well, you get back to me when you know. And yes, I'm meeting him. I don't know. Thanksgiving. My place. Because it's always at my place. Well... well, hell. It *can't* be your place, Mari, because you *brought me a dog.* Yes, yes it *is* your fault. Consequences, Mariana. Dogs have consequences. So my place will *have* to be safe."

And then Milo's voice grew low. Secretive. "Will *Garth* be there? I'll ask him. No—because, well, because I haven't. As far as I know, I'm like, you know, another dog. I don't see why not. I weigh less than Chad already. I could be another dog. Just, you know, one with very specific taste in television. Dogs do too. Chad loves documentaries about Africa and Australia. If Garth leaves him home alone, he leaves the TV on the *National Geographic* channel, and Chad sits quietly and gnaws his chewy and bones up on sharks. No, he doesn't get *boners* for sharks, he—oh, ha-ha. Yeah. I hear you. But yeah. I'll ask him. No, not Chad. He's automatically invited. Surprisingly enough, the dogs are easy, Mari. It's the *people* who are hard."

At this point, Garth—who had come in from work and who had been listening to Milo have this conversation from the foyer while Milo prepared dinner—dropped his toolbox with a thunk, on purpose, to let Milo know he was there. The thunk was Chad's cue too, because Chad didn't usually enter the living room before Garth thunked the toolbox. Sometimes dog training was as much habit as it was anything else.

"Gotta go. Garth's home and dinner's almost ready. No, I'm not the little woman—he cooks too. Yes. We're roommates. What was that word in German? With-the-boners? No. That's not it." His voice went flat. "You're hilarious. I'm not talking about that. Because it's too good to ruin with sex, that's why." Then, sullen, "No, I don't want to talk about that. Because it's super cringey and embarrassing. Look, I love you, Mari. Talk more soon."

And then he hung up and Garth was left with those little worms of unease that had occupied his stomach for, well, a month really, ever since he'd seen Milo running after Julia in his pajamas, looking unkempt and panicked and...

Alone.

Every little thing he'd let slip about his life, about Stuart, about sex—all of it had warned Garth that what had always been easy and natural and fun for Garth might not be so easy and natural and fun for somebody like Milo, who had been made to feel super uncomfortable in his own skin from a very early age.

Which was why Garth was always careful with moments like these. Milo was moving easily from Garth's refrigerator to his stove to his counter, and Garth normally would have simply come up behind him and pulled him close, nuzzling the back of his neck and kissing his cheek.

But Milo needed to see him first, to raise his head and smile. Or sometimes, when he was working at his desk, to raise his head and stare blankly until reality settled around his eyes again.

Then once he'd smiled, Garth would slip his arm around Milo's waist and kiss his cheek, savoring when Milo leaned into him, making happy little purring sounds in his throat and nuzzling.

Garth did that now and checked out the baked potato and hamburger thing in the casserole dish that Milo was about to put in the oven.

"Forty-five minutes?" he said hopefully, because he was hungry, and Milo grimaced.

"An hour and a half," he apologized. "My phone kept ringing, and I got started late. But I bought some *amazing* cheese this afternoon, and some of those club crackers and grapes. So we've got a... a whatsit. A charcuterie on a plate. I'll have that out in a sec if you want to wash up."

Garth nodded and regarded him steadily.

"What?" Milo asked, and Garth watched his ears turn red. He knew what was coming.

"Milo, I'll go shower, and you do what you gotta. And then I'll come back in here, and we'll sit at the table, and you'll let me eat an entire block of cheese, and then... do you think we might get to that question? The one you didn't want to answer Mari?"

Now it was Milo's entire face that was red. "You heard that?" he mumbled.

"Yeah. I heard the part about being squidgy and embarrassing, and I sort of get that. But... but someday, when you're ready, I was hoping to *get* to that sort of relationship. I need to know what we're dealing with here. Are you ace? Demi? Because you and I could have a beautiful intimate relationship with just some touching—and, well, a lot of lube and my fist—but some touching and some darkened rooms. I would *love* to be intimate and monogamous with you if that was the case. But... but I'm getting the feeling it's more than that, or *different* than that, and given what I know of Stuart, everything I can think of is awful. So can we talk about that when I get out of the shower?"

Milo blinked at him owlishly, and Garth hoped that this tactic would work. For three weeks they'd been with-the-boners, or whatever word Milo had been searching for, and while Garth had *never* expected sex in return for offering sanctuary, *Milo* seemed to be expecting sex. He kissed harder and more every night. He opened his mouth, arched his body sinuously against Garth's, seemed to crave Garth's touch as much as Garth craved his.

But Garth knew when Milo hit his discomfort threshold because his body would stiffen, he would take a step back and smile awkwardly, say something that sounded like a cross between "I'm sorry" and "thank you," and slide into his room.

Garth had made an effort to not kiss him on the couch for just this reason. The kisses were the absolute end of the night, and sometimes Garth wanted conversation too. In fact *often*, because when Milo started talking, he was something. He spent a half hour one night talking about the difference between Julia and Chrysanthemum, his still-lamented cat, and Garth had listened, fascinated, because Milo had pulled out his tablet and showed *pictures*, all of them drawn with Milo's fey intensity, of an amazingly fat, blow-dried brown cat with a perpetually vacant expression on his face.

Milo *missed* this cat, but he also had come to adore Julia, and Garth spent some of his time obsessing about Milo pondering the utter dichotomy of the two animals. Mumsy, as Milo called him, was by all accounts placid and absolutely calm and no trouble at all. Garth desperately wanted Mari's phone number to double-check this information. He wasn't sure Milo was a reliable narrator in the matter of his pets. The other part of that conversation had involved drawings of Julia that featured the oddly dignified but *very* strangely shaped "attention hound" Garth had come to know as a space-rescue dog, complete with a jet pack.

Garth loved the way Milo's mind worked, but he didn't always follow the gears.

So he didn't want conversation to end with kissing, but that's kind of what happened. Milo kissed him, turned red, and bailed.

Garth was coming to care for him more every day, but he was getting to the point where he really needed to know what was going on.

And as he dropped his clothes and hopped in his shower, he hoped what was going on still involved an invitation to Thanksgiving at Milo's.

Inconvenient

MILO FRETTED over the charcuterie board.

He'd been so excited about it—about the board he'd found in Garth's kitchen made especially *for* cheese, crackers, and fruit, and about the fancy little knife and the cheese he'd shopped for. Living here with Garth had been, well, *amazing*.

For one thing he'd gotten to know Garth so much better. His "dog-walking buddy" was a little grumpy in the mornings but perked up with his first cup of coffee. On one of Milo's trips to his neglected duplex for sundries, he pulled his french roast from the freezer and brought it over to brew in the mornings. Garth perked up *even more.* Garth was clean without being fastidious. He kept his work clothes and home clothes separate and usually took his boots off at the front door.

Very often he found Milo working at the kitchen table or cooking, kissed him on the cheek, and then went on to wash up. Their evenings were almost like evenings with Mari, including cuddling on the couch but, well… different.

Milo was aware—so very aware—of a warm, strong male body beneath his as they stretched out on the couch. He'd think, "Tonight. Tonight I'll keep kissing him in the hall and follow him to bed. Julia will have to sleep in her crate tonight. It's fine."

But they'd get to the hall, and the kissing would begin, Garth's warm mouth on his, the comfort of the evening seeping into his bones, and all those… thoughts, memories, would start buzzing around his head.

Jesus, Milo, I don't need you to like it. Just stop wiggling.

You know, if you had a bigger dick, mine wouldn't scare you so much. It's fine.

Oh, now you want sex—what a big old slutbag!

And while Milo was smart enough to try to evade *those* words, other words would show up, like, say, from his first college boyfriend.

Jesus, Milo, you're so fucking needy.

Or from his mother, who had no business in his head.

Milo, just shut up and deal with it. Your stepdad and I need you to not be a pain in the ass.

No, you aren't gay! Stop trying to get attention!

Fine, I don't care if you are *gay—nobody needs to hear about your drama.*

All of it, like flies, or worse, like *wasps* circling around his head until the one part of him geared for self-defense pulled a Julia-with-the-turkeys and barked at *everything* to get the thoughts away.

Which was when Milo shut down, stepped back, and slid into his own bedroom to hold his dog and shake until he could remember himself again.

And apparently by slapping away the thoughts, he'd slapped away *Garth*, and Milo was reminded, once again, of the consequences of letting a chunky, muscular id have its way with flocks of things that could be dealt with using some tenderness and common sense.

Carefully, he took a deep breath and started on the cheese board again. Julia had showed him how to deal with his problems in the worst possible way, but she was a dog. A good dog who deserved love and praise and lots of squeakies and some treats, but still a dog.

Milo was a person. He needed to find a better way.

"THE CHEESE board is great," Garth said softly as they sat at the table and snacked. "And the casserole smells wonderful. Did you get some work done today?"

Milo smiled a little and nodded. "Angela says hi," he said, recalling his Zoom conference. He'd taken Julia to work three times since he'd moved into Garth's house for the interim and had been warmed at how showing up at work with a dog as a security blanket seemed to make even his Zoom conferences more personal as well as more productive. "She wanted to thank you for watching out for me. Apparently weird, stalky ex-boyfriends scare *everybody*."

Garth nodded, obviously troubled. "The police have served his restraining order, and so far, the security system hasn't picked him up again since we, uhm, sent him our very clear message."

Milo couldn't help it; he snickered because the idea of Garth and Doug dropping trou and wiggling their asses was so much *fun*. He couldn't explain it. When he tried to make a statement, he hurt people. But the delivery of two pressed hams to Milo's ex didn't feel like a bad thing in the least.

"As soon as you're tired of me, I guess I can move back into my duplex," he said, but he didn't *feel* very enthusiastic.

"I'm not tired of you," Garth told him, sounding sincere. "I just... I don't know if you really want me, Milo. I mean, I swooped down to rescue you and, I don't know, I wanted to kiss you so badly. Maybe I should have waited. It's fine if you want to stay friends without kissing. I... I need to know, I guess. So I stop hoping for more."

Milo stared at him in mute horror, his breath coming in fast pants from his chest. "No," he managed. "No."

"No what?" Garth asked—but not unkindly.

And it seemed that all Milo *had* was Julia's example, because what he blurted next was almost a strike. "Don't give up on me!"

Garth rocked back in his chair a little, and Milo realized he'd probably shouted. "I'm sorry," he whispered.

Unexpectedly, Garth leaned forward and reached out to cover Milo's hand. "Okay," he said. "I won't give up on you. But maybe... maybe we should slow it down a little."

"No," Milo said, shaking his head. "No. I *like* the kisses. I *love* the kisses—"

Garth squeezed, and he stopped talking. "Then we won't stop. But we *will* get you moved back into your duplex. You can have some independence. Some breathing room. I'll come over for dinner some nights. You do the same here. You know, like two people dating. Not like a marriage of convenience. What do you think?"

Milo took a breath. And then another. "Okay," he said softly. "That would be good. We can date." He felt a smile flicker across his face. "But we can still cuddle on the couch, okay?"

"Sure," Garth said, nodding. "Sounds great. Just... just when I kiss you tonight, I want you to think about why you stiffen up. Why you stop. And you don't have to tell me. Not tonight. But, you know, maybe think about the words to tell me what's wrong. I get it if it's too soon after Stuart—"

Milo shook his head violently, suddenly angry to the point of tears. "I hate him," he whispered. "I hate him. I thought I loved him, but I hate that he's in my head still. It's not fair. I finally… *finally* meet a guy who's *worth* taking space in my mind, and I've got two years of *Stuart* in there, and he's screwing everything up!"

Garth swallowed. "Milo, look. Maybe that's the problem. Maybe the problem was that you were still grieving the relationship when I came along. Maybe we *shouldn't* be kissing—"

"Please," Milo whispered. "Please don't give up on me."

Garth nodded. "You keep saying that. Not kissing doesn't mean I've given up. I just need you to be comfortable with what we're doing."

"I am!" Milo squeaked. "I swear I am. Don't send me away!" He heard his voice and hated it and tried again. "I swear I'll do better, I swear!"

And suddenly Garth wasn't sitting across from him anymore. He was kneeling at Milo's feet, holding his hands. "Baby," he said softly, "you are doing great. I think you are doing the best you can. It's me who needs to do better. You're not ready for sex. You're not ready to live with anybody else. I should have seen that when you came here. I should have kissed you at your doorway and let you go. I should never have pressured you. It's my fault, do you understand?"

"You didn't pressure me," Milo whispered. Garth's eyes were bright and shiny, and Milo wanted to make it better. "You didn't. I wanted to keep you in my life, but I've got all these other voices in my head, and every time I swat them away, I swat you away too, and I don't want to hurt you, and—"

"Shh…." Garth kept rubbing his hands. "You're only going to hurt me if you don't tell me what's going on. What are you hearing in your head?"

"All the people telling me what a wreck I am," Milo confessed. "My college boyfriend, my parents, Stuart…. It-it's a mess in there."

Surprisingly enough, Garth chuckled. "I can hear that. Okay, then. Okay. I know what we're dealing with now. Don't worry. I like you in my life, Milo. I can be patient. Let's get you back in your house so seeing me is on your terms. Let's make a rule that the kissing needs to stop at the bedroom door, and that way you don't feel bad when it does. Let's slow this all down, okay? We've got stalky ex-boyfriends, and you've got voices in your head. You're cute, I like you, I can wait as long as you need."

Milo nodded and realized he could breathe again. "You really think I'm cute?" he said. Nobody had ever told him that. Stuart had always said, "You're okay, but I'll stay."

"God yeah." Garth reached up and brushed the bangs from his forehead. "I thought so that first day. If you're hearing voices that say you're not good-looking enough, tell them I said to shut up, okay?"

Milo nodded. "Okay," he said, and some of the clamor in the back of his head chilled out. "I can do that."

"Good." Garth stood heavily to his feet as the casserole timer went off. "How about you go clean up, and I'll dish us up some food. Let's eat in front of the TV, okay? The cheeseboard was a nice idea, but I think we can take a break from the heartfelt conversation, don't you?"

That night, as Milo leaned against him, Garth's arm over his shoulder, Chad and Julia at their feet, he felt a singular lightness. They would kiss—hurray! And then Milo would go to his room, and it would be *his* room, and he wouldn't have to make the terrible decision to share his body when he wasn't sure he was ready.

During a commercial break, without knowing he was going to do it, he reached out and paused the television.

"It hurt a lot," Milo said. "Sex, I mean. And Stuart said it was my fault it hurt, but I suspect it was because he didn't care. He only wanted me to stop moving so he could do what he needed to do. So part of me is really excited about kissing you and touching you and having sex. But part of me is afraid it'll be like it was with Stuart, and then you'll tell me it's my fault somehow for being bad at it. Or worse, when I like it and it all seems to be going well, that I'm… bad somehow, slutty or depraved, because I'm excited about it. And yes, I know I'm not, but I think if I heard your voice telling me those things, when… when you seem so much *better* than Stuart, I think it would break me."

Milo let out a breath then, aware that he'd said more on this subject during a commercial break than he'd said during his entire *relationship* with Stuart, and he'd done it because he'd been given the freedom to walk away. How weird was that? It was exactly the opposite of Julia, he supposed. Julia needed to be told what to do or sent to her crate, but then Julia was a *dog*, and Milo was a human, and the more Milo remembered that, apparently the better he got at being one.

Garth made a suspicious noise above him, and Milo glanced up and saw him wiping his eyes with the back of his hand. He tried to scramble into an upright position, but Garth shook his head and just held him— held him and cried.

"What's wrong?" Milo asked in a small voice.

"I hate that he hurt you," Garth said gruffly. "I hate that he hurt you. And I'm so glad you're here. I don't want him to ever hurt you again. And I'd die before I did the same. Thank you. *Now* I know what I'm working with."

"A complete and utter disaster," Milo supplied glumly.

Garth shook his head and turned to kiss his forehead. "A really amazing guy who's got some damage. I mean, my job is all about fixing damage. It's always worth it. There's always so much beauty inside."

And now Milo was the one who was making suspicious snorfling noises against Garth's side.

"Baby?" Garth asked.

"You think I'm beautiful," Milo whispered, and that was all he could manage. Garth just kept holding him while he cried.

EVENTUALLY THEY finished their murder show and got creakily up to turn off the lights and get ready for bed. Milo was *exhausted*, his head aching from his cry, his thoughts skittering away when he tried to rope them in. Emotions were *exhausting*; he should remember that.

Garth seemed to remember for the both of them, because when he paused in front of Milo's bedroom door, he said, "One quick kiss, okay? So you remember you're cared for. So you remember you're wanted. Then all the freedom in the world."

Milo nodded, not sure in his heart what that meant, but then Garth's mouth was on his own briefly, warmly, and Milo responded. Garth swept his tongue in and retreated, then kissed Milo on the forehead, and Milo's breath caught.

Freedom. And all he wanted with it was more.

But Garth turned him toward his door and said, "Remember, leave the door cracked so Julia can go outside. Good night, Milo."

"Good night," Milo whispered and did what Garth told him.

As he undressed and then brushed his teeth and washed his face, he felt a blessed numb exhaustion steal over him, protecting him from the big scary emotions.

But an ember of warmth had made its way into his chest with that kiss, and *that* kept beating warmly.

Oh, he kept thinking.

Oh.

A WEEK LATER, Garth helped him move his few belongings back into his duplex after dinner, and Milo wandered around, remembering how much he'd loved decorating it and how much Stuart had hated what he'd done.

As Garth brought the last of Julia's gear in and set it up in the kitchen, Milo had a sudden frisson of fear.

"You'll come back, right?" he asked, his voice pitching.

"Well, we'll meet tomorrow to walk the dogs," Garth said, but his smile was troubled, and Milo suddenly understood. He was worried too.

"You'll come for dinner tomorrow?" Milo begged. "You have to. We have to plan."

Garth's lips twitched, and his smile lost some of its trouble. "Plan what?"

"Thanksgiving," Milo said soberly. "I'm hosting, but you're coming, and Mari and her new boyfriend. And Doug if you want to ask him, but he's got a wife and kids, so probably not."

Garth shook his head. "Nope, Doug's going to his in-laws, and most of my other friends are doing family. My mom and dad are making noises about coming up—"

"They could come!" Milo said, knowing it was rash but not caring. "I"—his voice dropped—"I know I'm not an official boyfriend yet. But I'm an official friend, right?"

All of the trouble was gone now. Garth stepped into his space and lifted his chin. "Definitely an official friend," he rumbled. "A *very* special official friend. And I'll pass on the invite, and I'd love to come over tomorrow for dinner."

That ember that Garth had planted in Milo's chest the evening of their talk about what Milo needed and what Garth needed to give him, *that* ember lit up again, warmer and brighter.

"It's a date," he said, nodding. "An official date. With kissing afterward."

Garth's smile crinkled the corners of his eyes now, and Milo realized that was the *best* kind of smile, and he understood the appeal of laugh lines now like he hadn't when he'd been in high school and all the K-Pop boy bands had been the ultimate in ab-lick-able.

"With kissing afterwards," Garth promised.

"Can we kiss now?" Milo asked cannily. "To seal the deal, right?

"Yeah," Garth murmured. "I thought you'd never ask."

This kiss lasted longer than the kisses at Garth's house had, and Milo didn't mind. He was in his place now, his space, his floor, his walls, his art. And Garth liked those things about him and didn't tell him to change and had made sure this place was safe *for Milo*.

So Milo could let Garth around those places and around his body and much more freely around Milo's heart.

In fact, *so* much more freely, Garth was panting and sweating a little when he finally pulled away, and Milo realized that his groin actually *ached*, and he wanted *badly*, and the person he wanted was going to walk away and leave him, and this whole moving-out prospect seemed like a bad deal all around.

He made a sound, small and sad, and Garth pulled him close and kissed his forehead again.

"Milo, when you're ready, I will stay—or you will stay at my place—and we will finish all the kisses. We will undress, and touch each other's bare skin, and I will touch you so tenderly it'll make you cry, and then it will make you come, and I'll do it all over again until your body remembers *nothing* but how good it feels to be with me. That's a promise. I want your body, I do. So much. But I want your heart and your mind too. Can you wait? Wait until all the things agree?"

They do! They do! I swear they do!

God, Milo, beg for it why don't you. Jesus, how easy are you?

Goddammit.

Milo nodded miserably and, without meaning to, arched against Garth's thigh, whimpering when his erection ached more.

Garth's gruff chuckle was oddly reassuring, and he took Milo's hand and pressed it against the placket of his jeans. "Same," he said.

"But… but what are we supposed to do?" Milo groaned.

Garth whispered the next part in his ear, his voice rough and needy and explicit.

So explicit. Milo's mouth went dry, and he realized he'd started to dry hump Garth's legs like an alley cat when Garth cleared his throat and stepped back.

"Really?" Milo asked. "You want me to do that?"

"When you're done," Garth said soberly. "Text me tomorrow and tell me every detail."

Milo's mouth dropped open and heat swept up his body, and his cock leaked just a little on his underwear, leaving a cool damp spot under his jeans.

"That's more intimate than sex!" he squeaked.

Garth's smile was slow and sultry and did nothing to ease Milo's discomfort.

"God, I hope not," he murmured. He darted forward to give Milo a quick kiss on the cheek. "Call me later," he said. "See you tomorrow."

He left, leaving Milo alone in his house.

Alone to shower, to get naked and clean, to kick the dog off the bed, and to… to… could he do it?

He shuddered. There was nobody here. Nobody watching. Only him and Julia, and Julia was pretty discreet.

He and Mari had come in two days ago to air the place out and vacuum and dust, and his sheets were clean, and his comforter was the autumn-themed one Mari had given him two years ago.

Nobody had to know.

The freedom was almost as arousing as Garth's touch had been— but only almost.

BUT FIRST there was the moving back into his home, the sitting on the couch and manning his own remote control. He let Julia out and then threw her the squeaky numerous times and realized they'd not done this as much at Garth's house because Chad had been there and dog politics had taken precedent. Why chase the squeaky when making sure she, Julia, was getting more attention from Milo at any given moment was the goal?

Milo and Garth had continued to walk the dogs in the morning, and Milo took her on her own special loop while Garth was throwing the ball for Chad, but Milo realized now he should have been throwing her the squeaky too.

There were parts of living by himself that he needed to keep, he realized. He threw the squeaky down the hallway, angling it so it bounced off the wall and ended up in his office, and then listened for the scrabbling of her toenails as she changed directions and charged into the room. He heard her snuffling about, and then she came trotting back, her ears out in the crooked-airplane-wing formation with a totally different squeaky, one that had been here at the house while they'd been staying at Garth's, held proudly in her jaws.

Milo took it from her and rubbed her rump. "Okay," he said, taking the hint. "I get it. Garth is good, and you're starting to even like Chad, but it needs to be just you and me for a little while too."

He took the squeaky from her, and she wrestled him playfully for it, finally letting him win, and he threw it again and watched it go.

When she came back this time, she simply dropped it on the ground, then hopped up on the couch and stared at the television, which he'd paused on his favorite murder show. None-too-subtly she nudged his hand, and he hit the remote to play, then glanced back at her. She'd rolled over to her back, and he rubbed her tummy, laughing a little at her blissed-out expression, head lolled back, mouth parted ever so slightly in a smile.

She was a good companion, he realized. She'd made him stand up for himself at work, and she'd made him think about his actions, and now she was making him realize that the life he had, here in his own home, was not such a bad life after all.

He still missed Garth, but he also enjoyed the kind of night by himself he used to take for granted.

"Good girl," he said softly. "Good girl!"

AFTER TELEVISION, he took a shower and, feeling like a naughty kid, wore the towel to his bedroom instead of putting on his pajamas in the bathroom.

The air on his bare body made him shiver, but it also hit a spot… a sort of *sensuous* spot in his psyche. Stuart hadn't believed in being naked. You took off just enough clothes to have sex, and then you put them on again when it was done and you'd washed up.

Douchey college boyfriend had pretty much left before the jizz cooled.

In between the two, Milo had lived alone in this duplex and only masturbated when the loneliness got too much, and *then* it had been in his bed, with the lights off, under the covers, with nobody the wiser.

Garth would be the wiser.

Not that Milo would tell him anything he didn't want to, but Garth.... Garth *wanted* to know. So there was a naughtiness here, but there was also a freedom.

Nobody was going to condemn him for doing grown folks' business when there was nobody here to see.

So nobody saw him running to his room, because it was *his* room. And as he got there and glanced around, he realized it really *was* his room. Stuart had never decorated there. Milo had bought the furniture and bedding when he'd gotten the duplex—it had been his treat to himself when his trust had matured. The same with the living room. Stuart had complained about Milo's stuff, but except for the art, he'd never made any attempts to make the space *theirs* instead of Milo's.

So as Milo stood in his bedroom naked, he realized that he had *ownership* there. He had the *right* to be naked in his own bedroom.

The absolute power made him hard before he even thought of sex.

He pulled the covers back on his bed and gave Julia a stern, "Down, girl."

Her airplane ears went flat, as though he *must* have been mistaken, and then they drooped a little, and he pointed toward the door and said, "Crate."

With a little sigh, she curled up on the bed he'd put for her in the corner, and he figured that was a good compromise. And then, oddly enough, once she was situated, he was... alone.

He lay down on the bed and enjoyed the feeling of being clean and air dried and... alone. He wondered what he *should* think about when he did this, and while at first his thoughts went to Garth's kisses, those didn't make him feel sexy—they made him wistful. Suddenly he wanted to *share* this naked aloneness with Garth, and a little thrill danced through him as he realized that was *want*, and *yearning*.

He'd only ever felt these things—fleetingly—when he was being kissed or felt up, and he'd thought there was something lacking in himself that he didn't dwell on physical intimacy.

Now he *wanted* it. He *craved* it. And the freedom to want, the room to crave, *that* aroused him. He moved his hand to his cock and was surprised to find it had grown, was aching and hard, and suddenly he didn't need to think about sex, although the thought of Garth's hand over his own hand made him gasp. Suddenly the moment was all about *sensation*, and his cock was *hard*, and he was *stroking it*, and it felt better, aching, and his nipples tingled. He moved a hand up to pinch them, and *that* was exciting, and oh my God, his body was *amazing*! Look what it could do! He was panting, making little whimpers of excitement as he tightened his fist over his cock and pinched his nipples and then, oh wow! He propped his feet up on the bed and exposed himself to the air, and just that, the touch of the air on his cracks and crevices, it was barely enough, and then it was more than enough, and he let out a wordless cry as he convulsed on the bed and came.

And came.

And came and came and came.

With a happy little moan, he rolled to his side and squeezed the last of the fluid from his cock while pulling his covers up to his chin at the same time. A hoarse little voice in the back of his head whispered that somebody would be mad if he didn't wipe up the jizz, and then he reminded himself that *he* was the only one home, and *he* could wash his sheets whenever he pleased.

The lights were still on, but he was happy and floaty, and he left them on as he closed his eyes and fell asleep.

Eventually he'd get up and wipe down the sheets, put on his underwear, turn off the lights, and invite Julia to come lie down next to him, but for a little bit, the first hour, he dreamed about telling Garth and hearing Garth's warm, rumbly voice telling him he did okay.

Beautiful Torture

MILO'S BODY seemed unbearably far away and *far* too masked in a hooded sweatshirt and reasonably fitted jeans as they walked side by side, their dogs leading the way and Milo's voice confiding his evening's activity in a breathy whisper.

"And then," he said, pitch rising, "I *fell asleep*, and nobody told me there was a wet spot, and I left the lights on and… and I was *all by myself*."

Garth wanted to hug him, to whirl him up in the air and celebrate, but he wasn't sure what the dogs would do.

"That's awesome," he said, and Milo gave him a guarded look.

"You're not being snarky?" he asked, uncertainty suddenly lacing his voice, and Garth stopped, turned toward Milo, and held his shoulder with his free hand.

"I'm proud of you," Garth said softly, and at Milo's blatantly hopeful expression, he smiled and lowered his head to brush their lips together. "That was outside of your comfort zone, and you—"

Milo snickered. "Made myself damned comfortable."

Garth had to chuckle too. "Perfect," he said, meaning it. And then he had to kiss Milo again. This time Milo opened his mouth and answered the kiss, happy and anticipatory and greedy. They kissed hard, steaming the frosty November air around them, until Julia made a whine and tugged at the leash in Milo's hand.

Milo broke away and giggled before resuming their walk. But he kept his arm wrapped around Garth's waist and Garth kept his free arm slung over Milo's shoulder, and no, they didn't go very fast.

"So," Garth said, feeling warm and happy and really good about the decision to give Milo some space, "do you want me to bring dinner tonight, or are you cooking?"

"Oh my God!" Milo burst out, but not in a bad way. "You're coming over tonight! I'd almost forgotten. *I'm so happy!*"

Garth tried not to stare at him. "Uhm… yay?"

Milo shook his head. "No. I mean yay, because yes, you're coming over, but I'd forgotten that Mari's coming over too. And I know this is…." His voice dropped with a tinge of disappointment. "I was looking forward to more kissing," he admitted, "but Mari's coming over, and—" He shot Garth a sideways glance. "—you're getting important to me, and I wanted her to meet you."

Garth's heart sped up, and *he* almost jumped for joy. "Yeah?" he asked. He *got* how important this was.

"Oh yes." Milo nodded and gave him an adoring smile. "I-I mean, I hope you get along. I don't know why Stuart hated her so much, but she's coming over, and she's going to bring her new boyfriend, and I haven't met him yet. So you can meet them both, but mostly her, and…." He gave Garth another sideways glance. "I *really* want you to like her. I really, really do."

Garth let out a breath. "Listen," he said soberly, "I want to like her too. Because she's important to you. But you need to remember—even if we take one look at each other and growl and raise our hackles like Julia and Chad, we can learn to sit in the same room and behave. Do you know why?"

"No," Milo said, terribly concerned. "And why would you even suggest that?"

"Because I don't want you to panic," Garth said patiently. "Mari is your friend. She's your *sister*. Whether or not *I* like her, that doesn't mean you ever have to give up something you love for me. So I hope I *adore* her. But if I don't, remember that what matters is *you* adore her, okay?"

Milo scowled. "I'd rather you got along," he said darkly.

Garth crossed quiet fingers in the back of his mind.

"I'm sure we will," he said, hoping, hoping, hoping it was true.

"So it's like a job interview," Misty said to him the next day as he and Doug paused to hydrate as they worked on their respective tasks. Misty's patio office was taking shape nicely, and the drywall and wiring would be done within the week. Garth had been working on the small pond in the other corner of the yard, and while the chase games of three giant, rambunctious dogs might not have made the work go *faster*, it most definitely made it more entertaining.

Misty and Doug, after picking up on Garth's protectiveness over Milo on that first day nearly three weeks earlier, had been trying to gently poke him about their, in Doug's words, "January molasses romance" ever since.

They'd both cheered when Garth had admitted—with heated cheeks—that there had been kissing. They'd booed when Garth had told them that Milo had moved back to his duplex. Garth had given them both scowls.

"He's got a stalky douchebag of an ex-boyfriend," he said. "Milo needs to feel powerful, and he needs to be able to do that alone, and I'd be a *terrible* person if I got in the way of that."

"Well, yeah," Doug said, undeterred. "But don't you *like* him?"

Garth's grunt of frustration had pretty much said everything, and Doug had stopped giving him shit.

So now, when Garth told them that Milo wanted Garth and Mari to meet, there were opinions. Very strong opinions.

"Mm… no," Doug said in answer to Misty's "job interview" analogy. "This is more important. When I met my wife's bestie, I brought her flowers, paid for dinner, and volunteered to watch her dog when she was on vacation. I mean, Garth and I had already scared off her stalker, and she told me repeatedly that I got the job, but this—this was the ultimate test. It's like, 'Hello, this person is going to either be a part of your family or your greatest enemy. It all depends on the next three hours.'"

Garth stared at him, his stomach fluttering. "I hate you," he said. "Have I told you lately how much I hate you? Because if I wasn't godfather to your children, I would smother you in your sleep."

All the good feelings left over from Milo's ecstatic, *sexy* confession that morning had dissipated with Doug's words. *He was a landscaping manwhore whose only character reference was his dog!*

Doug gave him a sympathetic shoulder squeeze. "And I have probably done something in our past to deserve it," he said magnanimously. "But right now you need to plan to stop for flowers on your way to Milo's house tonight, and you'd better clean under your nails."

Garth grunted, and Misty regarded them both with puzzlement.

"That's so odd," she said softly. "I… I never put Jonathan through any of that. He was so handsome! So dashing! I guess I assumed he was too good for me as it was. My family lived in another state, and he

just, you know, became my world." Her gaze drifted off, and she toyed
with the diamond solitaire pendant at her throat. "I wonder...."

Doug and Garth exchanged glances. "Wonder what, Misty?" Garth
asked delicately.

What he wanted to say was, "No, your husband is unworthy of you, and
you deserve much better, and I bet you could get this house in the divorce,"
but the woman obviously enjoyed a comfortable life, and she hadn't let the
money make her mean, so he was just going to keep his opinions to himself.

She shook her head. "Nothing," she answered absently and then
seemed to focus. "You're a very sweet boy, and while you may have had
your wild days, I'm certain you've put them behind you. You stop and get
that young woman some flowers, make sure she knows you plan to treat
her best friend like gold, and I'm certain you'll have zero problems." A
smile flitted over the corners of her mouth. She wore a trace of colored
gloss on casual days, and Garth wished there was somebody there who
would appreciate her the way he, Doug, and Michael did.

Class A dame, all the way.

"I appreciate that," he said. "It had better go well. Milo's planning
on inviting us all to Thanksgiving."

"Oh, that's lovely," Misty said. She started to gather up the empty
water bottles and stuff them in a waiting recycling bag, but her voice had
obviously dropped, and she didn't sound as though *anything* was lovely,
anything at all.

"Misty?" Doug asked, just as Michael came out to take the bag
from her and set a tray of sandwiches down on the patio table that had
been set up for refreshments.

"It's nothing," she said, fanning her face. She gave Michael an
apologetic smile and excused herself to go wash up, leaving Doug and
Garth to continue eating as they stood, hopefully before the dogs caught
on to any human food being shared at this end of the yard.

"Michael?" Garth asked discreetly as she disappeared through the vinyl
doorway of the office/patio. "What's wrong? We mentioned Thanksgiving—"

"Her children won't be coming home for the holidays this year,"
Michael said softly. "Her two married daughters are visiting their partners'
families, and her son is going to school across country and saving his air
miles for Christmas. He's got friends, but...."

"But it's just her and Mr. Parcival," Doug said, and Garth could
hear the sympathetic platitude coming, but Michael shook his head.

"I'm going to gossip here," he confessed. "Mr. Parcival has been on business trips or working late for the past week. I don't believe she's had a chance to tell him there won't be any children for the holiday, and she's—"

"Oh no." Alone, Garth thought. Like Milo would have been if he'd let Stuart talk him out of having Mari in his life.

Michael nodded. "My own husband is going to be gone. He's an attending physician, and they volunteer one holiday a year to the residents so the residents aren't working *every* holiday. I'm quite used to Black Friday Thanksgiving, but this is the first time since coming to work here that she hasn't had at least a small dinner party for the holiday."

Garth said it before he had a chance to second-guess himself. "You know what?" he said. "Let me talk to Milo. I know he and Misty got along on that first day and"—he grimaced—"I hate to think of the two of you alone on the holidays. I'll talk to you tomorrow and set it in stone."

Michael's smile was amazingly warm. "That's very kind of you," he said. "I promise I can bring the most exquisite pies if Milo doesn't mind."

"Well, fine," Doug said. "Make *me* feel like an asshole because I've already got plans."

"We'd invite you too if you ever lost your mind and alienated your perfect family," Garth teased.

Doug grinned. "Well, yeah. I do have a pretty good thing going. That's fine," he said loftily through a mouthful of a homemade cheesesteak sandwich. "You all go do what you do. I'm gonna play with the girls while my wife and her bestie and her sister create magic in the kitchen. I'll be fine."

"I have zero sympathy for him," Michael said, eyes twinkling.

"He's even got dogs," Garth agreed. "It's disgusting."

"Hey," Doug said with a swallow. "I don't get any of Michael's pies. I think that gets me a *little* slack, right?"

Garth shook his head while Michael held his hand out in a "maybe/maybe not" gesture, and the three of them laughed.

And Garth made a mental note to get Mari flowers and to ask Milo if he could invite friends to their already tenuous Thanksgiving.

MARI TOOK one glance at the flowers from him in Milo's foyer and winced. "Lilies," she said in dismay.

"Oh no!" Garth said, catching her tone. "Are you allergic? Do you hate them? Did somebody in your family die?"

She peered up, her strong-featured face caught by surprise. "Oh no!" she said. "I personally love them, but I'm afraid they're going to have to live here at Milo's. They're toxic for cats. Milo, where's your vase?"

Milo looked up from the cutting board where he was mincing garlic. "Vase?" he asked, as though it was a foreign word. His glasses were steamed up, and his hair—as always—stuck out like a bird's nest in all directions, but the lines by his eyes, by his mouth, were relaxed.

He and Mari had cooked before, probably in this kitchen.

"Yes, Milo," Mari said patiently. "You remember—that pottery vase with the really neat blue glaze?"

Milo's relaxed, happy expression went carefully blank. "No," he said. "I'm sorry. I don't know what happened to it."

Mari cocked her head, and Garth sucked in a furious breath. "That's okay," he said. "I see a plastic pitcher on top of the fridge. Let's put them in there."

Stuart. Of course. Garth wondered how many of Mari's gifts Stuart had broken or disposed of while Milo ran interference.

What. A. Douche.

"Oh my God," Mari muttered, like she'd put two and two together. "Yeah, fine, the pitcher's a good idea." Obviously embarrassed, she set about putting the lilies in the pitcher and put them on the table. She also took Garth's side dish of pan-fried brussels sprouts and put it in a corner of the stove, probably to keep the heat from seeping out.

Garth felt the melancholy funk that had settled in the kitchen at the invisible presence of Milo's ex and wished Chad was the growly sort of nightmare who would eat Stuart's face.

Unfortunately, he'd left Chad in front of the television that night, figuring the big guy had about worn himself out with Misty's dogs.

Which reminded him!

"Oh wow." He smiled apologetically at Mari. "I'm sorry—both of you, I'm so sorry. But I was hoping I could invite Misty Parcival and her assistant, Michael, to Thanksgiving. I feel so forward. I mean, it's here in your house, Milo, but poor Misty, her kids all deserted her, and her husband has sort of forgotten to help with the planning, and Michael's husband is taking a resident's shift so the residents don't all have the holidays, and—"

Milo set the knife down and beamed at him. "Do you think they'd come?" he asked. "She was so nice to me. Mariana, she was *so* nice to me. That day, you know, the day they discovered the cameras? I've never had so many people over, and that Rick guy from work might come—his parents live down south—but I feel sort of grateful, you know? It was a shitty time, and everybody was... you know. Good people." He bit his lip. "We'd have to cook a lot of food, wouldn't we?"

"Nonsense," Mari said with a shrug. "We do turkey, potatoes, stuffing, and gravy, and everybody else brings something else." She glanced across the kitchen and the hallway to where an angular man with a ponytail, a wispy beard, and Birkenstocks, in camo shorts and a frayed T-shirt, was playing with Julia. "Isn't that right, Georgie? That way you can make some vegan dishes, and everybody gets to eat!"

Georgie gave a vague smile. "I've got a lentil bean/vegan cheese thing that's pretty yummy," he said and went back to rubbing Julia's belly.

"I can make my mom's bacon green beans," Garth said, happy to contribute.

"Awesome!" Mari grinned. "So yeah, Milo says they're good people. Ask them over. It'll be fun, right, Milo?"

Milo gave her a look of absolutely happy/stupid adoration. "Sure, Mari," he said. "We've never done anything this big before."

"Well, yeah," she said. "I mean, last two years, you came over to my place, right?"

Milo shrugged. "Well, it's always been you and me."

Garth saw it then, the sadness that crossed Mari's face as he went back to chopping vegetables—now it was onions—and he thought, *She knows. She's probably always known. But she hasn't wanted to give Milo up any more than Milo would have given her up.*

"Mariana," he said, feeling a little bit of wonder in his voice, "would you want to take a walk outside with me? I'll put Julia on the leash, and Milo can finish up here."

"Sure," she said, appearing relieved. "Milo's doing something secret with lemon, Dijon, garlic, and wine with this pasta, so let's let him be secret."

"It's the chicken, Mari," Milo said patiently. "It's called scampi." He glanced up at Garth and gave a tenuous smile. "Just because I've got a knife in my hand doesn't mean you can't—" His eyes darted toward Mari, and he blushed. "—you know."

Garth chuckled, moved in to kiss his cheek and brush his waist with a tender hand, and then moved back into the hallway for the peg where he'd hung his jacket after Mari had rushed in and grabbed the food and flowers.

In a few moments, they were outside in the brisk November dark, and Julia was giving a passable representation of a dog who might know how to walk with a leash.

"You knew," Garth said.

"That Milo was paying for my sister?" Mari denied. "Absolutely not." Some of her energy softened. "Although now that I've had a chance to get over not knowing, you know, it really *was* a nice thing to do."

"No, not that," Garth said. "Except yeah, Milo's possibly the sweetest guy in the world. But you knew Stuart was trying to get him to ghost you."

Her strong features—bold nose, square chin, full lips—settled into a scowl. "Oh yeah. I knew from the very beginning. And if Milo had started to fade away, I would have stepped in. But...." She gave him a helpless expression that Garth could tell cost her a lot. "You have to understand," she said. "He's always been so... so *Milo*. And his first boyfriend was a douchebag, and this guy at least, you know, called him back. Made him feel important. I thought, 'Hey, if Milo still stays my friend, then fuck Stuart's feelings.' I didn't expect to be the reason they broke up."

Garth grunted. "Mari," he said not sure how to say this right. "You weren't the reason they broke up. You're the reason Milo stayed *Milo*. The things Stuart was doing—the cameras, the coming by to fuck with Milo's mail, the trying to isolate Milo—those are *abusive* things. *Toxic* things. He... he didn't just try to isolate Milo, he tried to make him feel *worthless*. About everything. About his art on the walls, his choice in houses, his furniture, his *body*. You can't blame yourself for their breakup. Be glad there was anything left of Milo for Stuart to break up with."

Mari stopped short, much like Julia did, and stared at him. "What do you mean, his *body*."

Garth's cheeks heated. "Do you guys...? I mean, do you talk about sex?"

She shrugged. "I know Milo doesn't like it much, but you know, that's about all... he.... Oh God."

She swayed a little on her feet, and Garth put his hand on her shoulder and urged her on. "You can't pass out on me," he said, "because then we have to tell Milo we're having this conversation, and he'll be mortified."

"But I'm his best friend," she said, her feet moving seemingly on automatic. "How could I not know?"

"I think he was working super hard to not let you know how hard Stuart was working to break you guys up," Garth said. "So he wasn't going to complain about the sex thing, because that would give you a reason to—"

"Kill him," Mari said, obviously furious. "Oh God. *Oh my God.* What did that fucker say to my poor Milo? He's...." She turned a tearstained face toward Garth, and he thought, *Way to go, buddy. Way to ingratiate yourself to the best friend. You're traumatizing her!* "Fragile," Mari finished, breaking into his thoughts. "He's always been so fragile."

Garth thought about it. "Naw," he said, and she stared at him.

"What?"

"Look at him. He kept you as a friend. He kept your sister safe. He's been taking care of Julia like a champion. I know he doesn't always people well, but he's inviting lots of people to Thanksgiving. I mean, we left him alone with Georgie, whom I know he's never met before, and he's okay with it. He's tougher than you think. He just needs... you know. Room to grow. Like Julia. He takes her to the park so she can stretch her legs a little. He needs some time without an overbearing boyfriend so he knows who he is first."

"But...." She bit her lip. "Aren't you, like, *in love* with him?"

Garth held his finger to his lips, although her saying the words made his chest hurt. It would figure, wouldn't it? This was the first time since college that he decided to venture outside the realm of boom-chicka-wow-wow, and he was falling for a guy who *couldn't* be his boyfriend, at least not yet?

"I can wait," he said softly. "Like I said, he's sort of fearless. But right now, he's drawing cartoons of his dog, and he's afraid to show them to me because he's afraid I'll laugh the wrong way."

Mari chuckled wetly. "There's a *right* way to laugh at them, you know," she said seriously.

"His sense of humor is amazing," Garth agreed, missing Milo in his house, and the way Milo would sit with his tablet and work on his imaginative comics featuring Julia and Chad, and sometimes Daisy and Bruce, and sometimes an amazingly fat, fluffy cat apparently named Chrysanthemum, whom Milo still missed.

"And you care about him a lot already," Mari murmured.

"I do," Garth agreed. "Which is why I absolutely need you on my side. You understand that, right? You hold oodles of power over my head right now, because on your say-so alone, Milo will banish me forever, and…." He let out a breath. "And that would suck."

He was walking Julia with his outside hand, and to his surprise, he felt Mari's inside hand slip inside his. "I wouldn't get between him and Stuart," she said, "because I thought Stuart was what he wanted. But the more I think about it, the more I realize Stuart was all he thought he could have."

"He deserves so much better," Garth said fervently.

"I know he does," Mari said, nodding. "You just keep giving him space. You keep thinking he's strong but giving him help when he needs it. You keep treating my boy right and I'll be your biggest cheerleader. I'll buy pom-poms and a sweater that says Team Garth and I'll do the goddamned splits in Milo's living room whenever we end up in the same room together. Stuart was a douche. I'm mad at myself for not knowing how *big* a douche until…. God. What he's put Milo through. But he's a douche, and I hate him. You and me can be partners in hating Stuart, then, and we can take care of Milo."

"We won't tell him for a little while," Garth said.

"Nope." She leaned her head against his arm. "Thanks."

"For what?"

"For being a good guy. For talking to me like I matter in Milo's life. Milo's parents are assholes. I mean, *my* parents are assholes, and together we held hands and endured, you know? I know that's why all *my* choices have mostly been the horrible kind. And I figure that's why Milo just buckled down with Stuart to endure. But suddenly you're bringing me flowers and talking like Milo is important to both of us, and, well, you could have let Chad eat this weird little dog I brought him, and you didn't. Why didn't you bring Chad, by the way?"

Garth had to smile, because he suddenly understood why Mari and Milo probably spoke their own language. He bet Milo could have followed that ramble easily.

"Because he's a little bit larger than life," Garth admitted. "And I wanted tonight to be about meeting you and getting you to like me. It's hard to do when Julia keeps growling at him."

"Does she do that?" Mari asked in surprise.

"Sometimes," Garth said. "She's... I don't know where you got that dog, but she's sort of a misanthropic little asshole herself sometimes. She has definite likes and dislikes. And sometimes poor Chad falls on the wrong side of that line."

Mari laughed. "Milo thinks she walks on water."

And seeing that he was surprised Mari wasn't gliding on a six-inch cushion of air, given how much Milo adored Mariana, Garth could see how that worked.

"Well, seeing how Milo dotes on her, maybe someday she will," he said loyally. "I think in the hands of a meaner owner, she could have been a demon. But in Milo's hands?"

"Someday she'll be an angel," Mari said with satisfaction. "And someday you two will be married and run a dog shelter and make my heart beat faster because not all people are assholes and my friend Milo and his husband, Garth, are living proof."

Garth was torn between laughter and horror, but eventually he settled on acceptance. "That'll give us something to shoot for," he told her, and she seemed to think that was fine.

DINNER WAS easy after that. The conversation was mostly pet centered, which was great—pets were neutral and they didn't care if people gossiped about them or told their worst moments for a laugh. Apparently Mari's eight cats were forming a witches coven, and Mari would wake up sometimes staring into a circle of little furry faces casting a spell.

Georgie said—very seriously—that they controlled forces in the universe, and Milo and Garth met startled eyes over the table while Mari patted Georgie's knee indulgently and said of course they did.

After dinner, Garth and Georgie did dishes while Mari and Milo talked in the living room (and Milo muttered, "Garth and Georgie, Mari and Milo, Garth and Georgie, Mari and Milo," to himself as though he'd only now discovered alliteration), and for a few blissful moments, Garth got to catch his breath.

Georgie didn't say much, and when he did, he was sort of dreamy and unfocused—at least that was Garth's first impression.

Right up until Garth started drying the first round of dishes to put away in the cupboards.

"They're soulmates," Georgie said, his smile apparent under his scruff. "I've never heard soulmates talk until I heard them—even one side of their conversation."

Garth thought about it, and surprisingly enough he agreed. "I've never heard people fit so well," he said.

"Mari…. Mari talks about how lost she'd be without him. And I thought, at first, he didn't appreciate it. But then I found out about how he took care of her sister, and how it cost him a relationship, even with a douchebag."

"He'd be lost without her too," Garth said, surprised.

George nodded. "Soulmates," he said simply, with a sweet smile. "I'm so glad they have each other." Suddenly his eyes focused on Garth. "You understand, right? That they don't threaten us?"

Garth found himself smiling gently as he turned from stacking the plates in the cupboard. "Of course not," he said. "No more than the pets do. If Milo can love Mari or Julia or that cat he's so worried about, he might be able to love me."

Georgie nodded soberly. "Yes. Yes, exactly. Good. I was afraid that you'd be another Stuart. But you're an anti-Stuart, and we needed one of those."

Garth chuckled. "Or maybe I'm a dog owner," he said. "I wouldn't be happy at all if a lover got between me and my Chad."

Georgie's laugh was pleasant and reassuring, and at that moment, Mari called out, "Hurry up, you guys! We're going to do party games!"

"Party games?" Georgie murmured. "Like Trivial Pursuit?"

But Garth had heard Milo talking about a game system on his Xbox. "I think it's called Jackbox," he said. "And it's fun. Here, you wipe down the sink, and I'll wipe down the tables, and let's go see!"

THE GAMES were a blast; trivia, one-liner games, the program Milo had bought ran the gamut. Garth couldn't remember having such a good evening—or such a good date—in a very long time.

Finally Georgie yawned, and Mari took him by the hand and pulled him away, and Garth thought wistfully of Chad, who needed to be let out in an hour or so or the poor guy couldn't be held responsible for baying at the moon.

He sighed and stood and stretched, and Milo gave him an unhappy glance as he was putting away the game system.

"Oh no," he said. "You've got Chad at home, and...." He sighed. "I wanted some time alone with you. We didn't even get to plan Thanksgiving, and I guess it's grown!"

Garth chuckled. "Tomorrow?" he asked, and Milo grimaced.

"I go into the office tomorrow. Rick and Angela have instituted a 'go out for a drink' policy at a place that lets dogs sit on the heated patio, and my ad group is all in. I *think* it was in response to when I disappeared off the radar—a sort of, 'Let's make our group close so this doesn't happen again!' so I...."

"Have to go," Garth said, getting it. Relieved in fact. "Look at you, Milo. You have all these people in your life who want to be a part of it."

Milo gave him a shy smile. "You know... Julia helps, but so did you. I told you that, didn't I? Sit down! For a minute? I want to touch you."

Garth couldn't help smiling. This was the Milo he'd loved getting to know. "Sure," he said, parking himself in the corner of Milo's comfortable couch and extending one leg along the back of the cushions. He and Mari had taken their shoes off after their little walk, so he fisted his sock-covered toes in invitation, and Milo turned a shining smile toward him.

"I love how easy this is," he said, backing into Garth's arms with a sigh. "You never make me feel awkward about touching, and you never ask for more than I'm comfortable with, and you always make me feel like I have power. How are you so good at this?"

"Dog ownership," Garth told him dryly, although there was a kernel of truth to it. "You learn nonverbal communication, and you learn to give the dog some room to be a dog. It's the same with people. Give people the room to be themselves, and if they're going to be your friend, they'll find reasons to be close to you." He said this while pulling Milo against his chest and nuzzling Milo's ear.

Milo let out the slightest of satisfied whimpers, and Garth savored.

"I didn't tell you how you helped," Milo murmured, rubbing his cheek against Garth's shoulder.

"Nope."

"You… you forgave me. Julia was awful to Chad because I let her be, and you forgave me."

"You were a mess that day," Garth said, remembering it so clearly. "And your heart was in the right place."

"But I *was* a mess," Milo murmured. "And you were still kind. And it helped me realize that even though I was a mess and I made mistakes, I wasn't worthless. I was still a person. Still human. It made it so easy to trust you. To kiss you. To need to be held." He sighed and burrowed closer. "Do you think if we had dinner this weekend, and I brought Julia over, she would need her dog crate?"

"Absolutely," Garth murmured, something loosening in his chest that he hadn't known was tight. "But only for an hour or two. Then she could sleep on the bed if she promised to be nice to Chad."

Milo chuckled weakly. "An hour or two?" he asked.

"Or three," Garth said, moving his lips along the back of Milo's ear, wanting him so badly he wasn't sure if he could wait until the weekend but hoping it would be worth it.

"What're we doing while she's in her crate?" Milo asked suspiciously.

Garth chuckled. "Planning Thanksgiving," he lied.

Milo chuckled back and wriggled against Garth's swollen, aching groin. "That's not a turkey baster," he said cheekily.

Garth slid his hand under Milo's shirt and kneaded his chest. "And these aren't mashed potatoes," he teased, brushing his thumb along Milo's nipples. Milo made a helpless little squeak and wriggled some more before capturing Garth's hands under his.

"This weekend," he gasped, and Garth moved his hand back to the flat of Milo's stomach.

"Sure?" he taunted.

But Milo turned very serious eyes toward him. "I feel like I've waited my whole life to have sex that feels good," he said earnestly. "I don't want to rush it."

Garth nodded and felt very virtuous as he ordered his libido down. "Then maybe we can discuss Thanksgiving over text for the next two days," he said. "But I think Mari's right. Michael said he'd bring pies, Misty probably has a side dish she makes—a Thanksgiving potluck. People have been doing it for ages." His parents used to, he remembered.

In fact, he was pretty sure they were having one down south this year since he'd told them to hold off on traveling back to Fair Oaks, and his sister, who lived closer, was coming to them, as were some of their new friends.

"My parents always had a formal dinner," Milo murmured. "And we had to dress up in suits. And my stepdad invited his business friends, and my mom always told me to be seen and not heard. Until Mari and I bought a chicken at the grocery store and microwavable sides our first year at college, I had no idea you could have Thanksgiving and not hate it."

Garth's heart gave a painful throb in his chest. "I want good things for you, Milo," he said. "I want a dog who doesn't hate other dogs, I want you to have friends who care about you, lots of them, even work friends named Rick who sound like they're flirting with you—"

Milo snorted, and Garth kept going.

"I want you to have your art on the walls and a house you feel comfortable to live in." He felt a droplet, hot and thick, on the back of his hand, but his heart was full to overflowing, and he had to keep talking. "And I want you to have Thanksgivings and birthdays and Christmases where all your family and friends mix and mingle in a big loud noisy forgivable mess."

Milo's shoulders were shaking now, but Garth needed to say one last thing.

"But mostly I want you to spend day in, day out, comfortable in your own skin and knowing that the people who love you love you for exactly who is in that skin and don't need a different person or a better person or a perfect person to love the person you are. If me and Mari and Georgie and Misty and Michael and Rick and all the people in our world right now can help you feel that way, it's going to be a good Thanksgiving. What do you think?"

"I have no idea why I'm crying," Milo moaned against his shirt, following it up with a hiccup. "But don't leave until I'm done, okay?"

"Yeah, baby," Garth said, holding him tighter, nuzzling his temple as he sobbed against Garth's shoulder. "I don't have anywhere else to be."

The Mechanics of a Real Boy

"So," Rick said the next day as they sat at a place with picnic tables and a twelve-foot skeleton wearing a Hawaiian shirt and a pilgrim's hat, looking like a macabre master of ceremonies, in the corner of the patio, "That's a no on the date, but a yes on Thanksgiving?"

Angela was in the bathroom, and the rest of their team was still on its way. Milo, Julia, and Rick had been seated first. Julia had been given a small handful of dog treats by their waiter and was busy chomping away and eyeing the rest of the patrons of the restaurant with deep suspicion.

Milo nodded, studying the menu. "Exactly," he said, fighting the heat in his cheeks. Rick's suggestion that they go out sometime as more than friends had taken him by surprise. For one thing, his functioning gaydar had always been glitchy—he could have sworn Rick was straight. "I'm sort of seeing somebody." Oooh… he liked that. "Seeing somebody" sounded so grown up! Stuart had come over for a date and then started to move his stuff in because he'd assumed Milo wasn't going to say no. Why would he? He had no other prospects, and he didn't have a roommate—and that was almost verbatim. Compared to Garth, Stuart was such a child!

"Sort of?" Rick asked, sounding skeptical but not derisive. "As in, I've still got a chance?"

Milo glanced up from the menu—he was getting the pork-belly bao anyway—and shook his head. "No," he said. "As in this is a super-amazing guy, but he's letting me go slow. I just got out of a crappy relationship, remember?"

Rick's skepticism went up a notch. "*Letting you* go slow? Are you sure that's not code for 'seeing someone else on the side'?"

Milo remembered the night before, Garth's arms around his shoulders tenderly, the rather panicked note in his voice as he'd asked if he could invite friends to Thanksgiving, the sober grace with which he'd presented Mariana with flowers as he'd come into the kitchen. It suddenly occurred to him, in a wonderful, amazing way, that Milo *trusted* Garth's emotional reactions. Stuart used to say things like, "You should know I love you—don't be stupid!" right after he'd said something really cruel. Garth's reactions to the people around him were real. When he smiled or laughed, it was because he was responding to somebody, not because he thought he was better than they were. Garth was real, and people who were real didn't need to lie.

"He's a good guy," Milo said seriously, making sure he was looking Rick in the eye. It was important Rick knew that he'd been seen and heard. Milo knew that because he *hadn't* been a lot, and he knew it hurt. "I mean, a *really* good guy. The best. I don't think I could trust anybody else right now."

Rick grunted and sighed. "My fault," he said with a shrug that masked a little bit of hurt—but the kind Rick could recover from. "I should have asked you out when you first started with the company. You hadn't met Stuart then. I might have had a chance."

Milo laughed a little. "I'm sort of mad you didn't," he said, glad when Rick smiled. "'Cause I think we could have been friends after a breakup, and I might have been able to avoid Stuart."

That made Rick laugh outright. "What made you go out with him anyway?"

Milo shook his head. "I don't know. He was a client, remember?" Milo had almost forgotten. "He was just… persistent. And then…." Milo didn't want to talk about their first time in bed. Stuart had been plying him with alcohol all night. God, he'd even taken Milo out to a *club*, which had filled Milo with as much horror back then as it did now, and that was saying something. But he and Mari had been determined to go out and date after their college debacles, and Milo had kept thinking, *At least he wants me.*

"Then what?" Rick asked, almost gently.

"Then he sort of moved in. Assumed I didn't have a life, or friends. I was pretending I wasn't talking to my bestie anymore, because he hated her. We'd just reorganized at work, so we only went into the office once a week and… and suddenly he was my *whole* life. And…." Oh, this was weird to admit. "And I believed him. How twisted is that? I *knew* better, but I believed him."

"Oh," Rick said, nodding like this made sense to him, and as much as Milo preferred Garth's happy, easygoing company, he could suddenly see that Rick would have been a perfectly acceptable interim boyfriend who might not have tried to compromise Milo's entire sense of identity. "So when he left…?"

"I believed there was nothing left," Milo said, almost in wonder as he remembered that day nearly two months ago when he'd woken up to a pounding on his door and the realization that he smelled worse than a cat box. "And then Mari brought me Julia." And suddenly his day had been about walking his dog and how not to chase turkeys and how to keep Julia from trying to eat Chad. And about Garth. And about taking Julia to work, and how his coworkers really cared for him, and how even a weirdly sized Chihuahua/pit bull-looking creature could hurt people, and how Milo wanted to be better than his dog but needed to learn to people. And about Garth. And about Mari, and what Stuart had done to dick with Mari's sister's situation, and about cameras in his house, and how Stuart was a douche. And how Garth would work patiently to fix the situation and never, ever pressure Milo to think he was alone in the world without Garth.

"So Julia changed your life?" Rick asked, smiling.

Milo nodded. "And so did Garth," he added, feeling like that was important.

"And so did you," Rick said, eyeballing him up and down.

Milo blinked owlishly and remembered he'd worn jeans that fit today, and that he'd thrown out his "peanut butter" clothes, and that Mari had gone internet shopping and sent him a bunch of shirts and stylish zip-up hoodies and other "casual office" clothes that looked neither like a Sears catalogue from the 80s nor like he'd been vomited out of a stoner's college dorm.

Well, the clothes were nice, and Milo was grateful, but he was pretty sure they weren't the reason he felt this general sense of well-being as opposed to generalized anxiety, depression, and isolation.

"But mostly Julia and Garth," he said with certainty.

"But I'm still coming to Thanksgiving?" Rick asked.

"Oh yes." Milo smiled at him, grateful for the important conversation without any rejection drama. God bless people who could take "no" for "I'm sorry you're not that particular person" and not a complete takedown of their entire identity. Milo had never put himself out there with that level of aplomb—he could only respect people like Rick who did. "It's good to have friends."

Rick grinned. "Absolutely. And I understand there will be dogs there, so I get friends with dogs, and that is a *bonus*."

Milo grinned back. "And you'll get to meet Mari. She's got *eight* cats."

Rick gasped in delight, and by the time Angela and the rest of the group sat down, they were ankle deep in cat stories, because who *didn't* love a furry little love-bomb with claws and a superiority complex?

Nobody Milo wanted to know, he decided, and he and his work friends bonded over creatures large and small and some *very* powerful drinks that Milo could not possibly finish but enjoyed tasting anyway.

"SO YOU had a good time," Garth said over the phone as Milo stretched out on his couch and threw the squeaky for Julia.

"It was great," Milo assured him. "And then Rick drove me home in my car, and Angela took him back to his car."

Garth chuckled. "Enjoying a little buzz, are we?"

"This is *great*," Milo told him earnestly. "In college, there was only one way to drink. Do you remember that?"

"No," Garth said, "because it usually ended in vomit."

"*Exactly*!" Oh, Milo loved it when Garth understood him and didn't judge. "But this made me only a little bit wobbly, and now I'm all floaty, but I'm still okay."

Garth chuckled. "You sound *totally* okay."

"Stuart didn't like it when I drank," Milo told him seriously. "Not after the first time he got me drunk to have sex. I wasn't allowed to buy beer or drink wine, which was too bad, because Mari and I have this recipe for corned beef in beer that is *outstanding*, but Stuart thought it was too expensive." Milo belched and then sat up on the couch because he was suddenly tired. "When can I stop talking about him?" he asked, feeling the melancholy drunk part of the evening settle in.

"When you have memories that aren't him," Garth said softly.

"I'm working on it. I want it to happen *now*. Because every memory I have reminds me that I was stupid to let him move in, foolish to let him be in my bed, and a gutless insecure weenie to cry when he left. Every bad memory about *Stuart* is a bad memory about *me*, and I'm so over remembering bad things about me."

"Mmm…." Garth said softly. "It takes a whole lot of good memories to overwrite our software, Milo. I don't know what to tell you. Want to hear a good memory I have about you?"

"Yes," Milo said, suddenly shameless.

"I kissed you a month ago, in my house, and you looked at me with such wide eyes, I felt like all the crappy encounters, all the times I played seducer and walked into a stranger's house and did the sex thing, all of those were leading up to a time when I could kiss a guy I truly liked and he'd look at me like I wasn't a sleazeball. How's that?"

"Oh!" Milo said, his heart aching in his chest, making it hard to breathe. "You're such a good guy, Garth. You can't think bad things about yourself because of shit that happened when you didn't know the consequences. We all bowl for turkeys sometimes, right? Like Julia?"

"That's right," Garth said, his voice wrapping over Milo's aching heart like a warm weighted blanket. "And you were learning that you were stronger than you knew. That you didn't need someone who made you feel small. Good lessons, Milo. Think of it this way. Every bad memory about Stuart is a reason why you won't have *another* bad memory about Stuart. You know better now, just like I know better not to pretend real life is porn, and Julia is learning not to chase turkeys."

Milo grunted, sagging against the couch, his eyes half closed. "She'd still chase them if we let her," he confessed.

"Yeah, but analogies break down," Garth said. "She's a dog. Her self-awareness is limited to the squeaky and the crate. You're a person. You get to dream bigger."

"I want to sleep in your arms," Milo murmured, giving it up and turning on his side on his couch, facing the back. "And I want to have sex that doesn't hurt and doesn't make me feel dumb and worthless. And I think you'll be able to give me that. See? I want the squeaky, not the crate. I'm really just as dumb as my dog."

"Nope," Garth said kindly. "But you are going to be a lot more hungover if you didn't take some ibuprofen and drink some water. Did you?"

Milo grunted. "Would you believe Rick and Angela made me? I told them nobody was allowed to boss me around like that besides Mari, and they said they would call Mari and get permission if I didn't do what they said."

Garth's rumble of laughter echoed in his ear. "I love how you're opening yourself up to more people who can boss you around, Milo."

"It's the same reason I don't let Julia chase turkeys and you don't let Chad eat her for being a giant pita," Milo confessed. "It's 'cause they care about me. Isn't that funny? I thought Mari and Stuart were the only ones who cared about me, but Stuart left, and it turns out I'm actually sort of lovable."

That rumble got louder. "You are," Garth told him. "You're *very* lovable. And when you're sober, I'd love to boss you around and hold you in my arms all night."

"This weekend," Milo told him. "Next week is Thanksgiving, and I think a good weekend with you would be something to be thankful for."

Was it his imagination, or had Garth's breath caught? "Me too. I'll do my best."

"Everything you do is your best," Milo proclaimed as Julia hopped up on the couch and wriggled between the couch's back and Milo's front, licking his nose a little because he'd obviously forgotten the squeaky game. "It's all really good. Going to sleep now. Call you tomorrow so we can make plans for sex and Milo can become a real boy."

Milo didn't bother to end the call, so as he fell asleep, he heard Garth murmur, "You *are* a real boy, Milo. And you're as lovable as fuck."

LATE FRIDAY afternoon, as the early November sunset chilled the air to a crisp, Milo packed a sleepover bag for himself and one for Julia and was just about to load her crate into his little car when he got a text.

I got her a crate and bed for my house. You can leave that at home.

Milo—who had been entertaining thoughts about stomach butterflies—was suddenly much calmer about the next two days.

Should I worry about dinner?

No, because it's my turn to cook.

Did you really buy a crate? He had to ask. It was... it was practically a courting gift.

Yes. I don't want her to... misinterpret our activities.

Milo frowned. *Misinterpret?*

Milo, sex looks like fighting when you're a dog.

Milo glanced at his phone and smirked and then had a sudden thought. *Will there ever be a time when sex isn't funny?*

Dear God, I hope not. If you can't laugh at poking your thing in another thing and making that the be-all and end-all of your existence, you're poking your thing in the wrong places.

Milo smirked again and was about to reply, although he wasn't sure what he had that topped *that*, when his screen flashed again.

Stop stalling, Milo, and get your thing over here. I promise, whether there are things in places or we just go to bed holding each other, it's all going to be fine.

Milo gazed fondly at his phone and at the carefree selfie Garth had taken when he'd grabbed Milo's phone. It was out of focus and out of frame, and Milo thought Garth deserved better than that. *I need another picture of you,* he texted out of the blue. *So I can look at your face when you say these things.*

Okay, but after this, get moving.

Less than a minute later, the picture appeared: Garth's long, even features, the grooves next to his mouth from smiling, and the crinkles at his eyes from smiling in the sun.

Motivation, he texted back, and added the picture to Garth's number, then, upon consideration, made it his second screen saver—after Julia, because he figured Garth would understand. Then he tucked the phone in his pocket and got a move on.

BESIDES SETTING his knapsack down in the foyer next to Julia's plasticware bucket of food and bag of toys, arriving at Garth's was, well, perfectly normal. Although his temporary residence had been more about making sure Stuart wouldn't freak out when the cameras had been removed, Milo was pleasantly surprised to realize that Garth had given Milo freedom here. He'd worked at the kitchen table and cooked in Garth's kitchen, and while he wouldn't be sleeping in the guest room tonight, Milo *belonged* here.

So Milo took off his shoes and moved into the kitchen where Garth was draining some pulled pork into a bowl.

"What's for dinner?" Milo asked, checking out the various bowls in wonder. Tomatoes, onions, cilantro, lettuce, grated cheese, salsa, and what appeared to be a sour cream sauce, as well as the pulled pork, which smelled like cilantro and lime, all of it in separate bowls lined up on the kitchen counter, with a plate stacked with tortillas at the end.

"Make your own taco," Garth said, then gave Milo a sly glance. "The no-beans edition."

Milo snickered into his hand and tried to recover himself. "Look at me!" he complained good-naturedly. "I was a decently functioning adult, and now you came along and—"

Garth, who had set the bowl down and wiped his hands off on a towel, turned suddenly and captured Milo's mouth with his own. He placed one hand on Milo's hip, holding him but not pinning him, and used the other hand, smelling faintly of fresh vegetables and lime, to hold Milo's chin while he plundered Milo's mouth.

Milo moaned and opened, sliding his hands around Garth's waist and pressing them tighter. Oh wow! They were *here*. He hadn't realized it, but… but they were *here*. Where he could walk into this man's house and smile at him and get kissed by him and his body welcomed the touch. There was no fear here. He didn't think about pain or bothering Garth with his neediness or Garth kissing him only to find some way to humiliate him.

Garth had only ever touched him kindly, and Milo understood that would continue. He understood that in his *bones*.

Garth pulled back in surprise. "Milo, are you crying?"

Milo buried his face against Garth's shirt and snuggled. "I just really like street tacos," he said, hiccupping a little.

"And kisses?" Garth asked, nuzzling his temple.

"Especially with kisses," Milo agreed, and while Julia and Chad gave each other the side-eye as though they hadn't seen each other in a *week* instead of since the morning before at the park, Milo found peace in Garth's arms in front of the taco bar.

THEY DISCUSSED dinner *over* dinner, and both things were fun. The DIY tacos were delicious—the chivey, limey yogurt sauce was sort of the piece d' resistance—and they were also fun to make and fun to eat. It was hard to stay nervous when you were trying to keep your taco from dribbling all over your new henley, and they both laughed a lot as they mopped up.

And the discussion of Thanksgiving was awesome because Milo had researched turkey recipes, and Garth was planning to bring potatoes au gratin, and Mari and Georgie were doing salad and brussels sprouts and tofu. Add to that Michael's pies and Misty's plea to be the one to make the dressing, and Milo suddenly saw his little duplex as being filled to the gills with good smells and happy people.

"What's Rick bringing?" Garth asked.

"Angela and her wife," Milo told him, sounding baffled. "And they're all bringing sodas, beers, waters, and a shit-ton of potato chips." He smiled dreamily. "With onion dip. I *love* onion dip. I made it a deal-breaker."

"Wow," Garth said, sounding impressed. "This is gonna be some shindig."

"I know!" Milo said, surprised. "I actually talked to my tenant this morning to warn him, and… well, he's an older man, in his seventies, and he said he had an empty house, and he looked a little lonely, so, well…."

"So Jerry's coming too?" Garth asked, laughing.

"Yeah." Milo remembered the man's wistful reference to his wife who'd passed, and how he would be happy to hear the dogs in the backyard even if he couldn't see them. "In fact…." Milo grimaced. "I sort of volunteered you for something, and it may be something you'd have to undo, but I'd pay you for your time and everything, but—"

"Milo, it's fine. What do you need?"

"Well, Jerry said if I wanted to take away the divider between my backyard and his, he'd be okay with it as long as we kept it clean. And since Misty wants to bring the dogs, and Chad's coming too, that might be a thing we could do. If it didn't work over Thanksgiving weekend, we could put the fence back in place, but if you could—"

"Of course," Garth said. "That will be a much better space without the fence, and there's enough of us to go in back and police the area. In fact I can get you some inexpensive lawn furniture so a couple people can go out and sit if they need to. We can add some old blankets to keep warm if there's a cold snap, but you know how big crowds get—it's always too hot and too noisy inside for some people, and we can put the pickup equipment by the pipe where you put the droppings." Garth had installed one of those while Milo had been staying at his house, and Milo liked the system of putting the waste in a small septic tank and dropping in enzymes to turn it into dirt a lot more than throwing it in a plastic bag and chucking that in the trash.

"Yes!" Milo said happily. "That would work. Some chairs, a table, maybe one of those outdoor heaters—there's an outlet on the outside wall right before the backyard."

"We could rent a propane one," Garth said, "but I don't think it will be that cold next week. Let me ask Misty. She used to have outdoor parties in her yard, and I bet she has one you can borrow."

Milo bit his lip. "Do you think she'd mind if we—"

Garth shook his head. "Can't hurt to ask," he said. He pulled out his phone and set up a Notes page. "Let me get this down. I forget stuff if I don't put it in a list."

Milo blinked at him. "So do I," he admitted, cheeks pinkening. "I'm always too embarrassed to take notes in front of other people."

Garth cocked his head. "Why?"

Milo stared at his taco. "I don't know," he mumbled. "I think my mom sort of expected me to be perfect." It had felt that way, he realized. "Either perfect or invisible."

Garth nodded. "Did you want to invite her?" he asked, and Milo shook his head so hard he felt his ears wobble.

"No," he said, giving Garth a half-panicked look. "I-I don't want them near my house. They'd be as bad as Stuart!" His mother had been all frosty silences and his stepdad sardonic remarks. "They haven't called me since Stuart called *them* and told them I was abusing my trust. Once they found out it was a... a *domestic* dispute, they told me they were going out of the country until next year."

"Oh, Milo," Garth said softly. "I'm sorry."

"What about *your* parents," Milo asked, feeling his deficiencies as a son and a person all over again.

"Well, I told them I met somebody really amazing," Garth said. "And I wanted to spend Thanksgiving and Christmas with him, so I wouldn't be down this year. And since they're going on a cruise for Christmas anyway, that's fine, and I expect to be spammed by pictures. It'll be adorable."

Milo stared at him, suddenly *violently* aware of how much Garth had given him since they'd met. "You… you had somewhere else to go?" he asked. "And… and you *chose me*?"

Garth gave him a crooked smile. "Well, you know. I figure next year maybe you'll come down south to meet them. Is that okay with you?" His ears turned pink, and he appeared super interested in sopping up the rest of the yummy topping from his taco.

Milo swallowed and reached over to take his hand—the one not playing with his food. "I want to dream of that," he said softly. "I want to dream that this thing, you and me, it will stretch long, and it will get stronger, and next year I can take a trip to San Diego with you, and we can see what Julia does on the beach."

Garth glanced up from his taco leftovers and smiled. "She'll attack the waves, Milo. It'll be epic."

Milo grinned. "I… in a year so much could change. But maybe you and I could change to be even better."

Garth turned his hand over, palm up, and let Milo lace their fingers together. "Want to help me with dinner dishes?" he asked.

Milo bit his lip and nodded. "And then a movie on the couch?"

Garth nodded.

"And then *kissing* on the couch?" Milo asked, to make sure.

Garth nodded some more.

"And then *sex*…." He wrinkled his nose.

"In the bedroom, Milo. We're grown men. We don't have to have sex on the couch."

"Fan*tastic*!" Milo crowed. "I like a good detail check."

"Well, good. Before we clean up, let's have one for Thanksgiving, and then we can spend tomorrow getting it all set up. How's that?"

That, too, was just fine.

AND THAT month of living here, of getting to know Garth, of becoming comfortable in this home—it turned out to be a wonderful thing. It let Milo snuggle on the couch next to Garth's long body, and the night, which promised to be so momentous in some ways, was quite ordinary in others and progressed happily.

By the time the first movie was over, Milo had his hand under Garth's shirt and was rubbing his stomach, and then his chest. Garth had rucked up Milo's shirt and was dragging his fingertips along the small of Milo's back.

And Milo, who knew that tonight he wouldn't be stopping in the hall, wasn't worried. This man had put off his holiday for *Milo*. He was making plans for them *together*. And not once, in any of their conversations, had Garth made Milo feel like he wasn't important, or was invisible, or like his opinion didn't count.

Milo's opinion *counted*. And his comfort *counted*. And Milo, who used to anticipate sex like he anticipated getting his teeth cleaned—mildly unpleasant but necessary—was suddenly looking forward to being naked with the man on the couch who owned the big dog. Although the dog would not be naked with them at this time.

The movie ended, and Garth wielded the remote, switched the TV off, and then straightened up enough to catch Milo's mouth in a warm kiss.

Milo closed his eyes and fell into the kiss like he was falling into a lovely warm bath, and then….

Then he caught fire.

Garth deepened the kiss, and Milo whimpered, needing beyond comfort, needing *touch*, and Garth obliged. His hands were sure and steady—and *on Milo's skin*. Under his shirt, along his neck, probing the waistband of his jeans. Milo tried to wrestle his shirt off, sitting half on and half off the couch, and Garth backed away as Milo's hands flailed above his head.

"Easy there," Garth ordered, chuckling. He took the cuffs of Milo's new shirt and tugged, helping Milo get untangled and half naked, his chest fluttering in and out like a trapped bird's.

And then he realized that Garth could *see* him. They were in the *living room*, and the lights were still on, and he grabbed his shirt with an embarrassing little "Meep!" and held it to his chest.

Garth smiled grimly and tugged on the shirt. "You're beautiful, Milo," he murmured, moving closer. Gently, he traced his lips down Milo's shoulder, down the side of his arm.

Milo caught his breath and dropped the shirt, tangling one hand in Garth's thick hair instead. Garth changed the trajectory of his kisses and wound up on Milo's chest, bearing Milo back against the couch cushions while Garth explored. Milo still felt pale and skinny and un-amazing, but Garth seemed to savor each taste of his skin like wine.

Then Garth's lips found Milo's nipple, and savoring and embarrassment went right out the window.

"Ah!" Milo gasped, arching up into Garth's mouth. "What is that? What are you doing? Why does that feel so good? Oh my God—don't stop. Don't do that. Keep doing that! Oh… *oh wow!*"

Garth's gentle laughter probably should have killed him with mortification, but he was too overwhelmed, too *aroused* by the feel of Garth's mouth on his nipples.

"What in the world *is* that?" he demanded, pushing himself up on his elbows, damned near pointing at the tightly pebbled little bundle of flesh and nerves and whining, "Why does that feel so good? How is that even *possible?*"

Garth pushed himself up off the couch and reached a hand down to Milo to help him up. "It feels good because it's an erogenous zone, Milo," he said patiently as Milo stood right in the circle of his arms. "And if you help me turn off the lights and put Julia in her crate, maybe we can get to the bedroom and you can see how much I like having the same thing done to *me*."

Milo knew his mouth had fallen open, but he didn't care. "You *do?*" he asked.

Garth shook his head. "Listen, remember what we said about how everything Stuart said was a lie?"

Milo nodded. Words of wisdom. He lived by them now.

"Everything you learned about sex from Stuart was wrong. Dead wrong. Forget it all now." Garth smiled then, a supremely masculine, gloating sort of smile that would have made Milo blush, but he was already blushing all over. "By the time this night is over, your body won't even remember his name."

Milo grabbed Garth's hand and hauled him through the house, both of them turning off lights as they went.

WHEN THEY got to the bedroom, Garth glared at Julia, who had followed them into the room, and said, "Crate."

Julia paused and gave Milo the side-eye, but he nodded and said the same thing. With a sigh, she flounced into her crate, flopped to her side, and glowered at them balefully as Garth closed the latch.

Chad's big pillow was on the other side of the room, and the giant animal followed suit, lapsing into a happy snore as Garth dimmed the lights.

"Low," he said softly. "Not off. I want to see you."

Milo bit his lip. "I would rather see than be seen," he said frankly, "but I don't know how that would work."

Garth chuckled as he moved closer, his big rough palms cupping the pale skin of Milo's upper arms. "Milo, I enjoy you so much with our clothes on, why wouldn't I enjoy you with them off?"

Milo swallowed. "Skinny," he said, glancing down at himself. "Pale. Underdeveloped. Oh...."

Garth was running his lips along Milo's neck now, and then to his skinny, pale, underdeveloped chest.

"Delicious," Garth murmured before brushing up against Milo's apparently hypersensitive nipples.

Milo shivered and threaded his fingers through Garth's hair. "Wow," he whispered, and Garth grinned at him, his head level with Milo's stomach.

"Can I get you to sit down here," he murmured, straightening enough to guide Milo backward before pulling the covers down on one side of the bed to give him a place.

"Sure." Milo knew the drill. Without waiting for permission, he shoved his pants down and awkwardly toed off his socks, very conscious of Garth waiting patiently, an indulgent expression on his face. "What?" he said, glancing up, finally completely naked.

Garth lowered himself to his knees before Milo, rubbing his cheek on Milo's bare thighs. He didn't stare at Milo's groin or strip himself, he just... touched, palmed Milo's thighs, spanned his ribs, took in the lot of his body with tanned fingers, rough from outside work and unabashedly gentle on Milo's skin.

"Someday," he said softly, "you are going to let me unwrap you like the gift you are."

Milo *heard* his own swallow, and his eyes unexpectedly burned. "You say the nicest things," he croaked. "How... how do you say such nice things when we're naked in bed?"

Garth stretched his body upward, and Milo caught the hint, bending over to meet his mouth, to kiss him from a position of power, to give this incredibly kind man with the gentle hands and the unfailing good humor the attention he deserved.

Garth pushed himself up farther, and Milo straightened, and then they were reversed, Milo lying sideways on the bed, kneading Garth's bare chest with urgent, feverish hands.

"You like my body?" Garth asked, standing for a moment.

Milo nodded, unable to be coy or shy about it now that he'd been caught groping with such need.

"Then say nice things about me," Garth told him, unbuckling his belt and sliding his jeans and boxers down his lean hips.

Milo's mouth went dry. "Your… your belly button," he mumbled, overwhelmed. "It's *fathomless*."

Garth smiled, stepping out of his clothes. "That's new. Keep going."

"All the hair on your thighs is blond but your skin is *gold*. How does that *happen*?" He sat up, possessed with the urge to touch all over again.

"Lots of swimming in the summer," Garth murmured. "Anything else?"

"Hip bones," Milo said, running a finger from the delightful prominence down a diagonal. He stopped suddenly and glanced up to see Garth's eyes again. "Is this when I go down on you?" he asked, unsure.

Garth's hand, cupping his cheek, was suddenly so much warmer, more intimate than Garth's mouth had been. "Anything you want," he murmured. "Touch it, ignore it, taste it, stroke it—just don't hurt it, and I'll do my best to promise the same."

And again that glorious freedom. A slow smile stretched Milo's cheeks, and without looking, he raised his hand and explored.

"The skin is so soft," he marveled, fondling Garth's length in his palm. "I'm always amazed by that. Is that wrong?"

Garth closed his eyes and shook his head. "No. It's good," he whispered.

Milo tightened his grip the way he liked his own cock squeezed— not so it hurt, but so it—

"Ah!" Garth tilted his head back. "That's nice, Milo. Really nice."

Milo smiled and kept stroking and then lowered his head, staring at it for a moment. "It's pretty big," he said, not sure Garth was aware of that.

A rumble echoed up from Garth's stomach. "That's kind," he said diplomatically. "Any other notes?"

Milo grinned, that freedom expanding, giving him room to play. "Lickable," he said, and then promptly did that.

This time Garth's chuckle was tinged with a gasp, and Garth threaded his fingers through Milo's hair. He didn't grasp or yank or pull, simply cradled the back of Milo's head and let Milo do his thing.

Milo kept licking, wondering why nobody had ever let him do this before. This thing was *amazing*—he'd wanted to play with one for ever so long, but it had been like taking a ride in a friend's new car. Nobody ever let you drive. Stuart had loved to drive it right down Milo's throat, and that had been uncomfortable and humiliating. This was different. Milo got to *touch* and *taste* and *stroke* and *squeeze*, and as he did so, his own drive stick was swelling in his lap, and every time Milo took Garth's cock into his mouth and moved his head lower, that thing in Milo's lap responded like somebody was doing it to *him*.

And Milo was relaxed enough that when the head of the thing touched the back of his throat, he only needed to withdraw a little, not gag, not choke, and there was no humiliation because he was *in charge* and *powerful*, and oh my God, it tasted/felt *so good*.

Garth's fingers tightened a little in his hair, and Milo whimpered as Garth pulled out of his mouth. "Baby," Garth said, his voice choked, "you're going to make me come."

Milo felt like he'd just heard a perfect chord in his *cock*. "Really?" he asked, excited. "Can I? Please?"

And he lowered his head down, his mouth engulfing Garth one more time, and Garth loosened his grip on Milo's hair and placed his other hand on Milo's shoulder and made breathless gasping sounds while Milo worked his strokes longer and harder and swirled his tongue and tasted more, and more, and—

"Oh God!" Garth's fingers tightened again, but Milo didn't mind because Garth's hips were stuttering toward Milo's face, and suddenly a torrent of come hit his back teeth, and Milo could *taste* it, and he swallowed, and there was more, and Garth pulled out, taking over from Milo for one last squeeze, one last stroke, one last dig of his thumb in the slit, and this next spurt was surprising, striping Milo's cheek and his shoulder and his chest as Garth tilted his head back and cried out.

Milo stared up at him, joy like a sunrise in his chest and probably written across his face in come as well.

Garth was gulping air by the time he sank down to the bed next to Milo, chest heaving, body shaking, and Milo wrapped an arm around his shoulders and kissed the side of his neck.

"Wow," he said, not even able to remember the last time he'd been this happy. "You let me do that!"

Garth laughed helplessly. "You're really good at it," he said, still panting. But he was also still smiling as he turned to Milo and took his mouth, tongue busy swabbing and tasting, and Milo realized that what he'd just done was a shared activity, and he was almost giddy.

It was like sex was a *hobby* they could both participate in, like caring for the dogs. *Holy wow*! Best hobby ever.

And as Garth kissed him, bore him back against the pillows, and made him helpless and pliant, all thoughts of hobbies like dog walking and chess deserted him.

Garth's mouth was on his; then he was licking a playful strip across Milo's face, rinsing away the come, Milo realized, and he would have giggled, but he was suddenly so *very* turned on. Then Garth was working his way across Milo's chest, brushing his nipples barely long enough to make Milo need, to beg, until to Milo's surprise, he was flat on his back, his head on the pillows, his knees bent and his feet drawn up on the bed, legs spread wantonly.

He kept rocking up and back, his hard cock thrusting against air as Garth placed little kisses across his stomach, under his belly button, along his thighs.

Milo realized he was being teased and tried not to whine. "Could you…," he begged.

Garth pulled up, regarding Milo solemnly from between Milo's spread legs. Milo's glasses had disappeared, probably back in the living room, but nothing could be clearer than Garth's serious intent.

"Baby," he said softly, his breath blowing across Milo's dripping cock and making him squirm. "I *think* you want to bottom, but you said it hurt. Do you mind if I do some things to see if you'd like it?"

Milo had showered before he'd packed to come here. Very carefully. With this contingency in mind. But suddenly—albeit in a faraway kind of way—he was brought back to his usual experience in bed.

"Like what things?" he asked, and his hips rocked as he spoke, making him think that he was not as serious about self-preservation as he'd first assumed.

Either that or he trusted Garth *way* more than he'd *ever* trusted Stuart.

"I'm going to touch you in your no-no place," Garth said, the corners of his mouth turning up. "And if it turns into a yes-yes place, I'll keep touching you there."

Milo managed a dreamy, cheeky grin. "You're surveying me before you lay pipe," he said, nodding wisely, and Garth's throaty laughter as he reached up toward one of the solid wood bed stands on his side of the bed turned Milo on as well. They could *laugh* during sex—wow! Did everybody know about this? He was reasonably sure that if everybody knew about this, more people would be having lots more sex!

Garth fumbled around and was back quickly, and the cooling air left behind when he'd been gone had worked as a tantalizing touch, so Milo's entire no-no *area* was feeling *very much* yes-yes-yes!

And Garth didn't touch him between his asscheeks at first. Instead he teased Milo's cock with little licks and sucks that made Milo crazy, panting, begging, and then, just when he was at his craziest, he felt it.

A slickened finger there at his cleft, and he almost froze, but then Garth sucked his cock deep into the back of his throat, and Milo groaned.

When the finger teased his entrance, he thrust up against the back of Garth's throat and tried not to come off the bed.

Garth pulled his mouth away but kept his finger. "Yes or no," he gasped.

"Oh wow," Milo said, trying not to thrash. "It's good. Why is it good? It's—oh my God. I'm going to come. From that! Why? Why would I—oh wow! Garth!"

And he sounded a little afraid, even to himself, and the fingers of Garth's free hand twining with his helped to ground him, helped him breathe, as that other finger, the one sliding slickly into his no-no place, made fireworks go off behind his eyes.

He started to convulse, and Garth managed a miracle, sucking Milo's cock down his throat and keeping the one finger in his asshole while keeping their fingers twined.

Milo had mercy on him, releasing his hand and holding the back of his head as his entire body flew apart, like shrapnel made of white light and joy and come.

He was still shaking when Garth, wiping his mouth on his own shoulder, pushed up on the bed next to him and wrapped steadying arms around his body.

"That was…," Milo managed. "That was… oh God. God. Wow. *Garth*!" He turned his head in embarrassment and hid his eyes against Garth's chest. "Wow. Wow. How did I not know sex could *do* that?"

Garth's chest rumbled, but he didn't say anything, simply held Milo while he shook in aftermath.

Finally, when the spots were done dancing in front of his eyes, he asked in a small voice, "What… what do we do now?"

"Wash off if we want," Garth said, taking him literally. "Put on our pajamas. Let the dogs out to pee. Have some cookies and milk for dessert. Come back to bed. Maybe try again."

Milo nodded, all of that making sense although none of it was what he meant.

"I-I was thinking us," he said in a small voice. "That… that wasn't the sex people have when they're just friends."

"Mmm…." Garth nuzzled his temple. "That was amazing, Milo. We can make it even better. But you're right. We're more than friends. And before you ask, no, we don't have to move in together. We have sleepovers. Lots more sex. I think you'll be *surprised* at what kinds of sex there are that nobody has told you about. And about how good it can feel. But you and me have all the time to work on being you and me. Don't worry about it, Milo."

"Can I call you my boyfriend?" Milo asked, because he liked his titles to be secure.

"Sure," Garth allowed. "Can I call you mine?"

Milo smiled dreamily. "That would be *awesome*," he mumbled. And then he rolled over, burying his face against Garth's chest and staying there as his eyes closed, wondering if Garth would forgive him if he missed the milk and cookies portion of the festivities.

This was celebration enough right here.

An Extra Portion of Cookies

MILO'S BREATHING evened out as he fell asleep against Garth's chest, and Garth pulled up the sheet and comforter from the foot of the bed to cover their bare torsos.

Garth was pretty wide-awake—he *was* going to need to put on his boxers, let the dogs out for their last pee, and check all the doors and lights, even though he'd done that on the way to the bedroom out of basic habit. He waited until Milo was well and truly asleep, his breathing as soft and vulnerable as a rabbit's, before rolling out of bed, visiting the facilities, and getting dressed. He added an old sweatshirt because the night chill was starting to seep in and his thermostat was programmed to let the house cool after ten.

He left the light on dim, thinking anxiously that he didn't want Milo to wake up and freak out, forgetting where he was, and bent down to kiss a bare shoulder.

"Gonna let the dogs out," he murmured, and Milo's mumble in return made him smile.

Coulda been, "Fine," coulda been, "Fuck off," or it coulda been "Let's have babies together," but Garth was pretty sure not even Milo knew for certain.

Once he was no longer touching her human, Garth unlocked Julia's crate and opened the door, reassured when he heard her toenails clacking on the hardwood to follow him out the door.

Chad came soon after, and Garth spent a moment in the kitchen making sure their food and water bowls were full and even offering them both a soft treat from the bag. They knew this bag by now—this was a habit Garth had instituted with Chad long before Milo and Julia came into their lives, and the little nibble at bedtime was a time-honored institution.

After the treat, Garth opened the back door and gestured them both outside before closing it and knowing they'd both come back in via the pet door when they were ready. He wasn't sure why dogs needed the open invitation, but it seemed to make them happy.

That done, he reached into the fridge for the milk, and when he turned around, he was surprised to see Milo, in his briefs and the henley he'd worn over, getting glasses from the cupboard.

"Heya," Garth said softly, coming over to drape an arm around Milo's shoulders and kiss his cheek. "Thought you were down for the count."

"I was promised cookies," Milo mumbled, squinting a little. He did that a lot when he wasn't wearing his glasses, and Garth wondered about his prescription—he bet it was pretty strong. Milo needed help to see things like everybody else. It wasn't a shock.

"Cookies you shall have," Garth said, and by the time he'd retrieved them from the cupboard over the fridge—the one Milo needed a chair to reach, which made him feel bad—Milo had poured the milk in both glasses and perched himself on a stool at the kitchen island.

Garth set the cookies on the counter between them and leaned over, bracing his weight on his elbows. They each took a cookie from the box and began to eat, Milo dipping his in the milk first and then sucking the milk out of the softening cookie until the cookie fell apart.

Garth had never seen anybody eat a cookie like that. He was—as it was turning out to be with all things Milo—enchanted.

"How you doing?" he asked into the pleasant silence.

"I'm trying not to be embarrassed," Milo said, and sure enough, there went his ears. Pink as a carnation. "Should I be embarrassed?"

Garth leaned into him, enjoying his frowzy, sleepy heat. "Nope. We did grown-folks business." He allowed himself to preen. "And we weren't half bad at it for a first try. I'm sure we'll get better."

Milo gave him a shy grin. "*That*," he said with satisfaction as he selected another cookie, "is *very* exciting."

Garth chuckled and moved his feet so he was no longer leaning—he was completely in the sphere of Milo's warmth. "I'm glad you think so." And the sadness he'd been trying to keep at bay suddenly rushed in. He took a shaky breath and tried to breathe it out, but he wasn't surprised when it didn't go.

"What's wrong?" Milo asked, regarding him soberly over a disintegrating Oreo.

And Garth could have lied, but he remembered Milo and Mari and the lie that had lain between them for so long, and how mad Mari had been at the end of it. He decided to maybe try not doing that, even to save Milo some pain.

"I'm so sorry," he said after a moment, concentrating on his own Oreo. "I'm so sorry that you were in a relationship that took something that's always been so fun and so exciting for me and made it scary and embarrassing and painful." He bit off the softened half of the cookie and swallowed, barely tasting it. "I want so much better for you. For *us*. But I'm a little afraid."

He managed to glance up in time to see Milo staring at him soberly.

"Of what?" Milo asked.

"You're so bright, Milo. So talented. I'm a landscaper and a failed engineer. Most of my relationships have been sort of superficial. You're right—I've got a big dick, and some guys like to ride that and call it a day. I just... I'm afraid you'll see what an average guy I am—"

"Oh no." Milo had set his cookie down, and to Garth's bemusement he hopped off his stool awkwardly, allowing it to topple behind him, and threw himself against Garth with enough force to make him wobble. "No. No. Not average. Not average. *Perfect*. Kind. *Amazing*. I may be new at this—I *am* new at this—but I'm not so new that I'd throw away a perfectly good lover, a perfectly good *man*, because... what? He's handsome? And funny? And has a big penis? And takes the time to touch me and make me feel good in bed? No. No. No no no no no no no no.... You stay." He glared up at Garth, who wasn't moving anywhere, not with a suddenly ferocious Milo in his arms. "Stay!" he commanded.

In spite of the gravity of the moment, how hard it was to open up about the one thing he was really insecure about, Garth felt his mouth twist into a smile.

"Do you need to get me a crate?" he asked.

But Milo was immune to humor at this moment. "This house is your crate," he said, scowling. "And my house is my crate. And we will have play dates together and sleep over in each other's crates some nights and be alone others, just like you said. And someday—someday when I know what it's like to be alone and enjoy it but know, in my bones, that I'll enjoy being with you more, we can join crates or get a new crate or whatever. My analogy machine broke down because we're not dogs. We're people. And I care about you so much, and I will never throw you over because you have a big penis."

Garth gathered him up into his arms and kissed him then, leaving the Oreos and the milk on the counter to be cleaned up later. The dogs were still playing outside, and Garth trusted they'd come back in, but right now he had more grown-folks stuff to do, and it felt urgent and important and necessary.

This time their clothes seemed to fly off, and Garth was a little less gentle, letting Milo's urgency guide him. Garth wanted him *so badly*, and when Milo lay on his back and spread his legs, Garth grabbed the lubricant from where he'd left it on the end table and held it up for Milo to see.

"You're going to put that in the yes-yes place?" Milo breathed, undulating his hips on the bed in sheer provocation.

"Yep. And then I'm going to stretch you a little. It might pinch, so be ready."

Milo frowned a little. "But didn't you do that already? I mean, you only have to do that once, right, and then I'm all good?"

Garth almost fumbled the lube. "No, Milo, I have to stretch you *every time!*"

Milo's amber eyes blinked slowly, and his lower lip dropped. His erection softened a little, and Garth could tell he was processing. For a moment he wasn't sure whether to stop and give a lesson or keep going and show not tell.

"Keep going!" Milo demanded after a long moment. "I suddenly see how this could be so much better!"

Garth took a breath and shoved that burgeoning kernel of anger toward Milo's ex-who-would-not-be-named-in-their-bed far down beneath his heart, into his stomach, where it could be vomited up later, and instead he concentrated on the permission he'd just been given.

He gave Milo's cock a happy slurp, tasting a little bit of soap because Milo had obviously cleaned up, then progressed to operation yes-yes-yes!

It was *very* successful.

Milo, reassured that what had started out as a good thing would not suddenly turn on him when he was happy and aroused and vulnerable, relaxed even more, giving Garth access to his channel, giving him room to scissor his fingers, to stretch and work, while at the same time using his mouth on Milo's cock or frenulum or the base of his furry testicles to keep him distracted.

He knew Milo had endured enough when Milo started shaking.

"Can we… I hate to ask… can we… can you… oh please, Garth. Please?"

"Yeah," Garth murmured, pushing up so he was poised against Milo's entrance and gazing into Milo's wide, anxious eyes. "Remember," he whispered, kissing Milo's cheek, his chin, his lips. "If it doesn't feel good, *tell* me, and we'll fix it, okay?"

Milo's mouth flickered. "You can fix anything," he murmured dreamily, and Garth pushed gently against him.

And was welcomed in.

The blossoming of Milo's expression alone almost made Garth come. The feel of his silky flesh closing around Garth's erection made him shake all over. Thrust... thrust... thrust....

"Oh yes," Milo almost purred, sinking against the pillows. "Do that. More of that. It's like we're one person. Keep being my one person."

Garth pulled back just enough to thrust forward, and Milo gave a joyful cry of welcome.

And again. And again.

It never got to be pounding, bruising porn sex, and Garth didn't want that anyway. Not now. Not with Milo. Garth gave, and Milo received, and every thrust felt deeper, more perfect, more meaningful, until Milo grasped Garth's biceps and cried out, his body convulsing in orgasm.

Garth followed one thrust later, the climax rolling through him slowly, almost painfully, so all-consuming Garth's entire *body* caught fire with bliss.

He came to moments later, collapsed in Milo's arms, Milo's come slick between their bodies, Milo's happy little sobs breathy in his ear.

"Milo?"

"Y-y-yes?"

"Those *are* happy tears, right?" He had to make sure.

"Oh yes. You're amazing. Thank you. Thank you thank you thank you. I'm still shaking. It's like a gift. You gave me a huge gift, and I came, and that was a gift, and—"

Garth kissed him, pretty sure they could talk more rationally a little later. He barely managed to roll over and turn the bedside lamp all the way off, knowing the hall light could help Milo out if he needed it.

As he fell asleep, Milo still quaking in his arms, he heard Julia's toenails clack across his bedroom hardwood and her snuffling noises as she made herself comfortable in her new crate with her new bed.

On the other side of the room, Chad flopped over with a sigh, and their children were home, and Garth was home, and Milo was his home.

And he could sleep.

GARTH WAS starting to appreciate how Mariana could be a huge asset to his and Milo's relationship.

Milo had left reluctantly Sunday afternoon, the better to get some work and housecleaning done before he and Garth went shopping on Tuesday and for Garth to finish up his paperwork before working Monday at Misty's and then dedicating almost an entire week to Thanksgiving, including the work in Milo's backyard.

Monday afternoon found Garth missing Milo as he got home, but as they'd chatted at the dog park that morning, and texted over lunch, and Garth knew Milo had a busy night ahead doing basically what Garth had done at Misty's but on the computer. He needed to stay out of Milo's hair, and he didn't want to call Doug because Doug's kids were out of school this week, and the poor guy was probably pulling his hair out.

That left Mariana, and finally, *finally*, a chance to vent about Stuart.

"All I'm saying," he growled darkly, "is that some people could really benefit from a little specialized assassination."

Mari's cackle of assent reassured him on a core level. "I used to fantasize about dosing his special Columbian blend coffee with insulin," she said dreamily. "The only reason I didn't was that if Milo accidentally took a drink, I don't think Stuart would have called a doctor when he passed out."

"That's too peaceful," Garth muttered, moving about his kitchen to fix some leftovers for dinner. He and Milo had gone all out the night before and made a batch of barbecue pork noodles that he could eat for the next three days. "I know people who can lay concrete and don't ask questions."

"Ooh...." It sounded like Mariana was munching on a carrot. "I like the way you think. I honestly...." She sighed. "I mean, your best friend is supposed to find love, right? It's not my place to intervene. And when I thought Stuart was making him happy, I didn't. But I hated the guy. He was smarmy. He was fake. He never let Milo finish a sentence. He was condescending as fuck to both of us. But Milo would shrug and say it was fine, nobody got the perfect guy, particularly not him."

"Why *not* him?" Garth asked, the question ripped out of his chest. He would never forget Milo tearing down that hill in his pajamas, frantic that his small, weird dog would freak Chad out. So much good heart in that mess of bird's-nest hair and windmilling limbs. How could anybody think Milo didn't deserve somebody kind and considerate and... and *perfect*.

"Oh, I get it," Mariana said, sounding sage and wise and shit. "You had parents who *loved* you, didn't you?"

Garth gaped, dropping a spoonful of pork noodles on the ground and reinforcing Chad's secret belief that food came from heaven.

"Uhm, yeah," he said. "Doesn't... doesn't *everybody*?"

"You'd think," Mariana said grimly. "But no. And sometimes their lives have made their love as toxic as they are."

Garth let out a breath and had a moment of fear. Any sane person would, right? How much about his lover did he want to know? How much could he help with? How much did he just have to witness and know there was damage he couldn't fix?

But he and Milo that weekend.... Garth swallowed hard against the lump in his throat. He missed the guy already. He wanted Milo in the morning, in the afternoon, in the evening, and pressed up against his body at night. He sort of had to know everything if he wanted that, right?

"I'll take any examples you want to give me," he said after a long moment.

Mariana let out a breath. "It's like my parents," she said, probably because this was something she and Milo had bonded over. "My parents were *nuts* about my sister, because she looked like my dad. Me? I look like my mom's side of the family, so I'm no bueno. But Serena, she's fragile, and when she hit college, she gets diagnosed with schizophrenia. And suddenly my folks are convinced it was my fault. I was fourteen, and I had to sneak in the window of my own house because my father would scream at me that if I was a better person, my sister wouldn't be loony fuckin' tunes. So home's a nightmare, and I go hang out with Milo, because he says nobody bothers him at home."

"Did they?" Garth asked, heart aching.

"Nope. Nobody fucking bothered him at home. There was a housekeeper who left food in the fridge and a gardener who emptied the trash and kept the outside of the house looking lived in, and there was Milo's room, which was... well, clean but chaotic. He'd hung up art in there on every available surface. Picasso, Monet, Lautrec, anime, manga, random street artists—fuckin' *everybody*. And I walked in, and I could see it. He ate at one place on his desk and set his dishes there to bring to the sink when he was done. Kept it scrupulously clean. His clothes were neat in the drawers, but he didn't really care about them, so I had to go through and weed out shit that he'd outgrown in junior high while we listened to Boxer Rebellion on the computer. He had tasteful furniture and matching bedding and all of that fuckin' art. And while the holidays were sort of a shitfest for me—my dad literally handed me a twenty on Christmas morning and told me to get out of his sight—Milo had to show up in his best clothes and smile for his parents' guests and make excruciating small talk to people he'd never met before in his life. Can you imagine? For Milo?"

Garth's heart gave another terrible twist, like it was being wrung out between powerful, unmerciful, bony fingers.

"No," he said, his throat dry.

"So on the one hand," Mari said, "I hated my parents. I still hate them. I feel like that's the healthy option. But my sister never did anything wrong, and she was always kind to me, and as soon as I was old enough and had my shit together enough, I got the power of attorney to put her in a care home that didn't suck donkey balls, and you've seen how Milo helped me there."

And Garth could, with complete clarity, see why Milo would have thought that was necessary.

"But on the other," Mari continued, her voice dropping soberly, "Milo's folks gave him a trust that he came into at twenty-five, after he was out of college and had started making his own money. And he's been smart about it. Hired an accountant that he doesn't bother very often, invested in the duplex, lives like he wants. But when it comes to family, I'm it. His mother calls up sometimes and asks him to make an appearance at a holiday, but Milo's been saying no. And you know, it could be she wants to reconnect. His stepfather was sort of a cold fish, but I can see a mother wanting to know her adult son. But Milo got *so little* from the two of them when he needed *so much*, that I don't know if he's got anything, any padding, anything soft left for them. But when that Byron kid in college sweettalked his way into Milo's bed, Milo was practically one of those rats with the Pied Piper. And Byron was a douchebag, but me and Milo, we had sort of a pact, you know, to keep going. To not lose hope. So Stuart stalks him, and Milo's like, 'Okay. This guy must *really* love me if he's giving me attention,' but he didn't know—hell, neither of us did, 'cause it's not like I've got any track records, right? Neither of us could see that there's attention and there's *wrong* attention until Stuart walked away and Milo was alone in his own head."

Garth had given up on staying rational at this point, and had, instead, slid down his cabinets to join Chad on the floor. He hugged Chad's massive neck, and the dog tried to clean his face, hoping for more pork noodles, but Garth knew good attention from bad attention and, thinking about Mari and Milo, decided he was going to take the win.

"I'm sorry," he said hoarsely, and he heard a long pause and a sniffle on Mari's end.

"Yeah, me too. We were having such a great meeting of the minds here. I didn't mean to ruin it."

And Garth felt Milo's need then to make Mari one of his people. "You didn't ruin it," he said loyally. "We're on the same team here, right? We make Milo happy, we're happy. You tell me stuff about you, and we can keep you happy, and that'll make Milo happy. You're a package deal. I told you that when we first met. I get it more now. 'Cause you're right. I was loved. My folks were nuts about me and my sister. We still text every day, and they're down in San Diego. I've sent them about a hundred pictures of Milo and his dog, and he doesn't know that, but they do, because they want to know who I'm crazy about. But I never saw before that love's a skill as much as a feeling. That sometimes people need to be shown how to accept it so they can learn how to return it. I mean, with you guys, it started with each other, and then you both branched out into cats, and then you got him the dog. Maybe this last month and a half, he's been learning how to be toward *me* through the dog, you know? Like, the dog needs care and feeding every day, and people need tending that often too."

She gave a broken laugh. "Lucky me. I've got eight cats."

"Well, yeah, but your other human likes cats too. Maybe he's broken in the same places."

She gave a sobby sort of snort. "Yeah," she said. "Maybe. But right now, we're focusing on you and Milo. Your parents loved you. Milo's got to learn what that's like."

"I'm doing my best here," Garth said, and internally he was reminding himself he was in this for the long haul. A month and a half?

Early October to Thanksgiving? That wasn't particularly long if you were training a human how to accept love. He figured it would take Julia at least six months before she stopped giving Chad the side-eye every time they met. It would take Milo at least that long too.

"You're doin' okay," Mari told him. "Milo told me he totally understands sex now, and I've got to tell you, that's a helluva improvement over 'I don't know, Mari—it'll get better sometime, right?'"

Garth groaned, wanting to confide in her so badly.

"What?" she asked, her voice getting dangerous. "Why did you make that sound?"

"Stuart told him he only needed stretching the first time."

Oh hell. It was like he'd been possessed by Milo for a moment. The blurt had just *blurted*, and Mari's shocked silence proved to him that he'd gone over bounds.

"So," she said, her voice level at Barely Controlled Fury, "you say you know people who lay cement."

"Yup."

"I will keep my eye open for mob guys who like to pull fingernails."

"Me too."

She laughed a little. "Garth?"

"Yeah?"

"I'm glad we're on the same team."

"Me too."

Thanksgiving with Extra Turkeys

"BREATHE, MILO," Mari said sternly at ten o'clock on Thursday morning. "Breathe. C'mon now, take a breath and walk me through it."

Milo nodded and tried to stop running around his kitchen like Julia after the squeaky.

"Turkey's in the oven," Mari prompted, and Milo took over from there.

"Turkey's in the oven," he echoed. "Potatoes are on the stove. Garth brought over au gratin, already cooked, just needs to be warmed after the turkey comes out and is resting."

"Good," Mari prompted. "Keep going."

"You and Georgie brought the brussels sprouts, and you'll fry them in an hour."

"Good, and appetizers?"

"Chips and veggies are already on the table," Milo said dutifully. "Misty promised something delicious to go with her dressing—something about stuffing jalapenos with butter, cheese, and bacon, which cannot be bad. Michael's bringing pies. We have ice cream."

"That's great," Mari said. "And Rick and Angela?"

"Are bringing sides and drinks and more chips, and it doesn't matter what the sides are because we have plenty already," Milo finished.

"Yes. Exactly."

"But the plates—" He began to fret.

"I brought the heavy-duty paper ones, son. Your little four-count place settings aren't gonna cut it here."

Milo nodded. "Mari," he whispered. "What are eight people going to do in my house?"

"Ten," she whispered back. "Angela's bringing her wife, and you invited Jerry the neighbor. He's helping Garth with the fence."

"And four dogs," he said, his voice cracking. "*I'm an introvert, Mari—what am I going to do with four dogs!*"

She scowled at him. "You are going to calm down before I send you outside to go bother Garth. I'm in charge of sweet potatoes here, Milo, and they're almost done boiling."

"What else do you have to do with them?" he asked, distracted from his meltdown.

"According to Georgie?" She gave a conspiratorial, almost manic cackle. "We're going to *dessertify* them. Apparently this canned potato in a bowl thing that your parents did?"

"Yeah?"

"It's *bullshit*. I'm talking brown sugar, salted butter, cornflakes, pecans—it's damned near a cake recipe, and they call it *vegetables*."

Milo stared at her, enchanted.

"Can I watch you make this?" he asked, suddenly wanting to eat it every day for a week.

"Sure, baby." She patted his cheek. "Anything to keep you from running around the kitchen like a headless chicken."

Milo sat down at the kitchen counter and took a breath, enthralled when Georgie threw out instructions like, "I don't know how many cups, Mari—chop up *all* the pecans. Yeah. Now about two cubes of butter. Yes. Cubes. Honey, this is holiday stuff—if you don't gain five pounds it's not Thanksgiving. Good."

After some of that, Mari was working industriously on mixing everything, and Milo said, "I like him. He's a shiny penny."

"He is," she said. "And can I say the same about Garth. Did he tell you we talked the other night?"

"Yeah. He said it was about my care and feeding."

"Yup. We decided we're both on Team Milo, and we will make sure you're okay. I gotta tell you, I never got the same promise from Stuart."

Milo grunted. "Stuart is already embarrassing from a personal standpoint. As in, I'm embarrassed I ever cared for him."

"Naw, baby," she said, folding an obscene amount of brown sugar into the smashed sweet potato mixture. "Don't be embarrassed that you cared for somebody. Just remember that quote from that movie?"

"*Last of the Mohicans*?" he asked, because Mari had taken a Michael Mann class in college, and they'd seen everything he'd ever directed, and they could now quote his movies extensively, which wasn't saying much because the guy wasn't fond of dialog.

"Yeah, that one," Mari told him. "Remember? 'You are a man of a few admirable qualities, but taken as a whole, I was wrong to have thought so highly of you.' I mean, couldn't you *die*? That was such a good takedown. There was some culpability on her part, but mostly the guy was a shmuck. So that's you and Stuart. And now you and Garth get to go have ambiguous sex while the French invade the fort."

"Yay us?" Milo had never been sure of who won in that movie. "I'd rather have great sex in a bed."

"Oh, me too," Mari said, nodding vigorously. "Here, Milo—grab the glass dish. I already sprayed it. I've got to put crumbles on top of this, but first I have to dump it in the casserole dish."

Milo was calm now, and he could help get stuff ready with a cool head, but even more important, he could remember that people working together on the meal could be as much fun as having people in his house in the first place.

MISTY AND Michael arrived promptly at two, right when Milo and Mari were getting the turkey out of the oven. Garth took over with the dogs, escorting them past the chaos in the kitchen and to the backyard. The day was crisp and cold, so Garth had sprung for the heater and a couple of pop-up dog huts with old blankets in them. Michael was delighted at the setup and went out back to sit on a chaise, drink a beer, pet dogs, and talk to Jerry, who had been pleased as punch when he and Garth had finished taking down the fence and cleaning the yard.

Misty came into the kitchen and set her dishes on the stove and the counter and then started offering much-needed advice about what to do with the turkey once it had sat on the counter and rested.

Milo pointed out reasonably that the thing had been doing nothing *but* resting since he and Garth had brought it home. It had rested in the refrigerator and then rested in the sink in brine and then gotten its skin stuffed with garlic, rosemary, sage, and brown sugar and rested in the pan for the last five hours.

Misty's laugh had been sweet and not mocking, and she told them both about how leaving the meat on the counter to sort of stew and finish cooking would make it taste better, and in the meantime, could she help with anything else?

She was, as it turned out, a delight. She knew things that Mari and Milo did not about cooking, about having lots of people in the house, about being a host. She complimented Milo's décor, his art, and told Mari she looked darling in her bohemian dress with her loose bun and the wisps around her face. She asked about having eight cats, saying she'd have to find a bombproof cat who could put up with her two giant dogs. Mari said Georgie could find a cat that would put up with *anything*, and Georgie wandered by from setting drinks out on the dining table to confirm that.

They were having such a good time that when Rick and Angela arrived, lovely wife Michelle in tow, Milo wasn't panicking anymore. It occurred to him that everybody was working on this *together*. The plan had been for people to travel a buffet line through the kitchen and eat wherever comfortable. Angela suggested putting the snacks on the coffee table since the dogs were all outside, and then she and Rick did that while Michelle set up the drinks and plates. Georgie continued to drift in and out, doing super helpful things that Milo had not anticipated, like bringing dog snacks out to the guys in the backyard, who were apparently bonding over throwing balls to giant dogs and Julia. He even found Julia's favorite squeaky because the bigger dogs kept beating her to the ball.

"I like Georgie," Milo said. He was watching in fascination as Misty combined presteamed red cabbage, fried bacon pieces, red wine vinegar, and brown sugar into a pot on the stove. She'd done everything at home and then brought it to be heated. "That looks bizarre," he said frankly. "But it smells amazing. What is it again?"

Misty grinned at him. "German cabbage," she said happily. "Wait until you taste my dressing—it's a mess, but Michael and I worked on it for years, and now it's perfection."

"So you and Michael are like me and Mari," Milo said. "That's awesome."

Misty gave him a gentle smile. "I never thought about it that way, but yes. Michael was an employee at Jonathan's company when we married. Jon sort of ripped him out of the boardroom and threw him at me—'Here, help my wife learn how to have a big house.' He was *so* resentful at first, and I couldn't blame him. I kept leaving him alone to try to find another job, and in the meantime I was making a mess of the house. He found me sobbing over a half-cooked roast one day, right before a dinner party. I remember him throwing the roast away while I looked up emergency recipes—this was before the internet, mind you, so I was looking them up in Jonathan's mother's cookbook while she rang this tiny bell from upstairs, letting me know it was time for lunch. Michael stomped upstairs with a peanut butter sandwich and a glass of milk and told the old cow to be happy and give me a break, and then he came back down and researched housekeepers in the yellow pages while I tried to rescue dinner. I was so grateful. *So* grateful. I went to Jonathan and asked him to give Mike his regular job back."

Her face fell, and she stepped back from the pot and dried her hands on an apron she'd brought from home.

"What'd he say?" Milo asked gently, exchanging glances with Mariana because this made Misty sad.

"He said that he didn't know what to do. His board of directors had been trying to fire Michael for, you know, being gay, and Jonathan had just been made VP. He had no power yet, and his father was *awful*, and Jon had been trying to give Michael a chance to get another position. I-I told Michael that and, well, broke his heart, which was awful. But Michael? He stayed on. Helped me. Has been my friend. And I asked, and Jonathan's been paying him like an executive, with benefits. I spent our first three years together trying to find him another position. Michael's so smart. He's invested his and his husband's money—hell, he could retire. He just... he likes staying at the house and being my friend, and I love him like my brother, except my brother grew into a homophobic little shit, so I love him more."

"Why'd that make you sad?" Milo asked, ignoring the elbow in the ribs from Mari.

"I remembered, you know. That I'm mad at my husband for assuming and ignoring and neglecting, but he's not all bad. He risked a lot to give Michael a way to find another job, even if he couldn't change the rules back then. He has since. Once he had enough power, a big enough voice, he spoke up for women's rights, for Michael's community. He found ways for his company to give back, to give their employees credit for volunteer work—all the things he and I were passionate about when we were young and in love, he's stayed true to."

She sniffled, and Milo put an arm around her shoulder. He tried to think of anything about Stuart that he had admired or thought was awesome, and the only thing he could conjure up was "But he wanted me."

It occurred to Milo that he should have had better standards than that. Misty had. Her relationship with her husband had resulted in other relationships: Michael, a lifelong friend, her children, Garth.

Milo's relationship with Garth had resulted in, well, a house full of people happy to be here and this lovely woman, who had spent only a few hours in Milo's company but who had shed mom cells all over him and Mari and made them feel better about everything.

Bright as gold, pretty as a shiny penny or a rainbow, Milo had a standard for what his ties to the human world should give him. Garth had been right. Stuart who?

Within an hour he was outside, telling the "guys"—Georgie included—to come inside and eat. The dogs were all panting by this time, slow off the mark to chase the ball, obviously exhausted from play.

Julia gave Milo a perfunctory nuzzle, and he scratched her rump for a moment. When he stood, everybody else had gone inside, but Garth was right there, wrapping his arm around Milo's waist and kissing his temple.

"You smell like dinner," he said, smiling wolfishly.

Milo giggled, not self-conscious at all that it *was* a giggle. "You can eat me later," he said, warmed by Garth's happy guffaw. Garth had been right. Happy sex did wake up the naughty adolescent in everybody, didn't it!

"Seriously," Garth said, squeezing him tight. "How's it going in there?"

"So good!" Milo said, biting his lip. "Rick is being charming to Misty, Misty is trying to adopt Mari and hire Michelle, who apparently is an interior decorator, and Angela and Michael keep talking business strategies whenever he comes inside. The house smells *amazing*, and…." He tilted his head to rest it against Garth's shoulder. "And I'm super thankful for everybody in my life. How's that? I finally get why they call it Thanksgiving."

Garth turned so they were embracing fully. "I'm thankful for you too," he said in Milo's ear, and Milo's eyes burned because apparently happy tears were also a thing.

Together they walked into the kitchen and washed their hands before getting in the buffet line.

Milo was enjoying sitting in the living room and listening to all the people around him talking—and finishing off a second helping of those sweet potatoes that Mari had made because you couldn't *have* too much of those in your life—when the doorbell rang.

Garth tapped his shoulder as he stood up. "I'll get it, Milo. I'm ready for, uhm, thirds, anyway."

Milo smiled at him gratefully, and had just stood up himself—it was his duty, after all—when he heard an unfamiliar voice in the foyer.

"Misty!" called the man. "Misty, I tracked the car here. Are you inside?"

Misty rolled her eyes at Michael, who stood up with her. "Stay," she said softly. "This is him and me, and it's your day off."

Michael rolled his eyes and stood anyway.

"Jonathan?" she said, approaching the doorway, where a midsized, middle-aged man in Dockers and a button-down stood, a slightly askew trench coat over his shoulders and a scarf hanging on around his neck by a few inches. At Misty's voice, there was a rumble at the sliding-glass kitchen door, and Brutus and Daisy both started to howl. Michael hustled back to calm them down while Misty greeted her husband in the doorway. "What are you doing here? You said you were having dinner with your VP's."

"At our house!" Jonathan burst out. "And you're not there!"

Misty shook her head. "I left you with a housekeeper and a catering service. I had already made other plans, and I told you that. You're the one who assumed. You can't give me three days' notice, Jonathan. Not when I've been asking you for a month about our plans."

"But...." And Milo could read the hurt on the man's face. "But don't you want to have the holiday with *me*?"

Misty, in slacks and twinset, regarded him with composure, although her eyes grew shiny. "Of course, my darling," she said softly. "But I wasn't invited into your life until the last moment this year. The house is already your mother's, Jonathan. I refuse to be your last-minute nook-and-cranny girl."

Jonathan's mouth dropped in surprise, and now *he* was tearing up. "But you're my wife," he said, not mindful of the crowd gathering at the doorway to protect Misty. "You're… you're *my* girl."

She swallowed. "I defy you to think of a single moment in the last year when I was your girl."

He sucked in a deep, fractured breath. "I've been getting ready for retirement," he said. "We talked about that—"

"You talked about it," she said. "Have you heard what *I've* talked about in the last year?"

"You got dogs," he said and then frowned. "Are they *here*?"

Misty sighed, and for a moment she appeared helpless.

Garth stepped in to save her. "Mr. Parcival?" he said. "Would you like to come in and have some food? Nobody's sitting at the table— maybe you two could have a conversation there."

"We can go outside, Garth," Misty said gratefully. "I've got some cooked giblets for the dogs. I can mix them up with some kibble."

The crowd jammed into Milo's hallway parted to let them through, and Jonathan gave them all pathetically lost looks. Milo felt some hope for him then, since Misty seemed to feel he was redeemable, and figured the least they could all do was give the couple some privacy.

He was about to close the front door when he heard Misty exclaim, "Oh, Julia, *no!*" and then the scrabble of dog toenails belonging to an entire flock of dogs on his kitchen floor. He turned, door rebounding behind him, surprised when a man's voice said, "Ouch, Milo, you asshole, that hurt!"

Milo whipped around again, almost dizzy, and said, "Stuart? What are you doing here?"

Stuart stood in his doorway, holding a bedraggled, thin, pathetic Chrysanthemum in one hand and a grocery bag of cheap kibble in the other. Milo's first thought was that he had… faded, somehow. Stuart had always seemed to be made of bold lines and overbright colors. Milo would hide in his room to get away from all that brightness. But looking at him now, he seemed… ordinary. Small. An average guy in a wrinkled suit with thinning blond hair and a sour bracket in the corners of his mouth in lieu of laugh lines. How sad.

"Milo, I want you back. Here's the cat. Let me in." And with that, he shouldered his way into Milo's house full of people.

"No!" Milo cried, backing up anyway because… oh my God, his precious Chrysanthemum. "I mean, yes, I want the cat, but no—*Stuart*. I've got a *restraining order* against you. *Get the fuck out of my house!*"

"Aw, Milo," Stuart said, and at that moment, several things happened. Garth strode into the foyer, taking up the breadth of it with his shoulders, the four dogs following him, including Julia, who had no manners and was growling at the cat like Chrysanthemum was a new flavor of squeaky.

Chrysanthemum let out a frightened yowl, still carried *by the nape* in Stuart's scratched hand, and Milo had a terrified glimpse of the chaos four dogs and his poor abused baby could perpetrate on his house. Then Stuart shook the cat again, and Milo whimpered, unable to yell at the fucker when he was holding the cat hostage. Milo was losing all his power, all his resolve, when Garth proved he had the stuff of heroes.

"Milo, get rid of all these people and you and I can talk and—hey!"

Garth reached into Stuart's space, grabbed the cat by the nape of the neck, and drew him to his body, against his chest, wrapping his arms around the poor thing and sheltering him from the chaos. With one loud bark of, "Julia, Chad, *stay!*" he whirled out of the room and disappeared down the hallway, leaving Milo to face his ex without the hostage.

And suddenly Milo was furious enough to do that.

"Stuart, get out of my house," he said, his voice low and menacing. Julia and Chad picked up on the tone and started a toe-level grumble that told Milo they meant business and saw Stuart as a threat too.

"Milo," Stuart said, and he lowered his head and gave that sort of dimply smile that he used to get his way. "Look, baby, I forgive you for the restraining order—"

"*You bugged my house, you fucknugget!*" The scream came from Milo's stomach, and the grumble from the dogs turned into an Evenrude motorboat rattle.

Stuart paused and swallowed but did not step back. "Milo, I just wanted to make sure you were okay. If those guys hadn't found the system and—"

"And given my privacy back," Milo snapped.

"Well, you have to admit, you didn't do much for a month. I got worried. God knows what your little friend was going to do to cheer you up—"

Milo slapped him, and Stuart gaped. "Don't talk about her." His palm stung and his wrist ached, and that was the only reason he didn't do it again. "Don't talk about her or Garth. You keep their names out of your shitty, controlling, nasty mouth, Stuart. I'm done with you."

"But...." And Milo could see it. The moment it computed in Stuart's tiny brain that Milo meant it. "But Milo," he said with a condescending smile, "I'm all you've got."

That broke something in Milo's brain, and he wasn't sure what he was screaming in Stuart's face, spittle flicking from his lips with impunity, but whatever it was, Stuart turned red, then white with fury. In a moment, he was advancing on Milo, arm raised in retribution. He was bigger than Milo—smaller than Garth but still bigger than Milo—with wider shoulders and muscle mass from working out, and Milo suddenly knew he should be afraid, but he didn't care. Milo had *so* much more than this sad, slimy, pathetic excuse for a man, for a friend, for a lover.

And Milo hoped he said all that when Mari and Garth stepped smoothly between him and Stuart, Garth taking the arm readying to swing, Mari taking the other side. Together, they *dragged* him out the still open door, and Georgie, bless his quiet, helpful heart, was the one who slammed it shut behind them.

"SHUT UP, asshole, or we're going straight to the cops," Garth said smoothly. "We'll take you to the police station and dump your sorry ass in jail. Mari, where'd he get this janky polyester suit, anyway?"

"Scumbags 'R Us," she replied promptly. "Extraweenie size."

Garth chuckled, because she was referring to Milo's last screeching tirade delineating Stuart's inability to make love with an "amazingly tiny weenie" when Milo now knew it didn't have to hurt even with a "double-extra-large!" Ordinarily, Garth might have found comments on his erection size embarrassing, but seeing that it came with Milo's self-empowerment, he figured he could sacrifice a little dignity.

"I understand that'll fit him just fine," Garth said.

"I'll fuck you up," Stuart sputtered, struggling in their grip, but Garth tightened his hands, hardened from manual labor, and Mari executed a self-defense move, her comfy Doc Marten boot scraping right down the inside of his shin.

Stuart crumpled like toilet paper and whined as they dragged him to his truck. Mari searched his pocket and came up with his keys.

"The truck," she said in disgust, "with all the banners?"

Garth gave Stuart a pitying look. "We're gay, moron. Driving that thing is like saying 'Roaches for Raid.' I thought people like you were a myth."

"It's new," Mari said decisively. "Milo wouldn't have dated him if he'd seen that thing."

"Well, get it away from Milo's yard." Garth glared at the truck again and then glanced at Mari. "And search it for weapons."

Mari's eyes flew open. "Oh shit! Are we taking it to the police station?"

Garth grunted. "No, I got a better plan. Down Sunrise, right on Kiefer."

Mari chuckled. "Find the biggest field I can," she said. At that moment the chilly encroaching evening grew heavy with rain, and she smiled. "You throw that ball for Chad every day, don't you?"

"Every goddamned day," Garth agreed.

Nobody was out. Twenty minutes later Garth followed Mari into a turnout, a fuming Stuart at his side. The man had said nothing as Garth's workingman's truck, complete with scratches, divots, and chips in the paint, followed his pristine red Silverado into the boondocks and then jounced over an open field.

"Give me your phone," Garth said when they stopped.

"I'm not giving you shit," Stuart sneered, crossing his arms like a child.

"Give me your phone, or I'm dragging you out of this vehicle *by your hair*. And when I've ripped it off, I'll search your pockets and take your goddamned phone," Garth said, his fury boiling in his balls.

Stuart threw it at his head, but since he wasn't that strong, Garth figured the bruise would heal.

When Mari stopped, he asked her if she'd found weapons.

"Two of them," she said sourly. "One of them illegal in California."

"Great," Garth said cheerfully. "Now, keep the keys and lock the doors. Leave the vehicle on and shut them."

Mari chuckled and did that as Stuart gasped. "What in the hell? Give me back my keys—"

"9-1-1, what's your emergency?"

"Yes," Garth said pleasantly into the phone. "I'm calling on behalf of Stuart Jameson, from his phone?"

"Yessir, what seems to be the problem?"

"Stuart has been acting crazy, spouting off at the mouth about his ex-boyfriend, screaming about revenge because the guy left him. Anyway, I know he has weapons in his truck, and he went running out into the void screaming. I can't see him from the side of the road, so I have no idea where he is."

"And what's your name?"

"Byron!" Mari mouthed. "Byron Kilpatrick."

"Byron Kilpatrick," Garth said dutifully, knowing this was probably Milo's ex-douchebag from college.

"You stay where you are, Mr. Kilpatrick. There will be a police presence out there in a few minutes."

"That's a load off my mind, ma'am. I understand Stuart has a restraining order out on him, and I would hate to see him in jail because he violated it."

"Do you think he's violent, Mr. Kilpatrick?"

"I think he's a small-dicked sociopath, but I do hope he doesn't harm anybody in his way."

And with that, Garth turned and, without hitting End Call, pitched the phone as far as he possibly could into the empty field. Before Stuart could protest, Garth turned again and pitched his keys in the opposite direction. The ground around them was soft and powdery, the grasses growing in it straggly and brown. Good luck finding those objects, Garth thought grimly, particularly before the cops arrived.

"Shall we go?" he said to Mari.

"We shall," she replied. Then she glared at Stuart and said, "If you mention Milo tonight, we will put you in prison. Good luck evading the gun rap, asshole. By the way?" She held out her purse. "All your ammo will be in a dumpster somewhere in Sacramento. Enjoy."

And with that, they both hopped into Garth's truck. Garth ripped out backward, spinning a donut to get to the road and going back the way they had come. They passed five police cars, lights on, sirens screaming, on their way back down Kiefer to Sunrise, and Mari gave an evil chuckle while holding her chilled hands out to the heater.

"Think he'll rat us out?"

"Rat who out?" Garth asked. "Does he even know my fuckin' name?"

She laughed. "Nope. Do you think he's smart enough to get the license plate number?"

Garth shook his head. "He just sat there, arms folded, sniffling like we'd hurt him. Didn't even reach for his phone. I mean, think about it—he was all but abducted, and he didn't have anybody to call. God, what a fucking *void*."

"Milo's taste in men has improved so much," Mari said, patting his arm.

"We need to make sure Stuart gets arrested," Garth said soberly. "I mean, he seems pretty vacant, but some guys…."

"Yeah." She sighed. "It's never easy, is it."

"Not if it's worth it."

She leaned her head against his arm. "You and me, we make a good team."

Garth nodded. "If I ever have to make him a hood ornament, I'll call you for a tarp and a shovel. Doug will come with the cement truck. We can bury him under Misty's pond. It'll be fine."

"That's what I like to hear," she said. "A plan."

MARI TEXTED Milo on the way back, and they walked in, still shivering from the chilly rain, and discovered pie had been served, with hero's portions saved for the two of them. They ate standing in the kitchen while everybody gathered around to hear the story, which Mari told truthfully, because, as she said, they might need alibis.

Milo had cemented himself to Garth's side from the moment he walked in.

"I'm sorry," Garth murmured, wrapping his arm around Milo's shoulders, loving the rightness of him tucked in there. "I'm so sorry. I should have protected you sooner—"

"What are you talking about?" Milo asked, legitimately puzzled. "You took care of *Chrysanthemum*. Oh Garth, my poor kitty was in terrible shape. His fur was all bedraggled—Stuart had been feeding him commercial food, which gives him the runs. He smelled, and he was skinny." He gave a little smile and added, "Georgie made a run to his place for the appropriate food, and we bathed my kitty and wiped him down and put him back in the crate so he could sleep. You were so smart to put him there. The dogs can't bother him, and he's in the quiet and the dark. Julia's got a zillion places to sleep. She'll learn to share. But thank you. You... you trusted me to deal with Stuart, and you took care of my baby. It was wonderful."

Garth smiled into Milo's eyes, dazed and happy. They had work to do. So much work. Milo still needed time, time to trust in himself more and more, time to make his own decisions, time to adjust to the changes in his life and in himself. But for right now, it was Thanksgiving, and while Garth missed his parents, he had faith that this family here, these people with Milo, and Milo himself, would only enrich his life further.

There would always be loose ends—but that was what life was about. If fixing a backyard once was the end-all and be-all of growth and change, he would be out of a job.

On the Day of the First Christmas

"MEOW."

Milo opened one eye. "No," he said. Garth was snuggled in behind him, naked and warm, those delightful muscles in his thighs, stomach, and arms fully flush against Milo's softer, slenderer frame. He was not getting up.

"Meow." The bed depressed with a satisfyingly hefty weight, and a motorboat rumble started in Milo's ear, followed by the harsh pinpricks of biscuit kneading while Mumsy went to work on his primary job: poking tiny holes in Milo's skin.

"No," Milo mumbled again. "It's six o'clock, Mum. You don't get fed until eight."

"Meow." Chrysanthemum's blocky square head pressed against Milo's like the cat was trying to control Milo's body with his mind.

"Feed him, Milo," Garth rumbled. "Then we can sleep until nine."

Milo moaned slightly and sat up, clutching the cat to his chest, grateful he still had his T-shirt on from Christmas Eve. Mari had gotten it for him—it had little felt birds all over it like the song, and Milo both loved and hated it, as Mari had intended. He'd worn it, but he hadn't objected too much when Garth had gotten him to…. Well, it needed washing.

Which he only remembered when he stood up and realized he was absolutely naked from the waist down.

"My penis is cold," he said in a panic. "Mumsy, I'm not wearing any underwear. Here, Garth, hold him!"

"Only if you promise not to call the cat Mommy again."

But Garth threw his arm over Mum and touched noses. Chrysanthemum apparently recognized his savior from the day with too many people when he so unceremoniously arrived back in his former home. Garth had been Mum's favorite perch when Milo was busy tossing Julia the squeaky, and if Julia decided that *today* the cat needed chasing, it only took one command from Garth to change her mind.

Milo was still learning the correct tone of voice for, "Leave it!" to work. He usually ended up squeaking and yelling, "*Mumsy!*" and then Julia would do the unthinkable and *actually catch the cat.*

Julia had a couple of healing stripes across her nose and a newfound hatred/respect for Milo's once-placid Chrysanthemum, but they were learning to coexist.

Chad, for the most part, stayed out of it, although Chrysanthemum (and Milo) did notice that when the cat was curled up on The Chad, Julia left them both alone.

Animal politics, Milo was starting to realize, were more entertaining than real people-driven ones, and way more fun than TV.

But sometimes they were damned irritating. With gasping little breaths, Milo hauled his sweats up his hips and trotted through the house, wishing for the thousandth time that he had set his thermostat to go on at six instead of seven. He hadn't noticed at first because it had been summer, but Chrysanthemum's insistence on being fed early was *really* uncomfortable when it was sixty degrees in the house.

Like an ash-colored moth, the memory flitted of Stuart yelling at him to conserve energy because "they" were paying too much money in heating bills.

Milo frowned. Those were coming less and less these days, those flashes of living with Stuart, those moments when he forgot he didn't believe in the man anymore. Like a boogeyman from childhood, Stuart's power had begun to fade the moment Milo had stood up to him.

Of course the sixty days of jail time for being caught with illegal firearms while having a restraining order did help. Stuart had been in county lockup since Thanksgiving, and would continue to be so until almost February. Garth's friend, Doug, had contacts in the police department. Milo understood that the man who had gone into lockup was much different than the man who would be coming out. Did Milo think he'd been rehabilitated?

No.

But Milo was also pretty sure Stuart only picked victims who could be culled from the herd. Milo's herd was still going strong, and he and Garth were constant stars in their own solar system, so Milo would keep his eyes open, but hope.

In fact today they were hoping themselves right over to Misty and Jonathan Parcival's house. The two of them had made up, starting at Thanksgiving, and Jonathan had taken to throwing the balls for the dogs in the evening before he came in. Misty's book was coming along wonderfully, she said, and while she wasn't sure about shopping for agents yet, she mostly wanted to finish the manuscript.

Garth and Doug had finished her backyard modifications and her new porch office. It needed a space heater, she said, and Doug and Garth planned on putting sturdy blinds up before spring arrived and the Sacramento sun tried to cook poor Misty alive, but right now, she had a space of her own, and she got to share it with two big goofy dogs who thought the sun and moon rose with her smile.

Milo could tell Garth was happy that his friend was in a better place. And they were looking forward to a fancy Christmas. She'd told them both to dress nicely, to only bring themselves and the dogs, and to be prepared to sing.

Milo had hopes for one of those Christmases from TV where everybody sang carols, and Garth said it was very likely. Milo and Mari had been practicing their favorite Christmas tunes for the last two weeks whenever she and Georgie came by.

They came by a lot—sometimes one at a time, even, ostensibly because Georgie wanted to check on Chrysanthemum, but Milo was starting to suspect he just liked Milo's duplex. Then Georgie brought two shelter cats to Jerry next door, and Milo realized that he'd found another friend/victim, but since it meant Jerry wasn't alone anymore, that was fine too.

And Georgie *did* seem to enjoy watching movies or playing video games on their couch with Rick or Angela or Garth.

Knowing that Mari's boyfriend liked Milo as much as Garth and Mari seemed to like each other made Milo seven kinds of happy.

More. Good relationships gave you more people in your life, not less. It was very important to know.

"Ooh…," Milo muttered, running through the house. "It's a bit cold, it's a bit cold, it's a bit cold." He got to the kitchen and started rattling food in the bowls, not surprised in the least when he ended up dishing out wet food for *everybody*, although Chrysanthemum was the only one who got fed on top of the kitchen counter. Milo suspected Chad *could* steal his food if he wanted to go counter surfing, but Chad was much too well-mannered for that.

On Milo's trip back, he peeked into the living room where his small tree sat, lighted and glowing softly like a good Christmas tree should, and realized Garth must have put some presents underneath.

Milo was tempted to go see what he'd gotten—there were presents under there for Garth too—but he wanted to get back under the covers with Garth more.

"Let me in, let me in, let me in." He chanted when he got back to the room and charged under the covers, letting Garth devour him with the comforter, dragging Milo's chilled body right next to his again.

"Aww…," Garth mumbled. "I liked naked better."

"We can do naked later," Milo said. "Right now keep me warm, please. There is nothing sexy about cold feet."

Garth laughed, and Milo cuddled up to the laugh much like he'd cuddled up to Garth. It was hard to believe he'd never known that a boyfriend would make laughter sexy. Even sexual. All Milo's surprise about the adolescent sense of humor, and it was seeping in that finding sex humorous also meant it was human. Every touch was thoughtful, or sweet, or arousing, or funny. Laughter was one of the best parts of being a real boy, Milo thought, chuckling as Garth nuzzled his scruff against Milo's neck.

"Did you check under the tree?" Garth asked suspiciously.

"No," Milo said. "Too cold."

"You're not curious?" Garth asked, sounding hurt.

Milo turned in his arms. "I'll love it," he said without a doubt. "Because it's our first Christmas, and I'm stupid with love. I love Christmas, I love you, I'll love whatever you get me for Christmas—what?"

Garth pushed himself up on his elbow. "What you just said," he demanded. "Did you mean that?"

Oh hell. What *had* he just said? "I love Christmas," he muttered to himself. "I love you. Oh!" He smiled up at Garth, realizing the significance of that last thing. "Yes! Yes, I *do* love you. You're perfect. You're everything I wanted in a boyfriend. You make my life rich—as in, more people, more happiness, more laughter. You give me all that. I had no idea these were things I wanted, but you loved my dog when she was stupid, and you were kind to me when I was more so, and… well, you're amazing. I love you."

Milo grinned at him, proud and figuring that was the end of the discussion when Garth's sober eyes made him realize that no, there was supposed to be a whole other half.

Oh no! What if Garth didn't feel that yet? What if Milo had scared him? What if this was only sex—except *no*, it couldn't be, because he and Garth had so much *fun*, and they loved their days together, and it *couldn't* be only sex, it *had* to be more and—

"Don't panic," Garth said gently. "I love you too. I've loved you forever, Milo. I just... I had to know you were ready to hear it. Merry Christmas. I love you. I love you *a lot*. I want you to meet my parents this year, and maybe we can move in together when you're ready. I want you to bring Chrysanthemum to my house, and I'll get him a bed, and we can get a little dog pool for Julia and... and I don't care what your baggage is, I want it in my life. I love you."

Milo's grin back felt like it was going to take over his whole face, or even his whole body.

"Nine o'clock?" he asked, wanting to make sure.

"Yeah, Milo. Nine o'clock." Garth's face was right over his as Garth held himself up on one elbow. "Why?" He grinned wickedly. "You had something in mind?"

"I think I need to be naked again," Milo said, and then he sobered. "Because sex is awesome, and I think we need to use it to celebrate. What do you think?"

"Celebrate?" Garth asked.

"Christmas," Milo said. "Merry Christmas, Garth. Your love is, like, the *only* present I'll ever need."

"Tough," Garth murmured, brushing Milo's lips with his while he felt Milo's chest up under the dreadful Christmas shirt. "I got you new clothes and some walking boots and a swimming pool for your dog, and you'll like it."

Milo's laugh was low and guttural—and sexy. Yes! Milo Tanaka could be sexy and flirty and happy and naked with this man. "I got you a key to my house," he whispered. "And some other stuff, but the key to the house is the big thing."

"Aw, Milo...." Garth didn't say anything else. He captured Milo's mouth with his, and Milo knew his clothes were going to melt away like bad memories did sometimes, or tears in the rain, or candy under the tongue. When the right person touched you, with care, with forethought, there was no bouncing or screaming or running or panic. The time for bowling for turkeys as an emotional outlet was gone.

Milo was going to make love with the best man he'd ever met, and they were going to talk about a bright and shining future, and Milo could trust that someday it would be so.

Read on for an Excerpt from
The Twelve Kittens of Christmas
by Amy Lane.

Last Call

KILLIAN THORNTON wiped down the varnished wooden counter in front of him and fought the first yawn of the night. It was the Friday after Thanksgiving, and the rush had been fierce—lots of people celebrating their "friendsgivings" anywhere but in their own homes this year—and he was ready to clean up and go home.

"Don't do it," Suzanne, his night manager, ordered.

"Don't do what?" he asked, yawning.

"Don't do that, you bastard!" she responded with a yawn of her own. "Dammit, I still have to count drawers!"

Suzanne had been hired ten years ago straight out of college; she had an MA in history and no interest in teaching. She was smart, could talk customers down off a drunken soapbox and count a drawer at the same time. She also didn't hesitate to break out the baseball bat underneath the bar if things got rough, although they didn't often get rough in Catches. Catches was a chain bar—you could find one in most major cities in America, although usually they were found in big malls and shopping centers, along with BJ's and Cheesecake Factory. This particular Catches, though, was deep in Sacramento's midtown, maybe three blocks from Lavender Heights and sitting cheek by jowl between a mom-and-pop Mexican food place and a designer thrift shop—but right across from a Starbucks. There was enough unique and personalized business going on around them for the place to have grown a little character of its own, and for people to need the reassurance of a brand name while pub crawling through midtown.

"Go ahead and start," he said, moving on to polishing the brass fixtures. "Then we can go home."

Killian loved this area—lived less than two blocks away, in an old square apartment building with five units, vintage wood frames and floors that swelled and stuck in the summer, and wrought iron that had been painted over often enough to obscure the filigree patterns on the stair rails and the sconces in the upper apartment. He had a car, but he could walk anywhere: the laundromat across the street, the bodega a block down, the comic bookstore five blocks away, even the place he bought his shoes. All of it was close enough for a brisk walk under the Sacramento trees. What was left of them, of course, after the storms the year before.

Killian had been visiting a friend who'd worked at Catches, after he'd done two tours right out of high school. He'd come home rootless—his folks lived in the Midwest and had been happy to see the back of him—and lonely. The Army hadn't sucked entirely. Three squares, a salary, a daily goal. If it hadn't been for being in a war zone, it might have been great. But the war zone thing had been... frightening. He'd seen some action, and he'd hated it. Hated the casual disregard for life, hated the moral grayness, hated not knowing if he was going to be woken up by trumpeted reveille or mortar rounds. Hated seeing the civilians hurt, hated hurting the soldiers, felt like he had no business there to intervene but no choice but to help keep the civilians safe.

And then he'd just... left. Time served, sir. Go back to your business, go to school, get a job, nothing to see here, folks.

It hadn't sat right—guilt, anger, depression, the whole weight of it had rested on his shoulders. And he'd just come out to himself, if not the world. Going back home when he hated *everything*, including his own shadow, had not filled him with joy. Well, nothing back then had filled him with joy, but in particular going back to his fundamentalist family in the Midwest who wouldn't understand his feelings about the war or the military or other men—*that* had filled him with everything from horror to irritation to disgust. So he'd taken Jaime, who'd been stationed with him briefly in Kabul, up on his offer to come visit Sacramento in the spring, when Jaime said the sun was pleasant and not destructive, and there might be flowers on the hills.

He'd fallen in love with Sacramento—and briefly with Jaime, although that had been more of a starter relationship than the real thing. Before their sad but amicable breakup, Killian had gotten the job at Catches, and after it had gotten his own apartment nearby. Jaime had taken his savings and started his own bar up in Folsom, where he kept promising to ask Killian to come work, but Killian kept thinking that he'd miss the big sycamore tree in front of his apartment in the spring, or the way the breeze off the river could cool the whole place down in the summer. He'd miss the thick, honey-dripping light in the late afternoons in the fall or the boozy happiness of the pub crawlers on a warm Friday night. He wouldn't hear the women preening about their new looks as they left the nail boutique next door or be torn between the Starbucks across the street and the indie coffee place a block and a half down that he liked better. What if he never ate a dessert at Rick's again? All of these things, these moments, had rescued him when he'd come to Sacramento eight years before—they'd anchored him, filled him with quiet joy when he'd thought that was the impossible dream.

He couldn't leave them now. This city, this job, they'd served him so well.

And loneliness was such a small price to play for a little bit of peace.

But it meant that closing time at Catches had the same melancholy feeling as the Semisonic song. Nobody was ready to go home, but they couldn't stay there.

Tonight, though, things had cleared out rather quickly, with the exception of the kid in the oversized white sweatshirt and the skinny pants with the big denim jacket and trout-fishing hat sitting on the barstool behind him as he played one more spectacular round of darts.

Thunk. 25. *Thunk.* 50. *Thunk.* 100.

The kid with the slender, lithe body and the vulpine little chin with a wide gamine mouth—not usually Killian's type of face, but it was an *interesting* face, wasn't it?

Thunk. 25.

The kid who looked borderline familiar?

Thunk. 50.

"You got the drawer for me to count?" Suzanne asked, suddenly standing right next to Killian. "Don't you want to go home?"

Killian had been staring at the kid—twenty-two, twenty-three, maybe—throwing darts at the board with astounding precision.

Thunk.

"Wha—oh, yeah." Killian went to the old-fashioned register—a Catches staple—and hit the No Sale button, popping out the cash box along with the receipt he'd generated with all the night's transactions on it, as well as his first drawer count, done after the last—*thunk*—or, well, almost last customer had left.

Bullseye! Killian remembered who this kid was.

"Here's the drawer," he told Suzanne. "I'll polish some brass and wait until you count it out."

She snorted. "Puhleeze, Killian. Like your drawers are ever more than two bucks off."

Killian inclined his head modestly. He did like a clean count at the end of the night.

"Well, then," he said, "I'll wait to walk you to your car."

Suzanne was fit—as was Killian—but she also wasn't stupid. "How very gallant," she said. "I accept. I'll be back in a sec after I get this in the safe."

Killian nodded, because why use extra words when you didn't need to, right? And then turned his attention to Lewis Bernard, his upstairs neighbor's little brother.

Thunk. "Lewis?" he asked, timing the name carefully so as to not break the kid's stride.

Lewis, apparently, could multitask. "Hey, Killian." He yawned before bebopping to the dart board to pull out his latest round. "You almost done?"

"Yeah," Killian told him. "You weren't… were you waiting for me?" *That* seemed unlikely.

Lewis gave him a sheepish look that indicated the unlikely was true.

"See," he said with a sigh, "Todd wanted to, uhm, have some time with his girlfriend tonight—you know, Aileen?"

Killian nodded because he did know her—and Todd. Todd had been his neighbor for about four years—had been to movie nights and was, Killian thought fondly, a friend.

"Yeah, well, Todd never gets a night off—you know that-- and he didn't want his twinkie little brother around while they got their thing on. I guess it was true romance. Anyway—" He shrugged. "—I didn't want to go up until he texted me, and, well, I knew you lived in the building. I figured I'd walk home with you, you could let me in, and I'd hang in the stairwell until he remembered I didn't have anywhere else to go."

Killian squinted at him. "Did he just… *forget* you were here?"

Lewis made one of those faces where he squinched his lips together until his top lip touched the bottom of his almost hawklike nose. Killian wondered if he ever put a pencil in the space when he was a kid, bored at school, and then he put a dart in there and tried to make it balance, and Killian didn't wonder anymore.

"Lewis?" Killian prompted, and Lewis turned his head to the side with the dart caught lengthwise between his lip and his nose and smiled. The smile changed the curvature of his upper lip and the dart slid off, landing point first into the scuffed wooden floor with its own *thunk.*

"What?" Lewis asked, bending to pick up the dart.

"Did your brother forget you were here?"

"Mm… forget?" Lewis tilted his head, his shaggy blond hair falling into place with his every movement. "That's sort of a harsh word, don't you think? I, uhm, may have mentioned that he's already involved."

Killian squeezed his eyes shut. "Your brother forgot you need a place to sleep tonight," he said on a sigh. "No worries. You can use my couch."

Killian's place was small; all of the apartments in the building were small. The building was a large blocky rectangle with a peaked roof, and the two bottom apartments were built like crooked shotguns: The front door opened from inside the foyer, and the apartments consisted of long skinny front rooms connected to long skinny kitchens that led to a hallway with a bathroom and bedroom on one side and some storage cabinets on the other. Killian had never been in any of the upstairs apartments, but given there were three of them and a flight of stairs, he was pretty sure they were even longer and skinnier than the ones on the bottom floor, and two of them shared a bathroom.

"Really?" Lewis asked, eyes enormous. "That would be amazing. My brother's apartment is *small*."

Todd lived in the unit that *didn't* share the bathroom, thank God, but it still wasn't big enough for a guest. Particularly if….

"Does Todd even have a couch?" Killian asked, horrified.

Lewis shrugged. "He's got a nice recliner," he said, as though making up for his brother's shortcomings. "But you know the best thing he has?"

Killian stared at him, at a loss. "No idea."

"An address not in Texas," Lewis said, nodding sagely, and Killian sucked air through his teeth.

"Is that where you went to school?" he asked apologetically. Lewis's pretty, angular face sported two yellowing crescents of old bruises under his brown eyes, and he was half afraid to ask where those had come from.

"Don't get me wrong," Lewis said. "There are a lot of great things about Texas. Barbecue, nice people, country music, wide-open spaces. You know what's not great about Texas?"

"Fox News and bigots?" Killian asked, pretty sure this had been the reason Lewis had shown up to sleep in his brother's recliner.

Lewis put a finger to a still-swollen nose, looking glum. "Yeah. Got out of college, tried to get a job—had three different companies outside of Houston tell me they 'didn't hire my kind.'" He sighed. "I've got a degree in software engineering." He paused. "A *master's*."

Killian sighed. "Well, I wish you luck. You may have a better time finding a job here."

"And my parents' neighbors will quit signing petitions to evict them from the neighborhood," he muttered.

"Oh God," Killian said. "I'm sorry. High school must have been a *drag*."

Lewis nodded and touched his nose again—gingerly. "Bingo."

"Well, I can't solve any of that, and politics depress me. But you can sleep on my couch."

The way Lewis's face lit up right then, like Killian was his hero? Killian rubbed his chest, surprised at the warmth that look generated. It felt… potent. And *dangerous*. Like the opioids he'd taken sparingly when he'd fallen three years ago and broken his ankle. Like if he wasn't careful, he'd crave *more* looks like that. And *more*, and—he couldn't think about it.

It didn't do to need people like that.

"Thanks, Killian. That's kind." Lewis's voice had this sandpaper purr when he said "kind," and Killian had to fight that uncomfortable, needy sensation.

"I need to finish my closing shit," he said shortly, spinning away on his heel. "We'll leave when Suzanne's ready to go."

In the Cold and Dark

LEWIS WATCHED as Killian stalked back and forth across the bar, stacking the stools up off the floor, giving everything a final sweep. He even took a cloth to the windowsills and then got some Windex for the insides of the window itself. Lewis was pretty sure that the place had a deep-cleaning service that came in the morning—most bars and restaurants did—but Killian Thornton moved with a sinuous grace and self-assurance that said he'd rather he see it done right than rely on somebody else to do it.

Mm… muscles.

Lewis tried not to drool at his brother's downstairs neighbor, but it was hard. Lewis had shown up on Todd's doorstep the week before, after Glenda Dupree had discovered he'd blown her husband in the backyard when Lewis had been visiting his parents over spring break. Granted, Lewis hadn't known Richie Dupree, his brother's old friend from high school, had been married, and it hadn't been their first blowjob among friends, but this time another neighbor—a friend of Lewis and Todd's mother—had spotted them and apparently brought it up over the neighborhood pre-Thanksgiving potluck after Glenda had bragged about her Kitchen-Sink Hash Browns.

Glenda's shrieks had apparently burst eardrums across the neighborhood, and Glenda's best friend's husband, who had always carried a bigger torch for Glenda anyway, had led the charge across the Bernards' lawn to scream things like "pedophile" and "child molester" in Lewis's mother's face.

Lewis loved his mother. Glenda's best friend's husband had needed to have his nose set and to use the steaks planned for the day before Thanksgiving on his two black eyes. For that matter, Lewis still had a crooked nose and a couple of shiners himself.

As Lewis retreated into the house, more to get away from the hysterical screaming than to get away from the fight itself, his mother had given him a sympathetic look.

"Lewis…," she'd said helplessly, and he'd read everything right there in her face. She loved him. She and his father had supported him through his coming out, through his turbulent adolescence, through his Fuck yeah I'm gay! T-shirt wardrobe. But the political climate in their part of the country had gotten too damned violent for him to stay there while he looked for a job.

"I swear, Mama," he said, taking a towel from her and putting it to his bleeding nose, "I didn't realize Richie had gotten married."

She sighed and went to get him some ice. When she returned, she held it tenderly to his nose as he sat on the couch and then ruffled his hair. "It was Richie's fault for not telling you," she said, kissing his temple. "But that doesn't mean this place is particularly healthy for you right now."

Property values had sunk so low in their state they couldn't afford to move.

"Think Todd's got a couch?" he asked.

No, in fact, Todd *didn't* have a couch, but he still opened up his tiny apartment to his little brother. Todd worked nights at a movie theater and mornings in a book store and was on call as a special ed tutor, so they often ended up sleeping on Todd's queen-sized bed, just at different times. Todd would be gone in the morning, and he'd come home to sleep while Lewis was out looking for jobs and an apartment of his own.

The chance to see his girlfriend—take her out to a dinner, have some uninterrupted time with her—had meant a lot to Todd, who had grown up string-bean thin, with the lion's share of acne in high school. His skin was mostly clear now, and he'd grown into his height, but mostly he'd developed that kind of confidence that people got when they survived a miserable adolescence and were perfectly happy with themselves and therefor made the people around them happy too.

Todd didn't have much, but he'd opened it up to Lewis with a hug and a peanut-butter-and-banana sandwich and a "Hey, little bro, missed you." He didn't even bat an eyelash when Lewis told him about Richie. "Heh heh—shoulda known. He always *was* sorta crushing on you. I was too dumb to spot the signs."

That was Todd—laid-back in the extreme. If he'd forgotten to text Lewis after his date, it was probably because he'd fallen asleep, because the multiple jobs thing was exhausting. Lewis *probably* should have led with that when he was talking to Killian but....

But Killian had black hair with brown streaks from the sun, stunning blue-gray eyes with thick lashes, abs, shoulders, arms and thighs (abs and thighs!) of the muscular variety, and a rather sardonic, tight-lipped regard for other human beings. This was Lewis's third night in the bar, and he'd seen Killian be gallant to all the patrons, polite to the drunken come-ons aimed his way, and kind to the people who seemed to be in the bar because they were genuinely distraught. On Lewis's first night—Todd had brought him in as a sort of welcome-to-the-neighborhood—he'd inquired solicitously about Lewis's black eyes, had given Todd a reserved if friendly "Hey," and then had comped them both a drink as a rather sweet "welcome" gesture—after he'd checked Lewis's ID of course.

Lewis and Todd had snagged a table and sat with their beers while Todd gave Lewis the lowdown of the city and what he might be able to do with his degree. And generally? It had been a better hello than Lewis figured he deserved.

And watching Killian, brooding, polite Killian, work the bar had been the highlight of his night.

He'd almost swooned when he'd run into the man in the hallway the next morning. The aloof, polite nod, the "Let me know if you need anything," although it was clear Killian expected Lewis to be fine on his own, but still.... There was a sort of innate courtliness to the man that Lewis responded to.

He'd always wanted to be courted.

Lewis had an entire block-and-a-half walk home to make Killian Thornton think about courting *him*.

He kept playing darts, thinking he had to bring out his best game, and then it occurred to him that this man lived damned near in Lavender Heights, with its rainbow crosswalks, out-and-proud clubs, and happy mass pub crawls. If Killian Thornton played for Lewis's team, odds were good he'd seen *real* game, and not just the boy most likely to deflower jocks in the dorm of his state college.

Ugh. Jocks. Most of them didn't respect the equipment, and too many of them thought playing for the other team gave them a pass for not knowing the rules.

Someone like Killian—all of that repressed chivalry, that kindness, that *having his own apartment and a job*. Yeah, Killian might actually be out of Lewis's league.

All too soon, Killian's boss was clicking out of her office, dressed in her warm wool coat, with a hat. She had Killian sign the deposit slip for the night's take, which she tucked inside the cash register for the day manager, and together the three of them walked into the misty autumn darkness, the smell of woodsmoke thick in the air.

Suzanne sighed. "I know it's bad for the air quality, but I still love the smell."

Killian let out a chuckle. "Yeah, but now only rich people can afford fireplaces in the city, so that cuts down on emissions."

Suzanne gave a short bark of laughter. "You guys be safe on the way home." She looked at Killian meaningfully. "You hear?"

Killian nodded, and Lewis realized that bartenders got tips and the man next to him was walking home with a wad of cash in his pocket.

"Does that ever worry you?" he asked as Suzanne drove away.

Killian shook his head. "Naw. I've been mugged twice, and both times I just handed over my wallet and kept going."

Lewis gaped at him, and Killian gave a faint snort of laughter, like Lewis was too precious for words, and gestured with his shoulder for them to continue down the street. The silence was pleasant, but at the same time, Lewis racked his brains so as to not waste this perfect opportunity.

"I feel like I have to correct an impression here," he said, as their footsteps rang hollowly against the concrete.

"Hold up," Killian said softly, holding out his arm to direct Lewis away from a patch of wet leaves. "Those get slippery."

Lewis refrained from jumping him right then and tried to stick to the subject.

"My brother's a great guy," he said. "I mean, I know he forgot me, but God—he's so sleep-deprived I'm surprised he remembers to get up most days."

"Three jobs is a rough gig," Killian said, surprising Lewis because he obviously knew something about Todd's life.

"He needs to find one that can pay the rent," Lewis agreed. "But, you know, he deserves a night off. I was…."

"Also being a good guy," Killian said. "I get it."

And that was that. They kept walking, their apartment house looming nearer while Lewis almost hurt himself trying to think of a better subject to talk about. C'mon, c'mon…. Lewis was just about to try "Are you getting a Christmas tree," because wasn't *that* exciting, but when he opened his mouth a squeak came out.

Lewis stopped, and Killian stared at him.

"No!" Lewis said hurriedly. "That's not what I—"

They heard the sound again.

"What the hell is that?" Killian asked, sounding rattled for the first time.

"That's—"

And this time it was unmistakable. Crystal clear into the night came a pathetic little "Mew."

"Baby kitty?" Lewis asked, staring at Killian.

Killian looked around frantically. "Oh no," he said.

"Yes! I heard it!"

"But no," Killian told him, a hint of panic in his voice. "No. There is no kitten—"

"Yes, there is!" Lewis said excitedly. He listened again, turning toward the parking lot they were crossing in front of, where the sound came from. There was a retaining wall between the lot and the converted business building next door, and Lewis ventured into the shadowed area, the part cut off from the streetlight that sat in front of the bar half a block away. Lewis pulled out his phone, hit the Flashlight button, and swept it along the mess of wet leaves until he saw it.

"Mew."

"Aw," he said. "Baby. C'mere."

The light revealed a midsized marmalade kitten, maybe twelve weeks old. As he reached for it, he heard another "Mew," although the orange kitten had only regarded him with peaceful eyes as he reached for it. With another sweep of his phone, he saw the electric green flash. Huddled behind the orange kitten was a *black* kitten, blending in so thoroughly with the leaf mold that if the kitty hadn't been caught looking at the light, Lewis might have missed him again.

"Aw, guys!" he murmured, tucking his phone back in his pocket and reaching down to grab them. "Look at them!" he turned to Killian and without asking thrust one into Killian's arms.

"Wait a minute," Killian said, staring at the little black kitten in surprise. "Kid—"

"I'm twenty-three."

"And I'm thirty-two, and I don't have anything in the apartment."

"Do you have meat?" Lewis asked. "They're totally weaned."

"I've got turkey burger and tuna," Killian began, "but I was going to—"

"Great!" Lewis said, taking his own kitten and tucking it under his denim jacket to keep it from the cold. He noticed that for all his seeming reluctance, Killian had done the same with his black kitten, his arms wrapped around the creature protectively.

"But what about a litter box?" Killian asked unhappily.

"You've got a sandpit behind your building. Don't worry. I can rig something up." Lewis had seen some flat cardboard boxes, the kind they used for four sixpacks of soda or beer, hanging around his brother's dumpster that morning. He had a plan.

Killian puffed out a violent breath. "Okay, but kid—"

"Lewis."

"Lewis, we can't keep them forever. You've *got* to find a place for them, okay?"

Lewis grinned at him. "Oh, of course. I mean, you're just letting me crash on your couch, right? It's not forever. I'll totally have some place for these guys to go before I leave."

Killian stared at him. "Wait...." His brows were knit and his unflappable aloofness had been somewhat damaged, but he seemed to be trying to hang on to it with both hands. The kitten in his arms meowed and curled up, burrowing into his shirt, and he swallowed.

"Okay?" Lewis said, nodding like this was a done deal.

"Sure," Killian muttered helplessly. "Yeah. You'll find a home for them—I mean, there's a shelter not too far away, right?"

"Absolutely," Lewis said, nodding some more. Oh God. Oh God. This was gonna happen!

Killian looked down at the little black kitten, who was rubbing his whiskers against Killian's finger. "Kitten," he said, casting Lewis a baleful look, "I don't know if either of us knows where this is going."

The kitten started to nurse on the end of his finger, making biscuits against Killian's chest.

Lewis grinned at them both.

Kittens from heaven! Who knew?

SCAN THE QR CODE
BELOW TO ORDER!

Writer, knitter, mother, wife, award-winning author AMY LANE shows her love in knitwear, is frequently seen in the company of tiny homicidal dogs, and can't believe all the kids haven't left the house yet. She lives in a crumbling crapmansion in the least romantic area of California, has a long-winded explanation for everything, and writes to silence the voices in her head. There are a lot of voices—she's written over 120 books.

Website:www.greenshill.com
Blog:www.writerslane.blogspot.com
Email:amylane@greenshill.com
Facebook:www.facebook.com/amy.lane.167
Twitter:@amymaclane
Patreon:https://www.patreon.com/AmyHEALane

Follow me on BookBub

AMY LANE

SWIPE LEFT, POWER DOWN, LOOK UP

Busy soccer coach Trey Novak doesn't have time for the awkwardness and upheaval dating can cause, but when his cousin stands him up for a lunch date, he meets someone who changes his mind.

Dewey Saunders is dying to get a real job in his field and start the rest of his life, but a guy's got to pay rent, and the coffee shop is where it's at. When the handsome customer in the coach's sweats gets stood up, Dewey is right there to commiserate—and maybe make some time with a cute guy.

Trey's making hopeful plans with Dewey when his professional life explodes. He and Dewey aren't in a serious place yet, and suddenly he's promising to make sports a welcoming place for all people. When Dewey puts himself out to comfort Trey after an awful day, Trey realizes that they might not be in a serious place, but Dewey has serious promise for their future. If someone as loyal and as kind and funny as Dewey is what's offered, Trey would gladly swipe right for love.

SCAN THE QR CODE
BELOW TO ORDER!

AMY LANE

Sometimes the
best magic is just
a little luck…

THE
RISING TIDE

THE LUCK MECHANICS BOOK ONE

The tidal archipelago of Spinner's Drift is a refuge for misfits. Can the island's magic help a pie-in-the-sky dreamer and a wounded soul find a home in each other?

In a flash of light and a clap of thunder, Scout Quintero is banished from his home. Once he's sneaked his sister out too, he's happy, but their power-hungry father is after them, and they need a place to lie low. The thriving resort business on Spinner's Drift provides the perfect way to blend in.

They aren't the only ones who think so.

Six months ago Lucky left his life behind and went on the run from mobsters. Spinner's Drift brings solace to his battered soul, but one look at Scout and he's suddenly terrified of having one more thing to lose.

Lucky tries to keep his distance, but Scout is charming, and the island isn't that big. When they finally connect, all kinds of things come to light, including supernatural mysteries that have been buried for years. But while Scout and Lucky grow closer working on the secret, pissed-off mobsters, supernatural entities, and Scout's father are getting closer to them. Can they hold tight to each other and weather the rising tide together?

SCAN THE QR CODE BELOW TO ORDER!

AMY
LANE

WEIRDOS

Not all
dogs are
Lassie.

If Taz Oswald has one more gross date, he's resigning himself to a life of celibacy with his irritable Chihuahua, Carl. Carl knows how to bite a banana when he sees one! Then Selby Hirsch invites Taz to walk dogs together, and Taz is suddenly back in the game. Selby is adorkable, awkward, and a little weird—and his dog Ginger is a trip—and Taz is transfixed. Is it really possible this sweet guy with the blurty mouth and a heart as big as the Pacific Ocean wandered into Taz's life by accident? If so, how can Taz convince Selby that he wants to be Selby and Ginger's forever home?

SCAN THE QR CODE
BELOW TO ORDER!

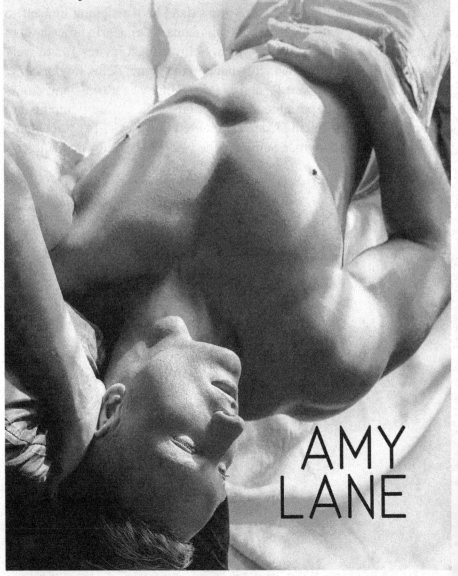

SHADES
of HENRY

AMY
LANE

A Flophouse Story: Book One

One bootstrap act of integrity cost Henry Worrall everything—military career, family, and the secret boyfriend who kept Henry trapped for eleven years. Desperate, Henry shows up on his brother's doorstep and is offered a place to live and a job as a handyman in a flophouse for young porn stars.

Lance Luna's past gave him reasons for being in porn, but as he continues his residency at a local hospital, they now feel more like excuses. He's got the money to move out of the flophouse and live his own life—but who needs privacy when you're taking care of a bunch of young men who think working penises make them adults?

Lance worries Henry won't fit in, but Henry's got a soft spot for lost young men and a way of helping them. Just as Lance and Henry find a rhythm as den mothers, a murder and the ghosts of Henry's abusive past intrude. Lance knows Henry's not capable of murder, but is he capable of caring for Lance's heart?

SCAN THE QR CODE
BELOW TO ORDER!

Bonfires: Book One

Ten years ago Sheriff's Deputy Aaron George lost his wife and moved to Colton, hoping growing up in a small town would be better for his children. He's gotten to know his community, including Mr. Larkin, the bouncy, funny science teacher. But when Larx is dragged unwillingly into administration, he stops coaching the track team and starts running alone. Aaron—who thought life began and ended with his kids—is distracted by a glistening chest and a principal running on a dangerous road.

Larx has been living for his kids too—and for his students at Colton High. He's not ready to be charmed by Aaron, but when they start running together, he comes to appreciate the deputy's steadiness, humor, and complete understanding of Larx's priorities. Children first, job second, his own interests a sad last.

It only takes one kiss for two men approaching fifty to start acting like teenagers in love, even amid all the responsibilities they shoulder. Then an act of violence puts their burgeoning relationship on hold. The adult responsibilities they've embraced are now instrumental in keeping their town from exploding. When things come to a head, they realize their newly forged family might be what keeps the world from spinning out of control.

SCAN THE QR CODE
BELOW TO ORDER!

FOR **MORE** OF THE **BEST** **GAY** ROMANCE

REAMSPINNER
PRESS

dreamspinnerpress.com